To Heal an Earl

Soldiers & Soulmates
Book 1

Alexa Aston

Dragonblade Publishing, Inc.

Text by Alexa Aston
Cover by Wicked Smart Designs

Dragonblade Publishing, Inc. is an imprint of Kathryn Le Veque Novels, Inc.
P.O. Box 7968
La Verne CA 91750
ceo@dragonbladepublishing.com

Produced in the United States of America

First Edition January 2020
Print Edition

Chapter One

Rumford Park, Kent—1800

Lady Charlotte Nott stood at the graveside of her beloved father, a terrible numbness spreading through her. The cold, gray February day already chilled her to the bone but it was the complete sense of isolation that now overwhelmed her.

She was alone in the world.

Her mother had died when Charlotte was barely two and she had no memories of her. She'd come to know her mother through the miniature her father kept on his desk. Every night, Lord Rumford retrieved the painting and brought it upstairs with him, placing it on his bedside table so that he could see his late wife's face first thing each morning. Charlotte remembered sitting in his lap when she was young and he'd be working at his desk. She'd hold the miniature in her small hands and wish that, somehow, her mother would come back to her.

Those wishes had never come true but she'd had the next best thing in one loving, attentive parent all these years.

And one very cruel, conniving half-brother.

Barclay was her father's son from his first marriage. He was a dozen years older than Charlotte and had never said a kind word to her in all her eighteen years. In fact, he'd been rather awful to her from the time she was a small child. Pinching her. Screaming at her. Even locking her in the cellar once. When she'd been found a day and half after she'd disappeared, she saw the warning look he gave her and so she never told on him.

She was still afraid of the dark.

Barclay resented that his father had wed again. The fact that Charlotte so closely resembled her mother gave him reason enough to hate her. Fortunately, he'd spent most of her life away at school, only home for short periods, and after university, he lived in the Rumford London townhome year-round. She and her father only went to London for brief periods and so even when in residence, she rarely saw Barclay. The most she'd been around him was last year when he'd wed Lady Leticia, who was a year older than Charlotte. She'd hoped during the various social events before the wedding that she and Leticia might become friendly if not true friends but Barclay had poisoned his fiancée against Charlotte.

And now the new Lord and Lady Rumford were her only living relatives.

Thunder grumbled in the distance and she looked to the skies, now darkening.

"Lady Charlotte?"

She turned and saw Reverend Bixby standing behind her, sympathy written across his broad, plain face.

"Yes, Reverend?"

"It looks like rain. You need to head home to Rumford Park."

Sighing, she said, "I know." She glanced back at the fresh grave. "It's just so hard to leave Papa."

He came and put an arm about her shoulders. "Your father was the best of men, my lady. He will be sorely missed by friends, family, and servants alike."

Tears misted her eyes. "Thank you. I should go."

The clergyman took her hand. "Send word if you have need of me, my dear. Mrs. Bixby and I would be happy to keep you company or share memories of Lord Rumford with you."

"Thank you," she said softly. "I appreciate your wise counsel, Reverend Bixby. Good afternoon."

Charlotte left the graveyard, the winter wind pushing against her back as she walked the two miles home. She'd told Barclay and Leticia that she wanted to stay a while with Papa and had assumed they would send the carriage back for her. Their thoughtlessness aggravated her but she knew to hold her tongue. Barclay had quite the temper and she didn't want to anger him in any way. Charlotte hoped they would return to London soon and leave her to her mourning.

It disappointed her that Papa would never see her wed. Charlotte was supposed to make her come-out this spring when the Season began and she'd so looked forward to all of the parties and gatherings. She'd known that she would seek her father's advice on which man to marry. Papa had always known what to look for in others. Now, he wouldn't be here to help her make the most important decision of her life. Her children would never know their grandfather. It was enough to rip her heart in two yet again.

Of course, now that she was in mourning, her come-out would be delayed until next year. She would take a year to mourn the greatest man she would ever know—and then hope fate would bring one just as good and kind into her life and allow her to marry him. She would appreciate a year of quiet at Rumford Park, knowing Barclay and Leticia would spend the bulk of it in London with their friends. It would allow her to mourn Papa in her own way.

The mist turned to drizzle and then a heavy downpour when she still had half a mile to go and by the time Charlotte reached home, she was wet, cold, and tired. And hurting. The ache within her was as physical as any pain she'd ever known. She didn't know how she would get through the rest of this day—much less all of the days ahead. Still, Papa would want her to not only go on living, but he'd want her to be happy. She decided in that moment that she would name her firstborn son after him, to honor the memory of the man who was kind and generous to all.

She burst into the house and quickly closed the door behind her, now so thoroughly chilled that her teeth chattered noisily. Graves, their butler, hurried toward her.

"Lady Charlotte, you'll have caught cold," he chastised. "You're soaked to the skin. I'll order a bath for you at once."

"Th-thank you, Gr-Gr-Graves," she said, allowing him to remove her sodden cloak.

"Go upstairs at once," he urged, his eyes darting to the staircase and back to her.

"What's wrong?" she asked.

He frowned. "You were to see Lord Rumford in the drawing room when you returned but, right now, you need to get in a hot bath."

Her stomach twisted. "I can quickly visit with him. I don't want you in any trouble."

"Just hurry," Graves said. "I'll see to the hot water."

The butler scurried away and Charlotte headed toward the stairs. She caught a movement but didn't see who it was until she reached the top and saw Barclay's valet hovering.

"I'll take you to Lord Rumford."

She sneezed violently and decided it was better to change before she did so. Being sick was a nuisance and she hated when others had to wait upon her when she was ill. "Thank you, but I'm going to get out of these wet clothes first. Please tell my—"

"You're to see Lord Rumford *now*," the servant insisted. "Follow me."

Charlotte did as requested, deciding to get the visit over with quickly. She clamped down on her teeth so they didn't chatter. She hoped whatever Barclay wanted wouldn't take long.

"Lady Charlotte," the valet announced as he led her into the drawing room and then closed the door after she'd stepped inside.

She saw Barclay and Leticia sitting on the far side of the room, close to the roaring fire, and made her way toward them, hoping to soak up some of the warmth from the blaze.

"You look like a drowned rat," sniffed Leticia as Charlotte approached.

"I'm very sorry. I got caught in the rain as I walked home," she apologized. "I can go change and come back," she offered.

"No," the new earl said firmly. "This won't take long." He set the newspaper he'd been reading aside and frowned at her.

Charlotte waited patiently for him to speak, though she started to tremble. She longed to move closer to the fire's heat but stood since he hadn't invited her to sit and likely wouldn't want the furniture stained with water.

"We need to discuss your living arrangements," he began.

She decided to help him since it was taking forever and she was dripping all over the carpet.

"I know I was to come to London for the Season this year with Papa. Of course, that can't happen now with us being in mourning. I realize I will need to put off my come-out for a year and I am fine with that. I'd actually prefer staying at Rumford Park until next spring."

"There's to be no come-out," Barclay said firmly.

"Yes, Barclay, I just said that. Mourning makes it impossible—"

"You'll address me as Lord Rumford," he demanded.

Charlotte knew that when younger family members assumed their titles that others in the family often changed the way they addressed them. "Of course, my lord."

"And I said there's not to be a come-out."

"I agree with you. I understand the need to mourn Papa."

He pushed himself to his feet. "You don't understand a bloody thing," he snapped.

She took a step back. "I . . . don't?" Apprehension filled her.

"There will never be a come-out for you," he hissed. "I wouldn't spend a farthing on you, much less on fancy ball gowns to clothe you."

"But . . . Papa . . ."

"Your precious papa isn't here anymore," he said harshly. "He coddled and protected you all of these years. *You* . . . the daughter of some third-rate opera singer. You're no better than the daughter of a whore."

Anger filled Charlotte. "Don't say that about Mama," she cried. "She was the most famous singer of her day. She loved Papa and he loved her. She gave up everything for him."

"Singers. Actresses. They're all trollops," Rumford growled. "And you're the mongrel she bore."

She tried to still her trembling, which had spread to every limb, whether from cold or fear, Charlotte didn't know. Still, she put on a brave front.

"I'm no mongrel," she declared. "I'm the daughter of an earl. A lady."

Leticia sniffed. "You don't have a coin to your name. And we are afraid our sons and daughters would be hurt by their association with you."

"How? I am a member of this family. I would never do anything to hurt my future nieces or nephews."

"You won't have a chance to know them—much less hurt them. Your reputation, thanks to your mother, is enough to see the Nott family totally disassociate themselves with you," Rumford said. "I want you gone from this house by morning."

Charlotte looked blankly at him. "Wh-wh-where am I to go?"

"You will be given funds for the mail coach that passes through the village. I suggest you travel to London and find work there." Her half-brother sneered. "If you can."

"I can't believe you would totally abandon me," she said, her voice wavering. Then Charlotte looked him in the eye and asked, "What would Papa say?"

He cackled like an old woman. "I don't care what that bastard would say. He stopped being my father the day he married your mother. I've had to put up with your presence all of these years—but no more."

"So, you'll turn me out into the cold?" she asked, her chin high, daring to keep looking him in the eyes.

"Gladly."

Rumford turned to the table and lifted up a bank note and handed it to her. "This is all you'll ever get out of me. As of this moment, you are dead to me. I never wish to see you again. Now, get out!"

Charlotte clutched the note, crumpling it in her hand. She turned and fled the room, hearing Leticia call after her, reminding her to be on the mail coach tomorrow morning.

Fleeing to her room, she saw servants toting buckets of hot water into the bedchamber. The last one dumped the bucket's contents into the bath and left.

From the doorway, she heard a throat clear and saw it was Graves. Charlotte burst into tears and ran to him, flinging herself at him.

"Tell me, Lady Charlotte," he said, stroking her hair.

The butler had always seemed more family than servant. Quickly, she told him how she was being removed from the family home—and the family.

Sorrow filled his face. "I feared something like this would occur. I tried to warn Lord Rumford but he wouldn't believe anything so drastic about his flesh and blood." He released her. "Your maid will bathe you and then I'll have a tray brought up for you. We'll talk," he promised.

Graves left and Charlotte's maid arrived, stripping the wet clothes from her and scrubbing her from head to toe as if she were a small child. Once dressed, her food arrived and she did her best to try and eat but could only pick at it.

A knock sounded and her maid entered again.

"Mr. Graves wishes to see you in the kitchen, my lady. I'm to bring you there now."

"All right," she said shakily and followed the girl downstairs.

They went through the kitchen to the servants' dining room, where she saw the room packed. Footmen. Maids. Scullery workers. The head groom. All eyed her with pity.

Graves stepped forward, a pouch in his hand. He handed it to her and said, "Lady Charlotte, you have always been a favorite with the staff, full of a gentle spirit and kind words for all you encounter. We have taken up a collection to help you once you reach London."

Tears blinded her and she blinked rapidly. "I cannot accept this," she protested, knowing what a sacrifice the entire group made on her behalf.

The butler placed a hand over hers. "You must, my lady. You'll need every prayer we send and each coin in that bag in order to survive."

Overwhelmed, she looked out at the people she'd known her entire life. "Thank you," she whispered and then wheeled and left before she broke down in front of them all.

In her room, she counted the contents of the pouch so she would know what she had. Not having any idea about how much things cost, Charlotte wondered how long she would be able to make it on the sum. She didn't know what a room's lodging might cost per night or how much a meal would be. She'd only used her pin money to buy ribbons and the occasional book over the years and hadn't a clue about the world around her.

She'd always had a calm, practical nature, though. Right now, she knew she should pack. It must be light enough for her to carry for she wouldn't have servants with her or coin to spare for others to transport her trunks. She opened her wardrobe and glanced through the dresses. Unfortunately, she only had a few and those were worn. Living in the country, she hadn't dressed up much, especially since she wasn't out in society yet. Papa had promised her an entire new wardrobe for the upcoming Season but she was to be fitted for it next week after they went to London. Who would have thought Charlotte would be arriving in the great city without her beloved father?

A footman brought her a valise and she packed three dresses into it, along with a spare pair of shoes and a night rail. She would place her comb and brush in it tomorrow. She went to the tray of food and forced herself to eat all that remained. She might not have the opportunity to do so in the morning since she needed to be in the village very early, waiting for the mail coach to arrive.

Charlotte lay on her bed, curled on her side, and cried herself to sleep.

Chapter Two

Oxford—1803

Danforth Grayson threw off his gown of colored silk and cap with its gold tuft, marking him as a Nobleman Commoner. His days at university had come to an end. What awaited him, he hadn't a clue. What he wanted more than anything was to have his brother purchase him a commission in the army. With England recently declaring war against France, Gray wanted to fight for his country against the threat Bonaparte posed.

Whether he could wheedle the large amount necessary from Seymour remained to be seen.

As it was, Gray had to fight his brother to release the funds to finish his schooling at Eton and then did battle again with Seymour in order to attend Oxford the past few years. Fortunately, Mr. Bonham, the Grayson family solicitor, had seen the tuition money earmarked for Gray's education spent in the proper places after the Earl of Crampton died five years ago. Thoughts of his father's death still left a bad taste in Gray's mouth. He'd arrived home from Eton after the Michaelmas term at sixteen to learn his father had passed away more than a month earlier. His brother had assumed the title, never bothering to notify Gray of what had occurred.

Gray had never forgiven Seymour for keeping him from their father's funeral and the chance to bid the old man goodbye. They'd had a huge row, with Gray proclaiming he'd never darken Gray

Manor again. And he hadn't.

Until now.

He'd written his brother, letting him know he was about to earn his degree and that he would arrive home for a short visit. As a second son, Gray was destined for the army and only hoped the earl would provide the funds for him to purchase an army commission. It would be impossible to do so on his own. Despite Mr. Bonham's help, the monies the solicitor had freed up so that Gray could finish Eton and continue on to Oxford hadn't been enough to survive on. He'd had to take on tutoring other students in languages and mathematics in order to eat and afford living space.

Of course, his closest friends in the world wouldn't have seen him cast out on the street or let him starve. He'd shared rooms with Reid Baker, Marquess of Medford, and Burke Nicholson their entire time at Oxford. Reid was always quick to accept any bill when they were at a pub and both he and Burke would offer Gray their castoff clothing, many times the items still in excellent shape, all so he would be adequately clothed. The two men had been his friends since they'd begun their schooling at Eton at seven years of age and were more brothers to him than Seymour ever had been.

Reid was a natural leader. Intelligent. Practical. Friendly to all without making many close friends. Every boy at Eton wanted to be on the pedestal Medford stood upon, admired by all for his strength and loyalty. Gray had gone home with Reid during many a holiday and was treated as family by the Duke of Gilford. Though the duke was against it and few peers of Reid's standing entered the army, his friend would be doing that very thing after a brief visit home.

Burke would also be joining the army. A third son destined for the church, Burke was a hellion. He went out of his way to ensure that his family wouldn't force him into the clergy and had long proclaimed he would make a career of the military. Burke was all charm and full of fun. Women wanted him. Men wanted to be him.

Gray couldn't have asked for better friends and hoped they would remain close for years to come.

He glanced at the small table where they always left a sheet of parchment in order to communicate with one another, reading the last line written by Burke. It told Gray to meet them at their favorite pub for a final meal in Oxford before they left in the morning for Kent. Reid had hired a chaise lounge to carry the three of them home. They would first drop Gray and then Burke before Reid made his way home to Gillingham.

Exiting the rooms, he hurried down the stairs and out onto the busy streets of Oxford. He traveled the three blocks to his destination and ducked inside, immediately spying his friends. Burke caught his eye and hoisted a tankard, a huge grin on his face.

"I see you've started without me," Gray said as he joined them.

"You're only one drink behind," Reid said, handing him an ale. He then held his tankard up. "To finishing our education—and friendship."

The three touched mugs and downed the cold brew. Gray wiped the foam from his mouth with the back of his hand and they took their seats.

"I've already ordered," Reid said. "All of our favorites."

"Is she one of them?" Burke asked, indicating a buxom tavern wench who saw she was the object of their attention and gave the trio a saucy wink.

"You'll have to arrange that on your own," Reid said. "After we dine."

They spent two hours eating and reminiscing about classes and professors and shared adventures throughout the years. People they'd known. Politics. Their love of horses and cards. Gray couldn't help but think that a curtain was being drawn on this part of their lives as they stood on the precipice of the next chapter that would come, one where they would become responsible adults.

He called for a final toast. "To Burke and Reid. My greatest friends and chief collaborators in mischief. You have stood by me as no others have in my darkest days. May we ever stay in touch and know we can call upon one another, in both good times and bad."

"Hear, hear," the two said in unison and they drank their fill.

THE COACH TURNED down the lane. Gray's stomach clenched, knowing he would soon see his brother again after five years of no contact.

"It's been a long time," Reid said as he gazed out the window.

Both his friends had been frequent visitors to Gray Manor during their early years. After his quarrel with Seymour, Gray had stayed with both of them during school holidays, trading off. He enjoyed Burke's noisy household, with two older brothers and four younger sisters but found going to Gillingham a nice respite, as well. Reid's young stepmother, only a year older than they were, had two small boys still in the nursery, so a quieter time was had when visiting there.

The vehicle pulled up to the manor and came to a stop. Gray steeled himself.

"Are you sure you don't want us to come in with you?" Reid asked, his brown eyes full of concern.

"I'd be happy to slam a fist into Stinkin' Seymour's nose," Burke offered.

They laughed at the nickname Burke had given the Earl of Crampton many years ago.

"No, I should do this alone. I doubt I'll be welcomed so I know the two of you wouldn't be," he replied.

"Why does Stinkin' Seymour hate you so much?" Burke asked. "In all these years, we've never talked about it."

Gray shrugged. "Father told me the best he could guess was that

Seymour blamed me for Mother's death. They'd always been especially close and after she died giving birth to me, Seymour took her death hard, blaming me for it."

"That's ridiculous," Reid said. "What was he, sixteen? I'm not saying he shouldn't mourn a mother he was close to but to blame her death on a newborn—and hold it against you all of these years? He was old enough to know better. Death in childbirth is but a fact of life."

"Stinkin' Seymour is a bloody idiot," Burke proclaimed. "We've always known that."

"Thank you both," Gray said. "I don't look at Seymour as my brother. That's a role the two of you play, not brothers by blood but ones by choice. But it's time I faced him after all these years."

Reid stopped him from rising. "If Crampton won't give you adequate funds to purchase your commission, Gray, I will. Or Father would be happy to do so. You know how he admires you. You could pay us back."

Gratitude at the offer filled Gray. "I know and I'm thankful for that option. I hope it doesn't come to that. Commissions are expensive and it would take years of an officer's pay to fulfill that debt to you or the duke."

He opened the coach door and jumped to the ground. "If I turn up at either of your doorsteps, you'll know things went poorly."

With that, he slammed the vehicle's door and stepped aside. The driver removed Gray's portmanteau from the top of the carriage and tossed it down to him. He caught it and watched as his friends waved from the window and the coach returned down the lane. Squaring his shoulders, he went to the front door and knocked.

When the door opened, it was Masters who greeted him, beaming from ear to ear. The longtime retainer had been a footman doing Gray's early years and then had moved into the role of butler about ten years ago.

"Master Gray, how good it is to finally see you again."

He shook hands with Masters. "Is that gray hair I spy along your temples?"

The butler laughed. "It is, indeed, sir. Just a touch of it. Do come in."

Masters took the suitcase from Gray and ushered him inside. He looked around the foyer and saw that nothing had changed. It was as if he had left only yesterday.

"Is the earl in residence?" he asked.

"He is," the butler confirmed. "Your carriage was spotted and he's received word that you're arriving. He asked to see you immediately."

Gray didn't know whether that was good or bad.

Suddenly, movement caught his eyes and he turned as a young boy ran up to him.

"Is this my uncle?" the frail child asked, his eyes large, shadows under them.

"If you are Rodger, then yes, I am your Uncle Gray. I haven't seen you since I held you in my arms. As I remember, you tinkled all over me," he said matter-of-factly.

"I did? You held me? I didn't know you were ever here."

"I was. And you did," Gray confirmed. "How are you, Rodger?" He offered the boy his hand and they shook.

"Very well, sir." He thought a moment. "Oh, you won't know about my sisters. I have two."

"What are their names?"

"Harriet is three. The baby is Jane. She was a year old last week."

Gray couldn't help but like this bright, eager boy and wished he would be able to get to know him and his two nieces. It would all be up to Seymour, though.

Suddenly, Rodger began wheezing and placed his hands on his knees, leaning over.

Gray's gaze met Masters and the butler mouthed, "Asthma."

He thumped the boy on his back lightly and after a few minutes, the fit seemed to pass.

"My lord, you should return to the nursery," Masters suggested. "You know it does you no good to become excited. Your uncle is to see your father now."

"Must I, Masters?" Rodger pleaded. "I want to talk to Uncle Gray some more. I don't know anything about him."

"Later, my lord," the butler insisted.

"Oh, all right."

Rodger reluctantly said goodbye and Gray watched his nephew trudge slowly up the stairs. Once he was out of sight, Gray turned and said, "How does Seymour handle the boy's asthma?"

"Not well," the butler said succinctly. "His lordship has never had patience for weakness of any kind."

"And my nieces? I'm sure Seymour's disappointed they're girls."

The butler's disdain was obvious but he remained silent on the matter. "We should go up to the drawing room, Master Gray."

Gray followed the servant upstairs and allowed Masters to announce him before he entered. The butler gave him a tight smile and a nod as he passed and closed the doors.

He spotted his brother on the far side of the room, seated next to his wife on a settee, and went to join them. His brother would be thirty-eight now and looked every year of. He'd gone to fat and his thinning hair had already turned iron gray from the family's chestnut shade.

"Good day, Lord Crampton, Lady Crampton," he said formally, knowing his brother enjoyed hearing his title. "I had a chance to speak with my nephew downstairs. He's a fine little fellow."

His sister-in-law nodded politely and then her gaze returned to her lap. His brother's face hardened.

"Why are you here?" Seymour demanded. "I thought you'd cut us from your life."

Gray kept his temper. "I regret the harsh words between us years ago, my lord," though he still felt his brother was at fault. "I was young and impetuous. I'd hope we could both be mature and set our issues aside."

"I won't support you, Gray. You're a second son and entitled to nothing," Seymour said flatly. "But despite that, I will do my duty to you."

"And what is that?" he asked, on edge.

"Father spoke of your desire to enter the military. Frankly, I think it's the best place for you. You were a spoiled, difficult child and I doubt you've matured any, despite all of those years of schooling."

Gray held his tongue, not willing to risk what Seymour might do if he spoke out against him and tried to defend himself from his brother's harsh opinion.

The earl reached for a rolled parchment sitting on a nearby table and thrust it at him. "When you wrote that you were coming, I prepared for your arrival. I've purchased you a commission in the army. Be warned that it's the last thing I'll do for you. I want you out of our lives. If we're lucky, some bloody French bastard will run a sword through you and gut you and you'll never return home. If you do live, don't bother to come to Gray Manor again for you won't be welcomed."

He clutched the commission in his hand, fighting the rage that filled him with his brother's cruel words.

"I am grateful for this, Lord Crampton," he said, holding tight on the reins of his temper. Though he had a thousand things he wished to say, Gray had gotten what he came for.

He never needed to see his brother again.

"Good day, Lady Crampton. My lord."

With that, Gray turned and strode from the room, leaving no regrets behind.

Chapter Three

Gray Manor—July 1808

CHARLOTTE GLANCED OUT the window, knowing Rumford Park would be visible from the road soon. The house sat at the end of a long lane which the mail coach would pass. She would have to squint but she knew the house would be there.

She'd been gone from it eight years.

A part of her wanted to be a poor match for the governess job she now headed to at Gray Manor, a place she'd visited a few times in her youth with her father. She remembered a boy close to her age, tall and friendly, with dark russet hair that shone red in the sunlight. Charlotte couldn't remember his name but did recall he'd been kind to her. Boys that age usually weren't nice to girls and his good manners had made a lasting impression on her. She wondered if that boy was now the Earl of Crampton, the gentleman she had scheduled an interview with. She vaguely thought there might have been an older brother but couldn't picture him. If there had been, he would be the earl instead.

The carriage came around the bend and, despite knowing how much it would hurt her heart, Charlotte looked wistfully at the beautiful manor home that stood in the distance as the vehicle passed by. Her throat grew thick with unshed tears, knowing she'd grown up at such an idyllic place. That she'd been an earl's daughter, hoping to marry a gentleman, and raise her own family in a similar setting. Instead, Barclay had tossed her from her home and the only life she'd known when she was barely eighteen.

Fate had led her to The Plummer Employment Agency, run by the whip-thin and bright-eyed Mr. Plummer, who placed impoverished gentlewomen in positions suitable to their backgrounds. Charlotte had thought her only choice would be to become a governess but Mr. Plummer insisted she travel to the far north to serve as a companion to the Dowager Duchess of Exbury. It had been the best place possible for her to heal from the emotional wounds inflicted by her half-brother. The duchess was in her late sixties and had lost her legs in an accident many years before. She possessed a fine mind and read voraciously. She'd taken to Charlotte immediately and they'd spent seven wonderful years together. Charlotte had become a part of the community, serving on church committees and singing in the local choir. She'd spent most every waking hour with the duchess—reading to her, discussing politics, pushing her in a wheelchair through the gardens. Bernice, as the duchess had Charlotte call her when they were alone, served as a grandmother to Charlotte. She still mourned for the friend she'd lost.

Bernice left Charlotte a small amount of money, not enough to live on, but it allowed her to take her time before choosing her next position. Unfortunately, she'd been fired from it within two weeks. She adored the little girl who was her charge but the girl's father had in mind for Charlotte to tutor him after hours in ways she found disgusting. When she refused to play his immoral games, she was sacked without references.

Her most recent position had lasted eight months but she spent all of her time trying to avoid the master of the house. The viscount wasn't in residence often but when he was, he made it abundantly clear that he was interested in her. He'd caught her several times, forcing unwanted kisses upon her, pressing his body against hers, his manhood jutting out. He told her of the things he wished to do to her in private, things that sounded so wicked and foul that they sickened her. Knowing the man planned to spend the entire summer at his country estate with his two small boys, Charlotte knew she wouldn't remain a virgin if she stayed. She resigned abruptly, knowing once again that no reference would be forthcoming.

She tried to explain all of this to Mr. Plummer in as vague a language as possible, not wanting to speak of such unspeakable matters, but he told her she was being too choosy. He said this position at Gray Manor would be the final one he would send her upon. Either she kept it or if she didn't, she wasn't to come crawling back to him.

If she would have known it was located so close to Rumford Park, Charlotte might have refused. She hadn't, though, and now found herself closer to home than she'd ever wanted to be.

The coach reached Wilton, the nearest town which was six miles from Rumford Park. From her best recollection, Gray Manor was another six or seven miles to the east of the town. That should be plenty of distance and she doubted she would ever see Barclay or Leticia. If they were invited to a social occasion at Gray Manor, Charlotte would remain locked in her room. The few times she might venture into Wilton, she suspected it would be places neither Lord nor Lady Rumford went.

The vehicle began slowing and she prepared to exit it. It came to a halt and the door opened after a moment.

"Wilton!" the driver called out.

"This is my stop," she informed him and was the only one to leave the mail coach, pointing out which was her valise that sat atop the carriage.

He handed it to her and tipped his hat before returning to the driver's seat and starting the team up again. Charlotte watched it leave her behind and then looked around. She was to be met but didn't see anyone so far. Venturing to the closest building, she remembered it to be a general store in which all kinds of goods could be purchased. She paused, her hand hovering above the door handle, and changed her mind about going inside. She didn't want to be recognized. If Mr. and Mrs. Simmons still owned the store, they would know her. Mrs. Simmons was a terrible gossip and she would spread the news that Charlotte had returned to the area—and how far down in the world she'd fallen. She didn't mind doing honest work to make her living but she didn't want to be viewed with pity or gossiped about by the residents of Wilton and beyond.

Instead, she returned to the street running through the village and after less than five minutes, a cart appeared with a man anxiously looking about. She waved and he came and stopped next to her.

"Be ye Miss Nott?" he asked.

"Yes, I am."

The man jumped down and took her valise. "I'm Sable, a groom at Gray Manor. I've come to fetch you."

He placed her luggage in the back of the cart and then helped her up, climbing beside her and taking up the reins again.

"Sorry I was a bit late. Lady Harriet disappeared again and I was helping look for her."

"And who is Lady Harriet?"

Sable glanced at her and looked away guiltily. "A daughter of the household. One of yer future charges if ye become the next governess. She's the older girl, at eight. Lady Jane is two years younger. A sweeter disposition but she does everything her sister does, which is plenty, indeed." He clucked his tongue. "Ye'll have yer hands full with them two, Miss."

Charlotte dreaded hearing that. She liked children but had never dealt with wayward ones. The charges at her last two positions had been sweet, quiet creatures. She resolved to make it work, despite what this groom said. It had to—because she had nowhere else to go.

"Have the girls been without a governess for long?"

The groom shrugged. "A few have come and gone. Tutors, too, for Lord Rodger, but he has none now."

Mr. Plummer hadn't mentioned a boy, only that two girls were to be her responsibility. "How old is Lord Rodger?"

Sable thought. "I suppose eleven now. Or twelve? He's a sick little thing. I doubt if ye'll be responsible for him."

"So, he isn't at school then."

"He has been in the past. Too sick to be there now, I reckon. He's rarely seen outside the house these days."

They rode in silence a few minutes and then he said, "The house is in a bad way. The housekeeper and estate manager left last week. The place is topsy-turvy."

"I see," she said, wondering what she was getting herself into. From what Sable had said, she would have two unruly charges and a possible sickly third one. The estate sounded ill-run. But she desperately needed this position. The last of Bernice's money wouldn't see her through a month now. Charlotte would have to make this work.

They turned from the road and, several minutes later, rounded a turn. She caught sight of Gray Manor, the stone edifice a pale shade of gray. The house was immense, even larger than her girlish memory thought it. She hoped she wouldn't get lost once inside, especially looking for Lady Harriet and Lady Jane.

Sable brought the cart to a stop and climbed down, handing her down and claiming her bag.

"This'll be the only time ye'll come in the front," he mentioned. "Unless ye have yer pupils with ye, of course."

"Of course."

Charlotte was used to the delineation between servants and residents and even lower and upper servants. While Bernice's companion, she had been treated well by the staff and the few visitors that came to see the dowager duchess, but once she'd become a governess, that had ceased. She'd learned a governess fit in neither above nor below stairs and had taken her evening meals on a tray in her room. The other two meals she'd eaten in the schoolroom with her charges. At the first household, she'd been Miss Nott. At the last, plain Nott. It was a long way from her days as Lady Charlotte, waited upon by so many.

Sable knocked and the door was answered by a man in footman's livery instead of a butler.

"This is Miss Nott," Sable said. "Here for the two young ladies." He handed the footman the valise. "A good day to ye, Miss."

"Thank you, Sable," she said, always one to express her gratitude even before she'd fallen upon hard times.

The footman closed the door. "I'm Smith, Miss Nott. Our butler, Mr. Masters, has taken ill and I'm filling in for him. You're to see Lord Crampton. He's in his study. Follow me."

They wound through several halls and Smith stopped. "I'll put your valise right outside the door, Miss. If you decide to accept the position, I'll bring it and you to your room. If not, well . . ." His voice trailed off, a worried expression creasing his brow.

"Let us hope Lord Crampton thinks I'm a good match for his children," she said.

Smith nodded and tapped on the door. She heard a voice bid him to enter and the footman announced her and then said, "Go right on in, Miss."

Charlotte entered a large room with several chairs scattered about and a desk covered with pages scattered everywhere. She shuddered at the mess and then looked at the man sitting behind it. In no way was this the boy she remembered. He would be close to her age and this man was at least forty years of age. Perhaps fifty. His complexion was florid, as if he'd just run a race. Sparse, gray hair covered his head. She guessed him to weigh over twenty stone and wondered how he even fit in the chair he was seated in.

"Miss Nott?" he said, his voice raspy.

She curtseyed. "Good afternoon, Lord Crampton."

"Have a seat." He indicated one in front of his desk and she took it.

"Usually, Lady Crampton handles these sorts of things. She is currently indisposed at the moment, giving birth to my child."

"Oh! Congratulations, my lord. How many children have you already been blessed with?"

The earl frowned. "Three have survived. Rodger, my oldest, is twelve years of age and my heir. He's down from Eton now. Has some health issues. You would need to spend a bit of time with him. He's bright and wouldn't need prepared lessons. More someone to discuss materials he's read. Until he's strong enough to return to school, of course."

"I'd be happy to do so, my lord. I myself read as much as possible and would love to discuss the classics with him, as well as current topics of interest. Does he speak any languages?"

"How would I know?" he asked, his irritation obvious. Clearing his throat, he said, "Your primary responsibility would be my daughters, Harriet and Jane." A sour look crossed his face. "They are girls but wild as geese. You won't be the first governess they've had. They've run off eleven others."

"I see," Charlotte said, her heart racing.

Eleven? How was she supposed to manage?

"Mr. Plummer said you have a genteel background."

"Yes, my lord. My father was an earl."

"Hmm. Well, you might be well-bred but it's going to take more than that to manage those little hellions. If they aren't under control soon, I don't know what we'll do. My wife has had several miscarriages and is no longer active. We need someone to totally take responsibility for the girls. Being around them isn't good for either of our nerves."

Charlotte began to gain a clearer picture. A self-absorbed father who seemed disappointed in the children he had. A sickly mother and brother. No family member spending time with Harriet and Jane. Governesses who allowed them to run wild, perhaps pitying them.

"The girls will need a firm hand," she said. "May I have your permission to discipline them?"

"Whatever it takes," he said grimly. "Are you up for the challenge, Miss Nott?"

"I would be happy to accept the offered position, Lord Crampton."

He rose and she followed suit. Before they could speak, the door burst open, a flush-faced woman pausing in the doorway.

"What is it?" Lord Crampton barked at the woman, who flinched.

"My lord . . ." Her voice broke as she entered the room. She looked to Charlotte and back to the earl. "My lord . . . the baby. He was stillborn."

The nobleman swore loudly, his hands crashing against the desk and sweeping papers off. They flew everywhere.

"And my wife?" he demanded angrily.

"She . . . Lady Crampton . . . she didn't live, my lord. She's dead."

A loud keening erupted from the large man. He turned an even brighter red than Charlotte thought possible and slammed his hands against the desktop, again and again. The servant backed from the room and disappeared, leaving her alone with her new employer.

Then the noise erupting from him became a guttural cry, something like a wounded animal would make. Lord Crampton's eyes bulged until she thought they would pop from his face. He clutched his chest, groaning loudly, and fell from his chair, hitting the floor with a loud thud.

Charlotte sprang toward him, rolling him so he faced up. His eyes stared straight ahead. She touched his throat and felt no pulse.

The Earl of Crampton was dead.

Chapter Four

Spain

GRAY ACCEPTED THE bundle of letters the corporal handed him and went about dispersing them to his fellow officers. Letters from home were the lifeblood to many, giving men renewed spirit to fight on. For two years after taking up his commission, Gray had never received one. It wasn't as if his brother would write to him, much less his sister-in-law. He had no other close relatives. He was fortunate to have been placed with both Burke and Reid and so he saw his best friends on a daily basis.

When the two finally learned that no one ever wrote him, though, they made sure that he received letters from England on a regular basis. His most frequent ones came from the Duke of Gilford, Reid's father, and Burke's mother, who constantly wrote to her brood of seven that had scattered across the land. Gray appreciate the small kindness his friends had been responsible for. It helped the loneliness that ate away at him. He didn't know what his state of mind might be like without having his close companions in his life. War, in all its brutality, was hard on a man's soul. Sometimes, Gray wondered if he had one left at all. He dreaded the day he would return to England—if this war ever ended—for he had no idea if he could ever live again in Polite Society.

He went about camp, distributing the large stack and bringing much joy, until he came to the final bit of parchment at the bottom of his pile. Surprise filled him when he saw his own name scrawled across the creamy paper, though it was addressed to Captain Danforth Grayson, not reflecting his recent promotion to major. The handwriting looked vaguely familiar but Gray had no idea who from home might be writing to him.

Returning to his officers' tent, he found it empty and sat upon his cot, breaking the seal and opening the letter. He glanced to the bottom before beginning to read it and saw it came from Mr. Bonham, the Grayson family solicitor who lived in Canterbury. He'd last communicated with the man when his final year of university tuition had come due. Mr. Bonham had made sure that the funds earmarked for Gray's education had been forthcoming from Seymour. He wondered what news the solicitor had and began to read the missive.

My dear Captain Grayson –

I hope this letter finds you in good health. Know that all of England counts upon men such as you to see Bonaparte squashed like the vile insect that he is. Your service is valued by your countrymen, including me.

I am sorry to be the bearer of terrible news regarding your family. Your sister-in-law, the Countess of Crampton, has passed away recently after giving birth to a stillborn son. Your brother, Lord Crampton, met the news of her death with such sadness that he, too, has left us.

Because of these unusual circumstances, I implore you to come home at once, not only to run the estate but to exercise your duties in regards to the children. Lord Crampton named you their guardian and they are in sore need of your presence at Gray Manor.

Your brother's will stipulated a generous, annual stipend to pay for your services to the estate if this day should ever come to pass. It is to be delivered every quarter to you. Monies have already been designated to run the household and country estates, as well as the London townhome, and those expenses are separate from what you will draw.

I know you have spent years in military service to your country, sir, but it is now time to return home and see to the duty of your family. Your nephew, now the Earl of Crampton, is but twelve years of age and so it will be some time before he reaches his majority and takes his seat in the House of Lords. The boy could certainly use your sage counsel and the estate, as well, needs a firm hand.

Send me word when you have arrived at Gray Manor and I will come to you as quickly as possible to discuss in detail the affairs of the family and your considerable responsibilities.

Your most humble servant,
Benjamin Bonham

Gray folded the letter, a myriad of emotions running through him. Shock at the deaths of both Seymour and his wife, along with their newborn. Anger at having to give up the only life he'd known as an adult, especially when Lieutenant-General Sir Arthur Wellesley was soon to arrive and a major campaign would be underway in Spain. How could he abandon his men and fellow officers at such a critical time?

If he were being honest, hatred also coursed through him, directed toward a brother who'd despised Gray the moment he appeared in the world. Their contempt for one another had only deepened after their father's death, as Seymour assumed the earldom. Gray recalled the last, bitter words the Earl of Crampton had spoken to him five years ago, expressing his hope that the enemy would kill Gray. He never forgave his brother for his callous comments.

And now, he was to become a father figure to the children of the very man he loathed with all his being.

Could he put aside the enmity that had existed between brothers and accept the responsibilities now thrust upon him?

Gray didn't know.

Oh, he would make sure the estate was being managed adequately. That its tenants were cared for properly. As for the children, he could hire the appropriate people to care for them, as well. He didn't know if he had it in him to be at Gray Manor with them, day after day, trying to be a parent to God only knew how many of Seymour's offspring. The last he knew, there'd been the oldest, Rodger, and two younger sisters, whose names he couldn't recall after so many years. The boy had so favored his father that it had been hard for Gray to look at the lad. Yet he remembered the eagerness of young Rodger and the frail child had wanted to get to know his uncle.

Would Seymour have tainted how his heir regarded his uncle? It wouldn't surprise Gray in the least if that's what had occurred.

He sighed, suddenly so weary that a fortnight of sleep wouldn't see him feel whole. He would do as asked. Sell out and leave the army. Return to England. He would go to Gray Manor and meet with Bonham to have a good idea what needed to be done regarding the estate. Make certain his nieces and nephews were surrounded by competent people who would manage them on a daily basis.

Then he'd go to London and reside in the city year-round. Gray Manor held too many memories for him. He didn't see a life there for himself, especially when Rodger would come of age and the estate would be his to do as he saw fit. It would be too painful to live at Gray Manor and run things in all but name, only to have to give it up several years down the line. This way, he could make a life for himself in London and only see his charges once a year. It was all he was willing to assume at this point after having lost too many men under his command. He didn't have anything to give and, in truth, would dodge this responsibility if he could.

He needed to find Reid and Burke.

Leaving his tent, he went to Lt. Colonel Baker's quarters. Reid could have gone by Medford since he was the Marquess of Medford, but his friend downplayed his noble connections. He entered and found Reid alone, pouring over a map on a large table.

"Strategizing? Hoping to impress Wellesley when he arrives?"

teased Gray.

"The future Duke of Wellington is an impressive man," Reid said. "England is lucky to have someone of his caliber coming to lead us in Spain." He withdrew a letter from his coat's pocket. "This is from him, the man himself. Read it."

Gray did and handed it back. "Wellesley makes several valid points."

"He does. And we'll be ready when he and his troops arrive."

"When who arrives?" Burke breezed in, his hair mussed. He raked his fingers through it to tame the wild locks.

"Wellesley," Reid said. "Where have you been?"

Burke grinned. "What if I told you scouting some of the enemy?"

"Bed sport with a foreign lass doesn't count for scouting," Gray observed dryly.

His friend's grin widened. "You never know, Gray. I say it's best to be prepared on all fronts."

He pulled the parchment from his coat. "I just received this." He handed it to Reid as Burke came around and leaned over his friend's shoulder. The two men read it at the same time. When they finished, both gazed at him with astonished looks.

"Obviously, I must resign my commission and take up the responsibilities for the Grayson family estate and whatever children there are. Three at the last count, before we left for war."

"At least the estate will pay you," Burke pointed out. "You'll be the Earl of Crampton in all but the title itself. Let that stick in Stinkin' Seymour's dead craw."

"I hate to abandon the two of you," Gray admitted. "Not to mention my men. I know what honor tells me I must do but returning to England and this situation is the last thing I would choose."

"Duty to family should always come first," Reid said firmly. "I would be gone from here the next day if I received word that my father had passed. These children need you, Gray. They've lost both parents in a very short amount of time. They will be hurting. They will look to you for comfort and continuity."

"What if I can't give it to them?" he challenged. "The oldest—the new earl—already favors Seymour so much. I fear it will be hard to look upon him and feel anything but enmity."

"He's not Stinkin' Seymour, Gray," Burke said. "No other bastard is and thank goodness for that. He's a little boy who needs to be taught how to be a good man." Burke placed his hand on Gray's shoulder. "I can think of no finer man to do so. Other than Reid, of course. We all know he's ten times the man we mortal men are."

The three laughed and then Gray said, "I will put in my papers today and leave in the morning for the coast. I'd prefer to participate in the upcoming battle but I suppose I can't afford to be killed now."

Burke chuckled. "That's the only thing good about being a third son. No duty or responsibilities to others. No need to wed. Don't worry, Gray. I'll fight for the both of us."

He nodded and exited the tent. Gray would be leaving the only life he'd known and the only family he had for the unknown.

GRAY GALLOPED ALONG the road on the rented horse and turned west, heading down the long drive that led to Gray Manor. It had taken him a week to reach Kent. He would send a letter to Mr. Bonham tomorrow, informing the solicitor of his arrival in England. He only hoped the man would come soon. He didn't know how comfortable he'd be staying at the estate.

He planned to ride the entire land tomorrow and take in the state of things in order to be better informed for when he met with Bonham. It would also to be prudent to meet with Masters, the Grayson butler. Servants knew everything that occurred in large houses and none more so than a butler or housekeeper. He didn't know who the current housekeeper might be but he had a deep trust in Masters and knew the retainer would be able to help Gray understand the situation.

Riding around the house, he went directly to the stables and was met by a groom he didn't recognize. Since he'd been gone from Gray Manor over a decade, that didn't surprise him.

"Can I help ye, sir?"

"I'm Major Grayson." He swung from the saddle.

The groom's eyes lit up. "Ah, yes, Major Grayson. Mr. Masters said ye'd be coming home. I'm Sable, the assistant head groom. May I take yer horse?"

"Yes, please." He handed the reins over. "I rented the mount in Dover and will need to see it returned." He mentioned the place where he'd gotten the horse.

"I'd be happy to take care of that, Major," said the groom. "I'm familiar with it since I grew up in Dover."

"Thank you, Sable."

Gray returned to the house, entering from the rear and cutting through the kitchens. No servants were in sight, which surprised him because the family dinner hour had yet to begin. Then he realized there was no family that would gather in the dining room with Seymour and his wife dead. Children would be fed in the schoolroom and put to bed. He paused and heard lively conversation coming from the servants' dining hall, along with the clink of forks against plates. Mrs. Rook, if she were still the family cook, must have moved up the time the servants ate. Not wanting to interrupt one of the few times they had a moment to themselves, Gray decided to head for the library. He wanted a good brandy and to sit for a moment and collect his thoughts before making his presence known.

He'd almost reached the library when a footman came into sight, a startled look on his face.

"It's all right," Gray said. "I'm Major Grayson. I'm expected."

Entering the library, he went straight to the crystal decanters and poured himself a drink. He sensed the footman's presence and turned around.

"You can let Mr. Masters know I'm here once the servants have finished their evening meal."

"Mr. Masters has been ill, sir. I'm Smith. I've been filling in for him."

"I see," he said, concern filling him. "It isn't anything too serious, I hope."

"Mr. Masters caught a nasty cold and then broke his arm. He's been laid up for two weeks. The doctor said he'll be fine. He's on the mend."

"I would like to see him first thing tomorrow," Gray said. "Would you send the housekeeper in once she's finished dinner?"

The footman shuffled uncomfortably. "We don't currently have a housekeeper. Mrs. Penney left a few weeks ago. Miss Nott is handling things now. Seeing to the running of the household and all."

"Why isn't there a housekeeper?" Gray demanded, worried with Masters down how the household was even functioning.

"She left," Smith said. "Abruptly. With Mr. March."

Frustrated, he asked, "And who is Mr. March?"

"The estate's manager. They left together. I'm mean *together*, if you understand. Mr. March found a new position in Cornwall and Mrs. Penney went with him straightaway." Smith drew a deep breath. "It's all right, though. Miss Nott is in charge of the estate."

Exasperated, he demanded, "Who the bloody hell is Miss Nott?"

"I am," a voice in the doorway said.

Gray turned and saw the most stunning woman he'd ever seen walking toward him.

"It's fine, Smith. I'll take it from here."

The footman looked at her in relief and hurried from the room.

Miss Nott—whoever she might be—came close to Gray. He was

two inches over six feet and she appeared about a foot less in height. She had a trim figure, with a good bosom and small waist, though the brown dress with cream cuffs looked hopelessly out of fashion. Dark brown hair was drawn away from the delicate bone structure of her face and fastened in some knot at the nape of her neck. She had high cheekbones and full, pink lips that were the most kissable he'd ever seen.

But it was her vibrant green eyes that stopped him in his tracks. They were vivid, bright as emeralds, and assessing him with a keen intelligence. He feared she would somehow find him lacking. The eyes stirred a memory somewhere deep within him, as if he'd met this woman before, but he couldn't think of any circumstances when that might have occurred.

Who could she be? With her regal bearing, she might be a duchess for all Gray knew. Was she some relative he hadn't known about, perhaps a cousin to his deceased sister-in-law who'd stepped in for a time to help out. Or—God forbid—Seymour's mistress who'd been set up somewhere in the house and now had taken it over upon her lover's death.

Finding his voice, he said, "I'll ask again. Who exactly *are* you, Miss Nott?"

CHAPTER FIVE

CHARLOTTE'S HEART BEAT rapidly as she studied the tall army officer. This was the man who'd been the boy she'd been acquainted with two decades ago. He was a few inches over six feet, with extremely broad shoulders and a narrow waist, accented by the uniform he wore. His dark hair gleamed with chestnut highlights and she knew it would be a deep, burnished red outdoors. High cheekbones that could cut glass gave way to a strong, steady jaw.

But it was his brilliant, blue eyes that gave her pause. They seemed to see right through her, down to the depths of her soul. His eyes also seemed haunted, as if he'd seen things he wished he could forget. She supposed the war had affected him greatly. He no longer looked like the boy she remembered, one who laughed easily. By the looks of him, this man hadn't laughed in years.

"We received word from Mr. Bonham, the family solicitor, notifying us that you would be arriving soon." She indicated a chair. "Won't you have a seat, Captain?"

"It's Major," he said abruptly. "Major Grayson. And shouldn't I be inviting you to sit?" He gazed at her steadily.

"I'm sorry if you believe I've overstepped my bounds," she apologized as she slipped into a chair.

He took one to her left, filling it with his large frame, his knees sticking out and almost grazing hers. He repeated, "Who are you, Miss Nott?"

Charlotte folded her hands and placed them in her lap. "I was hired by the earl as a governess to Lady Harriet and Lady Jane, as well as doing some tutoring of Viscount Warren, Rodger, the new earl."

"The boy's not at school then?"

"No, he's been much too ill to be away from home," she revealed.

"His asthma?"

She noted the worried look on his face. "Yes. You know about it?"

"I was made aware of it the last time I was home. Five years ago," he added just as she was about to ask. "He exhibited signs of it then. I felt sorry for the boy."

"His poor heath hasn't affected his mind. Far from it. He's one of the brightest lads I've ever been around. You must prepare yourself, though, for when you see him, Major. His health is quite fragile. The boy may never reach his majority."

Her words took him aback and she realized if Rodger died, this man would become the new earl.

He ran a hand through his hair, seemingly lost in thought for a moment, and then said, "The footman. Smith. He said something about you running the household. And he made a preposterous statement about you handling estate affairs, as well."

"Because I am," Charlotte said calmly.

"What?" he cried, disbelief written across his face.

"I arrived shortly after Mrs. Penney, the housekeeper, and Mr. March, the estate manager, vacated the premises. Without notice, I might add. They both abruptly quit and left for Cornwall, where Mr. March supposedly had gained a new position. Someone had to step in with the death of the earl and countess. It fell to me."

He rested his large hands atop his thighs and leaned forward. "To you. The governess. Running an earl's household and handling his entire estate."

Charlotte smiled. "A governess worth her salt can do anything she puts her mind to, Major."

"I don't see how a governess would know a thing about guiding a large household. It has nothing to do with how to comport oneself or how to read or do sums." His disdain for her was obvious.

She gazed at him a long moment, not wanting to explain how she'd run her father's household before she was ousted by her own blood kin. Her story was hers and she would keep it private.

Instead, she said, "I applied the lessons I learned and honed while I served as companion to the Dowager Duchess of Exbury, whose household I managed while in her employ. I know when silver needs to be polished and the best method to use to make the pieces gleam. I scheduled regular airings of mattresses and the cleaning of rugs. I planned menus and ordered food for the larders. I know when to rotate sheets and towels and how often to replace them. There's nothing I've left unattended during my time here, I can assure you, sir."

He looked taken aback by her description of various household duties.

"I also learned about farming and husbandry," she added, deciding to give him bare details. "I am knowledgeable enough regarding new techniques which I've read about in various tracts and would be happy to help you experiment with new breeding methods. I've also had time to meet with a majority of your tenants, as well as make observations regarding the books." Charlotte concluded with, "I will be happy to get you up to speed on the workings of the estate, Major, since it will be your task to oversee it."

Charlotte decided to keep quiet for now regarding her suspicions that Mr. March was bleeding funds from the estate. Major Grayson looked as if he already had enough to handle, based upon their conversation.

He shook his head. "You're no ordinary, run of the mill governess," he observed.

"No. I'm not," she agreed. "Tomorrow, once you've rested, we can go over estate matters and you can see the profit turned. I have a few ideas on how to make things more profitable. It would behoove you to hire a new manager, however, as well as a housekeeper. While I haven't minded stepping into these roles, there are only so many hours in a day. I don't wish to neglect my charges. They are the true reason I'm at Gray Manor."

She stood and he rose. "Shall I see a tray brought for you? And hot water sent to your rooms? I'm sure after living on the battlefields for so long that a hot bath would be something you might desire."

Charlotte suddenly saw the man peeling away the layers of clothing he wore and sinking into a tub. She felt a blush rise on her cheeks and dug her fingernails into her palms, trying to distract herself from such wicked thoughts, ones that had never occurred to her before.

"Yes. A bath and meal would be much desired."

"Knowing you were coming, I've had the earl's suite of rooms prepared for you."

Major Grayson frowned. "That's unnecessary. Besides, shouldn't my nephew take those rooms?"

"I have spoken with Lord Crampton regarding that and he wishes to remain where he is for now. I think he finds it comforting to have his own things about him and not reside in the chambers where his father did. We discussed it and with you gaining guardianship over the children, Lord Crampton thought those rooms would be more appropriate for you."

"I see," he said gruffly, and she wondered how close he'd been with his brother.

"I'm sure you know your way to your new rooms, sir. I'll have a meal and hot water sent up to you directly."

"Perhaps we can breakfast together tomorrow and you can begin filling me in on the state of affairs."

"No, I'm afraid that's not possible. I breakfast with the two young ladies each morning," she explained. "It's important that we keep to our routine." Charlotte hesitated. "They are . . . high-spirited children and have needed a steady hand these past few weeks. Especially with the death of the parents."

"How long have you been employed here, Miss Nott?" he asked suddenly.

She'd dreaded this question. "I came to work the day the earl and countess passed. I have been here close to three weeks."

She knew the information startled him and he tried to compose his handsome features.

"I see. Well, plan to meet with me before you dine with my nieces. I hope you're not opposed to rising at such an early time."

"Not at all, Major. I prefer an early start to my day."

"Then meet me at six-thirty in the small breakfast room," he ordered.

"Very well. I'll see to your tray and bath now."

Charlotte left the library, wondering if Major Grayson would keep her on.

Or not.

GRAY FINISHED THE food that had been brought to him. The leg of mutton was seasoned perfectly. The fresh bread and round of cheese were a welcomed accompaniment. Food in the army had been tasteless. He'd tried whenever he had a chance to find some local who would sell him something—anything—so he wouldn't constantly be thinking of filling his belly. Guilt flared within him, knowing he'd left his men behind to fend for themselves. He only hoped they would find a better commanding officer than he'd been. Though he'd had huge successes, it was the few failures that stood out in his mind.

And his nightmares.

Servants now came carrying a myriad of buckets. He'd almost

hoped the beautiful Miss Nott might supervise them but she was nowhere in sight. The outspoken governess intrigued him. When he thought of a governess, he pictured a colorless little mouse, one who floated on the edges of a family's life and never had much to say.

Miss Nott was far from that.

Once again, he thought of her tremendous beauty. The flawless skin. The perfectly-shaped oval of her face. The green eyes and full lips that dominated her face. The rich, shimmering hair that he would love to pull from its restraints. She'd only mentioned his nephew and the two girls, which led Gray to believe those were the only children.

"Your bath is ready, Major Grayson."

He looked up and saw all but one servant gone.

"I'm Parker, sir. I'll serve as your valet, as I did to Lord Crampton."

"I don't need a valet," he grumbled. "I'm perfectly capable of bathing and dressing myself. You'll have to find something else to do other than coddle me."

Hurt filled the man's eyes. "I see. Well, then I'll leave you to it." He turned and exited the room.

Gray stripped off his uniform, thinking he would need to purchase civilian clothes soon. He'd outgrown whatever he'd had from before his army days, the military training and subsequent fighting helping to fill out his frame with muscles he hadn't known existed. Sinking into the hot water, he eased himself down and rested his head on the edge of the tub. To be fully immersed in piping hot water was a luxury that he enjoyed for several minutes before taking up the bar of soap. He began scrubbing himself, the scent of sandalwood drifting over him.

After he'd washed his hair and body, he used two of the buckets sitting by the tub to rinse himself. Toweling off, he opened his satchel and removed its only contents, a second uniform, and placed it on. He'd need to see if Parker would brush the one he'd worn earlier.

Though he longed to fall into bed, curiosity led Gray to leave the earl's rooms and mount the staircase. He went to Masters' room and rapped with his knuckles on the door. Hearing the butler call for him to enter, he did so.

Masters sat in bed, a thick book across his lap. One arm bore a good-sized plaster from the wrist to the elbow. "Good evening, Major Grayson. Miss Nott informed me of your arrival. I hope everything is to your liking."

"It is." He indicated the lone chair in the room. "May I?"

"Certainly, sir."

Gray brought the chair next to the bed and sat. "I hear you've been under the weather."

The butler cleared his throat. "Yes, I have been. A nasty head cold that made me long to find a rifle and blow my head off. Not to mention this." He glanced down at the plaster.

"How did you break your arm?"

"It's of no consequence, Major. I should be up in the next day or two, back at my duties. Thank goodness Miss Nott arrived when she did. Mr. March's and Mrs. Penney's departure left us in a terrible bind. If not for Miss Nott, Gray Manor would have fallen apart."

"Tell me about her," he urged.

Masters frowned. "What do you wish to know? Miss Nott is incredibly efficient. No time is wasted under her watch and no task is left undone."

"Anything personal about her. Anything at all."

"She came from London. I believe Lord Crampton used The Plummer Employment Agency. Miss Nott has been both a companion and governess, though her references only made mention of the former. Her credentials satisfied Lord Crampton and he hired her on the spot. A good thing he did, with everything that followed."

Gray wondered why a governess would not have any governessing on her record and thought to ask her when they met in the morning.

"She was with the earl when he passed," Masters continued. "They had just concluded their interview and Lord Crampton had offered

Miss Nott the position when he received word of Lady Crampton's and the child's deaths."

"The babe was stillborn?"

"Aye, just like two others before. Lord Crampton was most anxious for another boy and so Lady Crampton became with child almost every year after the new earl's birth. With the boy in precarious health, your brother was eager to have a spare beyond his heir."

"It's just the boy and two girls?" Gray asked.

"Yes. No other children survived. Lady Crampton was practically bedridden the past few years, what with the attempts to bear another son failing time after time." Masters paused. "Because of that, things weren't always run well. I've done my best but Mrs. Penney let several things slide without the hand of the countess guiding her."

"And Miss Nott has stepped into the housekeeper's role, I'm led to believe?"

The butler nodded. "She has. Admirably, I might add. It was as if she were born to run a large household. And Mr. March left things in a muddle, as well. Lord Crampton depended upon Mr. March and I'm afraid the man neglected many of his duties. You'll have your work cut out for you, Major, bringing things up to snuff. Miss Nott will help you, though."

Gray was tired of the butler singing the woman's praises but held his tongue. "Is there anything else I need to know about, Masters, regarding the family or estate?"

"Not anything that Miss Nott—or Mr. Bonham—won't be able to tell you."

"I've never heard you quite so effusive, Masters."

The servant smiled. "Miss Nott has made a world of difference. The young ladies are almost . . . well . . . she has worked wonders with them."

"You've never been one to be cryptic before, Masters. What are my nieces like?"

The butler hesitated. "Quite . . . spirited. At least Lady Harriet is. Lady Jane is quieter and goes along with whatever her sister wishes."

Gray believed Masters wanted to call them brats but was too cautious to do so. It didn't matter. If the wonderful Miss Nott could do all the things Masters laid at her feet, surely educating two spoiled girls wouldn't be beyond her talents.

"What of my nephew? I hear he's home from Eton."

"Yes. School proved too much for Lord Crampton's health. Right now, Miss Nott is serving as his tutor but I'm sure you'll want to hire someone for him."

Gray rose. "I'll meet with the three children tomorrow. Thank you for seeing me, Masters."

The older man smiled. "It's a pleasure to have you at Gray Manor once again."

He replaced the chair and left the room, returning to those of the earl. He opened the wardrobe and found it empty, as was every drawer in the bureau. The ever-efficient Miss Nott must have removed all of his brother's items in anticipation of Gray's arrival. He'd hoped something of Seymour's clothes might have been left but no trace remained of the former Earl of Crampton.

The bedding had been turned back and Gray removed his clothing, placing it neatly over a chair. He preferred sleeping with nothing on, a luxury the army hadn't allowed. He'd had to remain prepared for attack at any moment. To slide between the soft, cool sheets and place his head on the plump pillow let him know for certain that he'd left his military days far behind.

If only he could leave the guilt for all the deaths he'd caused in the past, as well.

Chapter Six

CHARLOTTE DRESSED WITH care early the next morning, knowing she would start her day by seeing Major Grayson. She wanted him to take her seriously, which she knew would be hard. He seemed a traditional man in every sense of the word and she knew, though he would be respectful of women, he would be of a mind that they could do little on their own.

She was ready to prove him wrong.

Part of it was the challenge of showing him that women weren't emptyheaded pieces of fluff which she supposed in his world, many of them were. She'd never made it to London for her come-out Season but after having met some of the *ton* through her various positions, she could see where gentlemen might get that idea. Despite Bernice having a sharp mind, the other women in the households Charlotte had held a position in seemed happy to speak of nothing of consequence. A discussion on the most appropriate fichu was about as involved as they became on expressing an opinion regarding anything.

Not only did Charlotte want to show the military officer she used her brain as much as any man did, but she found herself attracted to him and wanted to prove herself worthy in his eyes. As if a man of the *ton* would even bother to look at someone in her lowly position. She knew it was foolish but everything about the man appealed to her. He was as different from his brother as the sun from the moon. She'd never been around an abundance of men and after her experience in her last two households, she'd never wanted to be around them again.

Until now.

She wondered what Major Grayson would think of her if he knew they'd once been childhood acquaintances from families of equal rank. She'd only seen him two or three times over two decades ago and knew he'd never recall her as she did him. Still, she knew who he was. He'd left a lasting impression on her back then and was equally impressive today in his officer's uniform and ramrod posture.

Charlotte smoothed her gown and left the bedchamber for her meeting with the major. She'd been in the room before, using it to supervise the polishing of the silver, which had been badly in need of attention. All of Gray Manor needed work and she hoped Mr. Bonham would free up the funds so that Major Grayson could see the home properly restored. She'd written the solicitor last night and went first to the stables. Finding Sable, the groom she considered most trustworthy, she entrusted him with the message, telling him it was to be delivered at once.

Entering the breakfast room, she saw her new employer already there, sipping on coffee, his plate already scraped clean. No footmen were present.

"Good morning, Major Grayson," she said pleasantly.

"Ah, good morning, Miss Nott. Please, have a seat. Would you like tea or coffee?"

She hesitated a moment and then said, "Tea would be nice. Is this the pot?"

"Yes."

Charlotte took it and poured some tea into an empty cup. She took a sip of the hot brew, letting it flood her with warmth.

"No sugar? Or cream?" he asked.

"No, thank you. I'm a purist when it comes to tea." She chuckled. "Coffee, on the other hand, needs all the help it can get to be bearable. I'm afraid if you saw me prepare a cup of coffee for myself, you'd ask if

I were having any coffee in my cream and sugar."

He looked at her for a moment and then burst out laughing. His laugh was deep and sinfully rich, the same as his speaking voice. She busied herself with another swallow of tea, hoping he wouldn't notice the heat she sensed flooding her cheeks.

"Tell me what I need to know before I write to Mr. Bonham," he said.

"No need to do that. I wrote to Mr. Bonham last night and sent a groom with the message this morning. I would expect Mr. Bonham will arrive sometime this afternoon. He is most eager to meet with you and discuss the property."

"Ever efficient, Miss Nott," he said with grudging admiration.

"I pride myself on being organized," she said. "As to what you need to know, I'd be happy to give you a tour of the house this morning and show you what needs to be done inside and out. It seems Lady Crampton was in poor health the past several years and the former Lord Crampton didn't care for household details in any sense. There are numerous repairs that need to be made. Items which should be purchased. I've already prepared a list for you."

Those blue eyes gleamed at her. "Of course, you have."

She ignored him. "As to the estate, I think you should see it firsthand before you consider looking at the books."

"And have you composed a list regarding this, as well?"

Primly, she said, "As a matter of fact, I have. Numerous cottages need new roofs. Fences should be mended. The crop yield has gone down thrice in the past five years. You should consider replacing some of the livestock. And then . . . there are the ledgers. Mr. March left the finances in a frightful mess. I'm very good with numbers, sir, and even these gave me pause."

He smiled. "Fortunately, I enjoy numbers a great deal. I used to tutor in mathematics during my university days, as well as serving as quartermaster for part of my military career. Do you ride, Miss Nott?"

"I do."

"Then perhaps you would accompany me about the estate and point out the things on your list."

"As long as it doesn't conflict with my duties to the children, Major."

He frowned. "I'm no longer a major. I sold out to come back to Gray Manor."

"Many military men retain their rank once they've returned to civilian life."

"I don't want to be reminded of the army," he said abruptly.

"Then perhaps you should think of investing in a new wardrobe, sir. Everyone who sees you will naturally revert to your rank when they address you."

"I thought of that last night. I noticed nothing of my brother's remained in his rooms that I might be able to use."

Charlotte had to bite back a smile. "If you were thinking you might wear something from your brother's wardrobe, I beg you to reconsider. It would take at least two of you to fill one of his coats. Perhaps two and a half."

"Seymour was rather large the last time I saw him five years ago."

"Was that before you left for the war?" she asked, her curiosity getting the better of her.

"I graduated from university and came home a final time before I left for the Continent." He paused and abruptly switched topics. "Tell me about the children. There were three when I was last here and it seems none have been added to the family during my absence."

She thought that statement odd. Wouldn't his brother have written him about affairs at home? From what Charlotte understood, Lady Crampton had several miscarriages and other stillborn children in the last few years.

"Yes, there are three. Viscount Warren—I'm sorry, Lord Crampton—is a very bright lad of twelve. He enjoys history and has a solid understanding of Latin and Greek. He is very advanced in mathematics. Taking after his uncle, perhaps?"

When Grayson said nothing, she continued. "He reads quite a bit. Any physical activity is beyond him at the moment. He's a sweet boy but a bit lonely. I gather he didn't make many friends at school. I have given him reading assignments and we've discussed those, as well as articles from various newspapers. I have him translating *The Iliad* now."

He steepled his fingers. "And the girls?"

Charlotte sighed, wanting to be diplomatic and not frighten him. "They are . . . an unusual pair. Lady Jane is quite solemn and wants to please those around her. She has a tendency to cry over small things. She idolizes her older sister and tends to allow Lady Harriet to talk her into unwise actions at times."

"You're saying Harriet deliberately misbehaves?"

"Not in so many words, though she doesn't always walk the straight and narrow. Lady Harriet is very lively. And very angry."

His features grew puzzled. "Why so?"

"From what I gather, she and Lady Jane never received much attention from either parent. It seems her mother was too ill and her father found girls, in general, a nuisance. In seeking attention, Lady Harriet believes outrageous behavior gains it. Hence, she has a tendency to do some fairly outrageous things."

Charlotte met the major's gaze. "She feels rejected, sir. She is a very bright little girl who needs love. I'm hoping you'll be able to give her love and attention in equal doses."

His face grew stony. "I doubt I'll spend much time with any of the children. That's what you've been hired to do, Miss Nott. It's your job to care for them and give them this attention you say they require."

"Are you serious?" she said, not bothering to hide her outrage at his words, knowing she should watch her own, though she appeared unable to do so. "You have three children—orphans—who need you, sir. Yes, they've had clothes on their backs and a good roof over their heads. They have adequate food in their bellies. But they are very lonely. They need you, their blood relative and guardian, to show an interest in them. I can teach them, Major Grayson, but you are the one who needs to love them."

It was as if a curtain fell over him. Charlotte could see him stiffening. Withdrawing. Her hopes for the trio having their uncle spend meaningful time with them faded and she stood.

"You haven't been dismissed, Miss Nott," he said, his gaze direct. "Sit," he commanded.

She slowly lowered herself to the seat, knowing she had gone too far—and that it might cost her this position. She couldn't afford to be sacked. She was a woman with very little to her name.

And nowhere to go if Major Grayson dismissed her.

"If you are to remain in my employment, you will practice decorum, Miss Nott," he said sternly. "While I admire your passion for your charges, you have overstepped with your too candid remarks. I am the guardian and employer here. I will make the decisions without your unsolicited advice. Is that understood?"

Her face flamed in embarrassment. "Yes, Major Grayson, I understand. Forgive me for my inappropriate remarks."

He nodded curtly. "That will be all."

"I must go to breakfast with the young ladies," she said formally, rising again. "Establishing a routine in their lives is very important now, especially since they have so recently lost *both* parents." She regretted the words the minute they left her mouth and waited for him to dismiss her on the spot.

Instead, he asked, When will you go over your massive lists with me, Miss Nott?" She heard the condemnation of her in his voice.

She regarded him coldly. "I assume you read, Major, so I will have them brought to you. You may see for yourself what needs to be accomplished. And since you're so talented with numbers, you may read through the ledgers yourself. As for the estate, I'm sure you're familiar with it and can ride it on your own. Good day, sir."

With that, Charlotte wheeled and left the breakfast room. Anger sizzled through her. She'd wanted this man to be the one to show the children their worth. Instead, he would have even less to do with them than their own parents had. Determination filled her. She would not see her charges ignored. She would redouble her efforts and give them everything she had.

She only hoped it would be enough.

CHAPTER SEVEN

GRAY COULDN'T BELIEVE the audacity of the woman. She'd dressed him down as if he were some naughty boy whose hand was caught in the cookie jar. The nerve of someone of her class addressing him in such a manner flew all over him. Who was she to tell him he needed to love total strangers? She should keep her opinions to herself. Already, she'd proved to be dictatorial, involving herself in everything at Gray Manor. Her sheer arrogance unnerved him.

And despite all of that, he wanted to kiss her senseless.

The color had risen in her cheeks as she'd berated him, making her even more attractive—which Gray hadn't thought possible. It had taken everything in his power to keep from leaping from his chair and silencing her, his mouth on hers. Even now, the thought of that caused desire to shoot through him.

He rose, placing his napkin on the table. He wasn't about to let some bossy little no one tell him how to manage his own life. He knew what his brother's will stipulated. He would see his nephew and nieces had the proper care. That Gray Manor and Seymour's other estates were managed properly. Then he would leave and visit once a year. Miss Nott could send him a monthly report regarding the children's progress.

"Love them," he murmured and snorted. Gray didn't love anyone. Well, perhaps Reid and Burke. They were more family to him than his own brother had been. He'd foolishly loved his men once, at the beginning of the war, and then discovered it too painful as more and more of them died in action. He came undone every time he had to write a letter home to the family of a fallen soldier. For his own sanity, he'd divorced himself from feeling anything for anyone other than duty and responsibility to the soldiers placed in his care. Even then, his disappointments and poor decisions which got too many of them killed haunted him. He'd resolved to care for no one, least of all three brats with whom he felt no connection.

Gray left the breakfast room, determined to meet his unruly nieces and speak to the new Lord Crampton before Mr. Bonham arrived. Once he got this over with, he doubted he would need to see them again before he left for town.

He assumed the girls and the tyrannical Miss Nott breakfasted in the schoolroom. He always had at a young age. Gray made his way up the flights of stairs, nodding at a few passing maids who looked at him nervously. Perhaps he should gather the servants and guarantee them they all would maintain their positions. Unless some of them were as careless in their work as the former housekeeper and estate manager had been. Drat, he'd probably need to speak to Miss Nott about the work ethic of the servants in the house and those who worked in the stables and on the estate. The thought of that conversation rankled him, having to depend upon the woman, but knowing her knowledge would streamline matters.

He reached the schoolroom and paused outside the open door. Though he believed eavesdropping beneath him, for a moment, he wanted to see the lay of the land before he stormed inside.

"Do you think our uncle will like us?" a soft voice asked, uncertainty obvious.

"Of course Major Grayson will like you," Miss Nott reassured her charge. "Both of you are exceptional young ladies, intelligent and kind. What's not to like about you?"

"Jane's kind. I'm usually not," another girl said, her tone harsh and full of stubbornness.

"You are kind when you wish to be, Lady Harriet," Miss Nott said. "You should choose to be so more often. It's important to make a good first impression on your uncle. First impressions can be lasting ones."

"What will we call him?" Jane said.

"I suppose Uncle. I don't know his Christian name. I'm sure when you meet him later today, he'll tell you how you should refer to him."

"He came from the war. I'll bet he's killed all kinds of people," Harriet said gleefully. "I'll ask him about it."

"You'll do no such thing," Miss Nott admonished. "War is an ugly thing, Lady Harriet. Major Grayson will not want to be reminded of it. Yes, he most likely has killed in the name of king and country, but it would be impolite to discuss it with him."

"I don't think he'll like me," Harriet proclaimed. "No one does."

"That's because you make a point of deliberately misbehaving. And since I've come, I believe you've conducted yourself in a much better manner. After all, you were sorry for Mr. Masters' injury. That counts for something."

Her words took Gray aback. Harriet had something to do with Masters' broken arm? No wonder the butler had brushed the matter aside.

"He'll like Jane. She's sweet. Unless she's doing what I tell her to do."

He heard sniffling and Miss Nott said, "No need to cry, Lady Jane. We've talked about this."

"What if Uncle doesn't like me?"

"Well, he's never met you. He'll have no opinion formed of you beforehand. Both of you must do your best to be your best. It's something you should always strive for," Miss Nott said. "You can start, Lady Jane, by being responsible for your own actions. You are old enough now to know right from wrong. The next time your sister wants you to do something you're uncomfortable with—something you know is wrong—simply tell her no."

"I can do that?" Jane said, wonder in her voice.

"Of course, you can," Miss Nott insisted. "We are all responsible for our own actions. Just because Lady Harriet tells you to do something doesn't mean you must blindly follow her and do her bidding."

"But I'm older than Jane," Harriet insisted. "She should follow my example."

"Only if it's a good one, my lady. Besides, I have a feeling your days of unruly behavior are coming to an end. You are a strong little girl, Lady Harriet. I don't just mean your physical strength. You need to act as a leader and as an older sister should by being a good example to Lady Jane. I'm sure your uncle will be pleased and proud of you, once he gets to know you."

"You won't tell him how awful I've been?" Worry echoed in Harriet's words, touching Gray.

"Why should I? Major Grayson should get to know you himself. From this moment on, Lady Harriet, you and Lady Jane will conduct yourself as members of the Grayson family should. Be kind and courteous to all."

"Even to servants?" Harriet asked, clearly perplexed by that notion.

"*Especially* servants, for they wait on you and do things for you that you don't even think about."

"Like what?" Jane asked.

"First, you're wearing clean clothes today. Not only did someone make those clothes for you, but they washed and ironed them. Washing is a long, dreary business. Clothes don't magically appear in a wardrobe. The same with your clean linens and towels. And your baths. Think of how long it takes for the servants to heat the water and haul it upstairs."

"That's a lot of work," Jane pointed out and Gray found himself smiling.

"It is. That's why you should be nice to your servants. They devote their lives to caring for you. And you should be kind to everyone around you, not just your friends and family."

Jane started sniffling again and Miss Nott asked, "What's wrong, love?"

"I like Rodger. I do. But Mama and Papa weren't nice to us at all." She began crying and Gray sensed movement in the room. He supposed Miss Nott moved to comfort the girl.

"Jane's right," Harriet said. "Neither Mama nor Papa were nice to us. They didn't care about us at all. I heard Papa say girls were useless things and he'd wished we'd never been born."

Gray winced hearing the vile words, knowing it was exactly the kind of thing Seymour would voice. The fact Harriet had overheard it cut him deeply.

"Papa didn't really like Rodger much either because he's sick all the time," Harriet continued.

"Not everyone has loving parents," the governess said softly.

"Did you, Miss Nott? Did your parents love you?"

"I suppose Mama did. She died when I was very young. I have an impression of sitting in her lap as she rocked me and sang to me."

"Oh, that's why you sing so well, Miss," Harriet said. "You got it from your mama. Are we going to keep singing?"

"Yes, my lady. Now that your uncle is here, he will assume the bulk of responsibilities and hire the appropriate people. It will give us more time for all of our lessons, including singing and music ones."

"And riding?" Jane piped in. "You promised we could learn how to ride."

"Definitely riding. It's an important accomplishment for a lady."

"I don't know if I'll ever learn to sing or play the pianoforte well," Harriet complained.

"A lot of practice is involved. You'll need to exercise patience. The same with riding. You won't become an expert immediately but after time spent in the saddle, you'll feel more comfortable."

"What about your papa, Miss Nott?" Jane asked. "Did he love you?"

Gray leaned closer, curious as to the governess' answer.

"Oh, Papa loved me a great deal. I believe he tried to make up for me having only one parent. We spent a great deal of time together and he taught me many things. He is the best man I will ever know. I miss him every single day."

"Do you miss being away from him—or did he die like Mama and Papa?" Harriet asked.

"He passed away some eight years ago, when I was barely eighteen."

"What about your brothers and sisters?" Jane demanded. "Did he love them, too?"

"I only have a half-brother."

"Half?" Harriet cried. "How can a person be a half-person?"

Miss Nott laughed, a throaty laugh that caused Gray to want to see her but he remained just out of view so he could learn more of her past.

"No, silly. My papa was married to a lady who gave birth to my brother. She died several years later and Papa remarried. That lady was my mama. That is why we are half-siblings because we come from different mothers."

"Do you miss your half-brother?" Jane asked.

Silence filled the room and Gray waited for her reply.

"No. He never liked me, much less loved me."

"Why not, Miss Nott?" Harriet demanded. "Everyone at Gray Manor loves you."

"Not everyone. My half-brother . . . well, he was unhappy when Papa married again. And he grew even more unhappy when I came along."

"Was he mean to you, Miss Nott?" Harriet asked fiercely. "If so, I shall find him and box his ears."

The governess laughed merrily. "And I would pay a ha'penny to see that. Yes, he was a bit mean. It doesn't matter, girls. I doubt I'll ever see him again."

Gray would like to do more than box the man's ears. He heard in Miss Nott's voice more than she was revealing to his nieces. The hurt was obvious. She had no one in the world, other than her charges—and it was obvious she cared about them a great deal.

"Come, we've spent far too long on breakfast. Let's set the dishes aside and begin our work."

"And then go see our new uncle?" Jane asked hopefully.

With that, Gray stepped into the room. He hadn't tried to picture the girls as they spoke but it was clear from the moment he saw them that they were Graysons. Both had the startling blue eyes and chestnut hair that were a family trait.

"Good morning," he said genially. "I thought I would come to the nursery and meet my nieces."

"Schoolroom," Harriet corrected. "We are beyond the nursery."

Miss Nott shot her a warning glance and Harriet smiled prettily. "What are we to call you? Miss Nott has said you are Major Grayson."

"I'm no longer a military officer. I am plain Mr. Grayson." He smiled at the girl, who gazed at him inquisitively. "You shall call me Uncle Gray."

"Is your name Gray Grayson?" Jane asked timidly.

Gray pulled out a chair and sat, most of him spilling out of it since it was built for children. He lifted Jane into his lap. "My given name is Danforth Grayson but my friends have always called me Gray."

Jane smiled up at him shyly. He could see the girl had a sweet disposition and wouldn't be half the challenge her sister was.

"I like it," she said. "Uncle Gray."

He turned to Harriet. "Will Uncle Gray do for you, as well, Harriet?"

"You know my name?"

"I do. Rodger told me."

"You've already been to see Rodger—before us?" Harriet asked, a bit put out.

"No, meeting the two of you was my first priority. Rodger told me he had two sisters when I last visited Gray Manor. I was off to the war and came home to say goodbye after university. Rodger was quite proud of being a big brother and told me you, Harriet, were three and that Jane had just had her first birthday."

"Why have you been gone so long?" Harriet demanded. "Didn't you want to see us?"

"Because I've been fighting for England, Niece. Bonaparte doesn't take time off from battle and neither could I."

"Have you seen Bonaparte?" Harriet asked, her eyes round with wonder. "Is he the monster everyone says he is?"

"I have not seen him in person and, yes, I believe anyone who wants to take over all of Europe and have us bend our knee to him is a monster."

"Will he win?" Jane asked, her voice small.

"No," he reassured the girl. "It will take time because France has thousands of soldiers and a good stockpile of weapons, but I do believe that Bonaparte will be defeated someday."

"Do you miss the war?" Harriet asked, her eyes cutting to her governess and back to him as she skated along the edge of polite conversation.

"I miss the friends I left behind," he admitted. "My closest friends, who are like brothers to me, are still in Spain. We've been friends since we were all seven years old and met at school that first day."

"That's a long time to be friends," Harriet pointed out. "You must be old." She caught herself and said, "But not as old as Papa. He had gray hair and was very fat and old."

"I am sixteen years your father's junior. That makes me twenty-seven."

"That's more than twenty years older than me," Jane said. Then she looked at Miss Nott. "How old are you, Miss Nott?"

Gray leaned down and whispered, "Never ask a lady her age, Jane. It's not done."

"Why not?"

"Because most women like to keep certain things private," Miss Nott responded. "However, I will tell you that I am six and twenty." She looked at Gray. "Would you like to have the girls read to you, Mr. Grayson?"

He noticed she now referred to him without his title. "Yes, Miss Nott, I would enjoy hearing them read and seeing how advanced they are."

"Miss Nott says we're very smart," Harriet confided to him. "We're learning Latin, like Rodger. And geography and history."

"And Miss Nott is teaching us pianoforte," Jane said eagerly. "And to sing."

"What about riding?" he asked, remembering they seemed eager to do so.

"That, too," Jane said, nodding her head. "Papa didn't have time to teach us and none of our governesses wanted to try." She whispered, "I don't even think they knew how to ride."

"Oh, I'm sure they did," Harriet said airily. "But Miss Nott is very patient. She will be able to teach us when no others could."

"So, you like Miss Nott as your governess?" he asked. "The reason is, I must decide what is best for the three of you since your father appointed me your guardian."

"Oh, we love Miss Nott," Harriet assured him matter-of-factly. "You must keep her on. She already knows everything about Gray Manor."

"I see," he said solemnly. "Well, let's hear how well you read and what else your governess has been teaching you."

He spent another half-hour in the schoolroom as the girls showed off their knowledge. They were both bright and eager to please him. If he hadn't known Harriet was a problem child, he never would have guessed it.

"I think we've taken up enough of Mr. Grayson's time. It's only his first day here and he has to see to estate business, my ladies."

"Will you come back?" Jane asked, and he saw the hesitation in her eyes, knowing she believed he wouldn't.

Something pulled hard on his heartstrings and he found himself saying, "Yes, Jane. I will certainly want to see your progress. I must go visit with your brother for a while now. We don't want to leave him out."

"Rodger's very sick," Jane said, her eyes misting over.

"I'll see he gets the very best care. Even if I must send to London for a physician, we'll do our utmost to see him well."

"You're nice, Uncle Gray," Jane said solemnly. She looked to her sister. "I think he likes us," she whispered, as if Gray couldn't hear what she said.

He saw the smile tugging at Miss Nott's lips as she turned away and busied herself with stacking books on the table.

"Miss Nott, would you be able to give the girls an assignment and accompany me to see Lord Crampton? I'd like to hear about the progress he's made with his studies."

She hesitated a moment and Harriet said, "It's all right, Miss Nott. We will be perfect angels. We can work on our drawings."

"That's a very good idea, Lady Harriet." She looked to Gray. "Your niece is a very talented artist. At some point, she will require a drawing master. It won't take long for me to teach her all I know regarding art."

"I'll certainly consider it." Gray rose, glad to stand after sitting in the cramped little chair for so long. "Girls, I will see you later."

"Maybe you can help us with our riding lesson," Harriet prompted, shooting her governess a pleading look.

"We'll see," he said and held a hand out toward the door. "After you, Miss Nott."

"Thank you." She swept past him and into the corridor.

Chapter Eight

Charlotte wondered who the man was that accompanied her to young Lord Crampton's room. Not an hour earlier, he'd expressed no interest in the children after she'd begged him to lavish love and attention upon them. Yet he turned up only minutes later and charmed both his nieces with a smile that tugged at her heart. After a rough start, Harriet had proven to be on her best behavior, while Jane had taken to her uncle from the start. Knowing he still had so much to read through and prepare before Mr. Bonham arrived, the man still insisted on going to see his nephew now.

She hadn't been around many men in her life but Charlotte decided she might never understand the ones she encountered. Especially Mr. Grayson.

"Is Rodger in his room this time of day?" her new employer asked.

"He's there every day, Mr. Grayson," she replied evenly, trying to fight all the wild emotions running through her and calm herself. "He is as close to bedridden as one can be. I've insisted he get up and walk about the room twice a day with my help, just to keep his limbs working. Mr. Parker, who served as the former earl's valet, also helps the young earl to bathe and dress daily. I feel it's important that he gets up and tries to have some semblance of a normal life, even if he remains in his room."

"You make it sound dire."

"His health is most fragile. I warned you that unless great improvement is seen, Lord Crampton may not reach his next birthday, much less his majority."

"What doctors have seen him?" he asked as she paused in front of the boy's room.

"Only the local village doctor, to my knowledge. And one at Eton, who insisted the lad return home. You mentioned bringing in someone from London. I feel that's a splendid idea." She paused. "Shall we?"

"Be my guest."

Charlotte knocked and entered without waiting for an invitation. She'd learned the boy's voice sometimes was quite hoarse and he had trouble speaking. As she'd established once she came to Gray Manor, an older woman sat in a chair near the boy to keep watch over him.

Lord Crampton's eyes lit up and he gave a feeble smile to his guests. "You're . . . my uncle," he said, placing a palm over his chest as he grimaced.

"I am," the older man said. "How are you, my lord?"

The boy coughed and then took a few, quick breaths.

"Careful, my lord," warned Charlotte as Mrs. Minter rose and came to stand on the other side of the bed. "Breathe slowly and steadily as we discussed."

"Your chest hurting you, my lord?" the servant asked softly.

"A little," the boy admitted.

"Lean back against your pillows. I'll fetch you some nice broth." Mrs. Minter excused herself, leaving Charlotte and Mr. Grayson alone with the boy.

"I'm very sorry to learn about your parents' deaths," Grayson said.

"Miss Nott says . . . they are in a better place." He looked to the governess. "I was . . . able . . . to get another passage . . . done." A smile lit his face.

"That's excellent, your lordship," she praised. Turning to the boy's uncle, she said, "Lord Crampton has an excellent command of Latin and Greek."

"Is that so?" He took the boy's hand. "I enjoyed languages myself but preferred mathematics over all else."

Lord Crampton frowned. "I like . . . history. The stories. Miss Nott . . . knows . . . many stories of . . . famous people." He began coughing again and she placed her hand against his forehead.

"No fever. That's good. You've spoken enough, my lord. Perhaps your uncle might do the talking for the both of you. He could tell you about his life in the military."

The lad nodded. "I remember you came. Here. And left."

Charlotte retreated to the chair and watched Mr. Grayson sit on the edge of the bed. His hand still held the boy's, giving her a good feeling. Maybe he'd spoken rashly before, not having any children of his own. She hoped that to be the case and that he would continue to show interest in the trio.

They spent a quarter hour together as the older man told of training mishaps as he readied himself to go off to war. The boy smiled the entire time his uncle spoke.

Mrs. Minter returned with a steaming bowl of broth and Charlotte said, "We should wrap up this visit."

"Will you come back?" the boy asked, sadness in his eyes. "I . . . don't see many . . . people."

"Of course, your Uncle Gray will come back," Charlotte assured the lad. "But he also has an estate to run and we must let him get to that."

"Thank you. For coming."

Mr. Grayson rose. "I was delighted to see you, my lord."

"Could . . . could you . . . call me Rodger?"

Charlotte watched the man's features soften. "Of course. I'd like that. Now, get some rest, Rodger."

He looked to her and she accompanied him from the room.

Once the door was closed, she said, "Thank you. He needed that.

Desperately. Very few people come to see him. Conversation is quite hard due to his shortness of breath and the constant coughing."

"He looks just this side of death. He's far too thin. Those dark circles under his eyes look permanent. My heart went out to him."

"I'm glad to hear you have a heart, Mr. Grayson." Charlotte began walking down the corridor quickly, regretting her comment.

It didn't take her companion but a few strides to catch up with her. He caught her elbow, stopping her. She looked at his hand on her arm and then glared at him. He removed it and she had to lock her knees to keep from collapsing in a heap. No man had ever touched her beyond her father—until Viscount Waverly.

And yet Danforth Grayson's touch was as if fire singed her.

"You seem to freely speak your mind, Miss Nott. More so than any servant I've heard."

She flushed with embarrassment. "I'm sorry I was rude previously. I merely felt someone had to speak up for the children. They're lovely creatures, every one of them, and it's a shame how they were treated by their parents. I'd hoped, as their guardian, that you would change things in their lives. Let them know they are loved and they make a difference in the world."

His eyes shuttered once again and she could sense him withdrawing into himself.

"You ask quite a bit of me, Madam."

She boldly searched his face. "You have done your duty to the crown, Major Grayson. I only ask you to do your duty to your own family and see your blood kin not become lost children."

"Where else were you a governess, Miss Nott?" he asked suddenly, causing her stomach to clench.

"Why would you ask?" she retorted, showing a confidence she didn't feel. "Your brother felt I was suited for the position."

"I haven't been able to locate your references. I know you mentioned serving as companion to the Dowager Duchess of Exbury for several years. What other positions have you held?"

She licked her lips nervously, deciding she would only reveal as much as she had to. "I served for a brief time as governess to a young girl, aged four. Then I was assigned to Viscount Waverly's children. He had two young boys. I believed Lord Waverly preferred a male tutor for the boys before they went off to school and so I found myself available to come on at Gray Manor."

His eyes bored into hers. "How long were you at each household?" he asked evenly.

"Two weeks. And then eight months," she said, her head growing light. "I understand if you think I am not experienced enough for Lord Crampton but I assure you that I can work with him and the two young ladies."

When he didn't reply, Charlotte decided to throw herself on his mercy. "Please, Mr. Grayson. This is a good situation for me. I will do whatever you ask in order to maintain it."

Her words caused her stomach to roil. Would she really do anything in order to remain at Gray Manor? She remembered the horrible things Viscount Waverly whispered to her, slobbering over her as he pinned her against a wall.

And then Charlotte knew she wouldn't be able to stay on if that was what was required of her.

Before she could speak, he took her hand, startling her. She gazed into his eyes, the blue so rich and deep, and became lost in them for a moment.

"What's wrong, Miss Nott?" he asked softly, his large, warm hand dwarfing hers. "You seem distressed."

She bit her lip. "I won't do just anything to stay in my role. That was wrong of me to say." Charlotte swallowed and continued to look him in the eyes. "I was forced to leave both of my previous positions because of . . . unwanted attention. If I were allowed to stay, then I," she paused and took a deep breath and expelled it, "then I would have to perform certain duties for the master of the house, as well."

She pulled her hand from his. "I wasn't willing to do so—and I won't here either, Mr. Grayson. I want to do what I was hired to do. Look after the three children. If you want more from me, I must tender my resignation."

He captured her hand again, making her heart pound wildly against her ribs. "My dear Miss Nott, I would never ask you to do anything that didn't fall within the scope of your duties with the children. You've already done so much for those at Gray Manor." He squeezed her hand and released it, leaving her oddly bereft. "I am sorry you faced such . . . complicated situations alone."

She felt her mouth tremble. "Thank you, sir. It's just that . . . if this situation doesn't work out, I'll have to find a new agency. Mr. Plummer was quite clear that he would refuse to place me again if I returned to London after only a brief spell."

"You have a home here for as long as you like, Miss Nott," Mr. Grayson said firmly. "I think you are doing an outstanding job with the children. Even the very unruly Harriet."

"She doesn't mean to behave badly," Charlotte said quickly. "She did want to make a good first impression upon you."

"And she did," he assured her.

She nodded. "I am happy to stay as long as you wish, Mr. Grayson. And I apologize for being too forward. You will maintain the relationship you wish with your nieces and nephew. I should never have ordered you about."

He gave her a slow, lazy smile that caused butterflies to explode in her stomach. "You remind me of an experienced general, Miss Nott. Very qualified and capable. Skilled. Productive. Methodical. And one who would do anything for his men. I can give you no higher compliment. I hope you will stay at Gray Manor for many years."

"Thank you, sir," she said, her voice quivering. "I must see to the girls now."

With that, she marched off on shaky legs. As she returned upstairs, she pushed aside all thoughts of Danforth Grayson from her head.

For now.

CHAPTER NINE

GRAY ENTERED THE room he still thought of as his father's study, though he knew Seymour had used it for the past decade. The last time he'd stood here was when he'd learned of his father's death and burial while he was away at school. Already, the desk had been a mess, typical of Seymour's carelessness. Gray had thought his father might spring forth from his grave if he could see what his older son had done to the room that had always been the older man's sanctuary.

As expected, the ever-efficient Miss Nott had put things to rights, though. He could picture her here, sitting where he now sat, combing through the papers and making the neat, orderly stacks that greeted him. He wondered where he should begin.

A knock interrupted his thoughts and he said, "Come."

Smith, the footman filling in for Masters, approached him. "These are from Miss Nott, sir. She said you were to review them."

"I'll bet she did," he said under his breath and then accepted the pages from the servant. "Thank you, Smith."

Gray decided these were the most important things to look at—because Miss Nott deemed them so.

He couldn't help but pity her—a stunningly beautiful, intelligent woman forced to earn her living among men who were cads and sought to take advantage of her unfortunate circumstances. He knew how hard it must have been to reveal her past experiences. Anger sizzled through him, thinking of unwanted attention being forced upon her. He tamped down his ire. Miss Nott wasn't his concern. She wasn't his to protect. She was there to protect the children. As long as she did so, he would have no complaints regarding her.

But the thought of another man kissing her drove him to distraction. Because *he* wanted to do the same. Ever since he'd first seen her, he'd yearned to kiss her. Gray pushed aside the thought of Miss Nott, soft and pliant in his arms, as he kissed her until they both flamed with desire. He shook his head, clearing away the image. That was the last thing he should do. He owed it to her to conduct himself as a gentleman would. It wasn't only expected but he felt he owed it to her after those of his sex had blatantly disregarded society's rules and used their positions to try and bend her to their wills.

Gray raked his fingers through his hair and then focused on the first list prepared in her neat, precise hand. It was in regard to the status of the house itself. What repairs needed to be done and the order of importance. What goods needed to be replaced throughout the household. The list also contained her assessment of the work habits of those inside the house. Who should be let go and who should be promoted, as well as who should be retained in their current positions. He was surprised at the thoughtful, complete picture it gave him of Gray Manor, as he learned things that might otherwise have taken him months on his own to discover.

Putting it aside, he took up the next batch of pages, all regarding various aspects of the estate. Gray pored over it, seeing in his mind's eye everything Miss Nott referred to. Once again, she ranked items to be accomplished by prioritizing them. Her assessment was practical and showed a deep knowledge of estate affairs.

Where had a governess learned of such things?

She'd mentioned running the household for the Dowager Duchess of Exbury. Had the dowager duchess taken a young Miss Nott in hand and personally trained her? Possibly. Still, it didn't account for the next report she'd prepared regarding crop rotation and husbandry on the estate.

Miss Nott remained a mystery to him.

His stomach growled noisily as a knock sounded on the door. Smith came in and informed him Mr. Bonham had arrived from Canterbury. Gray heard the clock chime and asked the servant to bring tea.

"And find Miss Nott," he added. "She should be here for this meeting."

"Very good, sir." Smith indicated for Mr. Bonham to come in and left.

Gray rose and greeted the solicitor. "It's been several years, Mr. Bonham." He offered his hand.

"Yes, indeed, Mr. Grayson. I apologize for not coming sooner. I had a funeral to attend. One of my clients. And might I express my condolences for your loss, as well."

He indicated that the man should take a seat. "We don't have to pretend among ourselves, Mr. Bonham. Seymour's death meant nothing to me. He hated me from the moment of my birth and even told me during our last meeting that he hoped I'd die at our enemy's hands."

The solicitor winced but quickly recovered his composure. "Yet here you are, Mr. Grayson, selling out and taking on the responsibilities of family for your brother and his late wife."

"Someone had to do it," he replied. "I was the only one available. As it is, I'll see to getting things running smoothly again and then retire to London. I'll stay in the city most of the year."

The solicitor studied him. "You don't plan to stay at Gray Manor then?"

"No. The children will remain with Miss Nott. I would prefer to be elsewhere. But don't worry, Mr. Bonham. I will see to my duties and earn every penny of my stipend. I'll call for regular reports from my employees. Speaking of that." He picked up the pages he'd studied for the last several hours. "Miss Nott's work. Her recommendations will guide me for what's to be accomplished."

Bonham smiled. "Ah, Miss Nott. I don't know what Gray Manor would have done without her steady influence the past several weeks."

At that moment, the door opened and the governess entered. Both men rose and Gray thought that he'd never done so for a servant. Yet she seemed so much more than that.

"Smith said you wished for me to meet with you," she said, her low voice calm and steady. "It's a pleasure to see you again, Mr. Bonham."

"The same, Miss Nott. I was just singing your praises to Mr. Grayson here."

The tea cart had followed her in, pushed by a maid who stood waiting for instructions.

"Bring it to the group of chairs," Gray ordered. "Shall we adjourn there?"

The three took their seats and he asked Miss Nott to pour. It didn't surprise him when she did so with grace and confidence. More and more, he grew curious about her background. He loaded his plate with sandwiches and sweets, having had nothing since early morning.

Settling back in his chair, he said, "I had a chance to review your recommendations, Miss Nott. Has Mr. Bonham seen your list?"

"I have. I only had a few recommendations to add," he said.

They spent an hour discussing what work needed to be done at the house and on the estate. Miss Nott wasn't shy about expressing her opinions and he found himself agreeing with her on everything. Some of the work could be done by men in the nearby village, while others would need to be brought in from Canterbury. They came up with a plan of action, Miss Nott taking notes for them as they came to an agreement.

"I'll duplicate these so that you both have a copy to refer to."

"That would be most appreciated," Mr. Bonham said.

"We should also discuss hiring a new housekeeper and estate manager," she added.

"I would like to interview no less than three candidates for each position," Gray stated. "I want to get the most qualified person for each post."

"I've used an agency in Canterbury," Mr. Bonham offered. "I can go there first thing tomorrow and then the day after bring those candidates to Gray Manor to speak to you in person, Mr. Grayson."

"Yes. Arrange that, Mr. Bonham. And Miss Nott, I'd like you to sit in on those interviews. You have a working knowledge of the house and estate and your contributions would be invaluable."

"Of course, Mr. Grayson," she said.

The clock chimed and she looked to it. "It's five o'clock. I read with the girls from five to six every afternoon and—"

"It's important to maintain a routine," Gray finished, smiling at her. He looked to Bonham. "I've told Miss Nott that she would have made a fine army officer with her discipline and love of order."

The solicitor chuckled. "I do believe you're correct. If Bonaparte saw Miss Nott coming, he would surrender immediately."

She stood and the men followed suit. "I'll keep that in mind in case governessing doesn't work out for me," she said lightly, her magnificent green eyes lighting with mirth.

After she left, Gray asked, "I haven't seen any records for salaries. How much is Miss Nott paid?"

Bonham named a figure and Gray winced. "Only that per quarter?"

"No, sir. That is per annum."

"That's ridiculous. Especially with all she's done to help get the estate into shape. Triple that figure—and that is what she should earn each quarter."

"Of course, sir. I can prepare a list for you of the other servants' compensation."

"Do so. I need to know if they're as severely underpaid, as well."

The men spoke of a few other matters and then Bonham took his leave. They arranged for the Grayson coach to be at his office at nine o'clock the day after tomorrow in order to ferry back prospective workers to be interviewed. After shaking hands, Bonham departed, leaving Gray alone—but not for long.

Smith appeared again. "Mrs. Rook would like to discuss something with you, Mr. Grayson."

"I can see her now."

Within minutes, the rotund cook with abundant white hair appeared. "Thank you for seeing me, Mr. Grayson."

"What's this about, Mrs. Rook? Menus? Until we hire a housekeeper, you're free to prepare what you like. I've never been particular and after army rations for the last several years, I'm happy with anything you put on my plate."

"Miss Nott has seen to the menus until now. I'd prefer she keep doing so. Such a lovely young woman, Miss Nott."

"Anything else?" he asked.

"I'd like to see what time you'd like dinner served each evening, Mr. Grayson. It will only be you."

"We're in the country, Mrs. Rook. Early is better for me. I know my brother preferred dinner at eight but you can push it up an hour at least. No, let's say half-past six. That will allow the servants to eat at a decent hour and get to bed."

The cook beamed. "Thank you, sir. We'll start tonight. In the small dining room, if that suits you. Let me know if there's anything you fancy. It's good to have you home again. You've been missed."

Gray didn't know about that. He didn't think of Gray Manor as home anymore. He was glad he'd informed Bonham of his plan to remain in London most of the year. He could supervise things from there easily.

It would also keep the delectable Miss Nott out of his sphere.

He returned to the desk and sat at it, contemplating the scope of the various projects that would soon begin. Once they'd begun and he had the right staff in place, he would retreat to London. It would be easy to come down periodically to check on things. Besides, with the wonderful Miss Nott in residence, he wouldn't be needed that much.

The clock's chiming let him know it was half-past six and he went to the smaller of Gray Manor's dining rooms. Seating himself, a footman served him the first course of soup. After a few spoonfuls, he thought it would be lonely each night dining alone. Turning to the footman, he asked, "Does Miss Nott eat with the other servants?"

The footman shook his head. "No, sir. Mrs. Rook sends a tray to her room each evening. It's not like a governess eats with the others. They never have."

Once again, Gray felt sorry for her, a woman caught between two worlds of upper and lower, fitting in neither place. He thought of how lonely she must be and how she'd mentioned missing her father every day. He'd been lucky enough to have Reid and Burke in his life for years on a daily basis and couldn't fathom how isolated Miss Nott had been for her entire adult life.

"Send for her," he ordered. "Let Mrs. Rook know that Miss Nott will be dining with me each evening while I'm in residence."

Startled, the footman said, "Yes, sir. I'll see to it now."

Gray went ahead and had almost finished his soup when Miss Nott arrived. The color was high in her cheeks and for the first time since he'd met her, she looked uncertain of herself.

"You've asked me to dine with you tonight, Mr. Grayson?"

"Yes. And every night." He indicated the chair on his right. "Have a seat, Miss Nott."

She moved toward it but remained standing. "I'm not sure if this is quite appropriate."

"Why not? You have to eat. So do I. You're not eating with the other servants."

"No, Mrs. Rook has a tray brought to my room for the evening meal."

"I'm alone. You are, too. After a day spent in the company of children, I would think you would long for some adult conversation. I would like that, as well, Miss Nott. Did you eat with the duchess when you served as her companion?"

"Yes, but that was different," she said reluctantly.

"How so?"

The blush on her cheeks deepened. "It just was," she said stubbornly.

Gray dug in his heels, determined to win this small battle. "I'd prefer to have companionship during dinner. We will be able to talk of your lists and what progress is being made inside the house and out on the estate." Looking to lure her in, he added, "By dining together and discussing it then, it wouldn't take away any time from your pupils during the day."

She thought a moment and then conceded. "It would be an efficient use of time."

With that, the footman came and pulled the chair from the table and Miss Nott seated herself.

"See to the next course," Gray said and the footman removed his soup bowl and left the room. Looking to the governess, he said, "Dinner will be at half-past six each evening. That way, it won't conflict with your reading hour with Harriet and Jane."

"Thank you. It's my favorite part of the day," she shared. "That and strolling through the gardens after dinner." She paused. "I hope you don't mind that I make use of them."

"Not at all. It's been many years since I walked through them myself." He smiled. "Would you allow me to accompany you tonight?"

CHAPTER TEN

CHARLOTTE DIDN'T KNOW what to say. Already, Mr. Grayson had flustered her. She rarely felt out of control in any situation but this man had her at sixes and sevens. Her time in Gray Manor's gardens had come to be her haven, a place away from all of the demands placed upon her. She drank in the solitude while enjoying a bit of nature. Still, she didn't want to seem churlish. After all, it was the family garden. And Mr. Grayson had proven to be an enigma, one Charlotte was interested in solving.

"Yes, I'd be delighted to have your company this evening," she replied, her attention focused on the empty spot in front of her. She didn't trust herself to look into his hypnotic eyes.

The footman returned with their next course and also brought her a wine glass. He poured the liquid for her and then stepped back toward the wall. At least someone else would be present during their evening meals together. Then she almost laughed. Mr. Grayson didn't view her as a woman. It wasn't as if she were alone with him and tongues would wag. She was the family governess. No more, no less. He'd also promised to be a gentleman with her. While she appreciated his words, a small part of her longed for more from him. He was the kind of man any woman of the *ton* would have been attracted to, with his handsome looks and tall, broad frame. The kind of man Charlotte had thought she would one day wed and have children with.

She forced such idle thoughts from her mind. She was employed by Mr. Grayson. They were to discuss business and the children. They had no relationship beyond that—and never would.

"Shall we talk about the upcoming interviews?" she asked. "What are you looking for in the new housekeeper and estate manager?"

They spent the rest of dinner going over the things that he felt were most important for both positions, as well as the fact that he wanted someone with experience assuming both posts.

"I'm not saying they would have to have run something as large as Gray Manor but I can't see elevating someone unless they truly know what they're doing. Things have been lax for far too long as is it. The estate needs someone dependable. A person who can commit to serving the family indefinitely."

By now, they'd finished eating and the footman brought a tray with port and a cigar. Mr. Grayson waved it away.

"None for me. I've never been one who enjoyed a cigar."

Her father had been much the same, not liking the way tobacco lingered on his clothes and stained his teeth. Charlotte almost mentioned it and bit her tongue. She was a governess now. It did no good to speak of things from long ago.

The footman removed the tray from the room and Mr. Grayson helped her from her chair.

"Are you still interested in a stroll through the gardens?" he asked.

"Yes. I'd like that."

They went outside. The warmth of the August day still lingered in the night air as they reached the gardens. Suddenly, he took her hand and tucked it into the crook of his arm. Surprise filled her. For a moment, she closed her eyes and inhaled the sweet smell of roses, wishing things could be different. Charlotte opened her eyes and almost withdrew her hand but thought it would be rude after he'd made an effort to treat her graciously.

Strolling down the paths, he asked her about the various flowers. She pointed out gladioli, delphiniums, and dahlias and explained how all were mid-to-late summer flowers.

"You enjoy gardening?" he asked. "You seem quite knowledgeable on the topic."

She had once upon a time but that time was long gone.

"My father liked flowers. He taught me about them." Let him think her father was a gardener on some lofty estate. The truth, if it came out, would hurt too much. She had seen respect in his eyes for her knowledge. She couldn't bear to see it replaced by pity at how she'd fallen in society.

"My father taught me nothing about this estate. As a second son, I was never destined to be in charge and gain the title. I was always meant for the army. That's why all of this seems so foreign to me. Seymour was brought up knowing he would become the earl someday. Unfortunately, my brother was more interested in the fortune that came with the title and not much for running an estate."

"I know you haven't had the time but I do want you to examine the ledgers closely."

"What am I to look for? I told you I enjoy numbers but it would help me to know what you wish me to see."

Charlotte hesitated. If she were wrong, she wouldn't want to have accused a man falsely. "Just let the numbers speak to you, Mr. Grayson. If you see something amiss, then we may discuss it."

"You're speaking in riddles, Miss Nott," he said, exasperation apparent in his voice.

She shrugged. "Then we'll see how skilled you are at solving riddles."

He laughed. The sound was rich and vibrant and it made her wish to always make him laugh.

"You are certainly a governess, Madam, even when conversing with adults."

She knew he meant to tease her but his words pained her all the same. It just let Charlotte know how far she was from the almost-debutante she had been. Nowadays, she was practical. Competent. Useful. Wearing her plain clothes. No jewelry. No ribbons in her hair. She was as far away from that naïve schoolgirl than she'd ever been.

Mr. Grayson halted and turned to her. "Have I upset you in some way, Miss Nott?"

She would have to watch herself. This man was much too observant. "No, Mr. Grayson. Not at all. Once a governess, always a governess, I suppose. Even with adults. I will try to refrain from attempting to teach you lessons."

Without warning, his large hands cupped her cheeks. Charlotte's heart slammed against her ribs. She ceased to breathe as his thumbs stroked her face gently.

"I will always be happy to learn your lessons, Miss Nott. You have much to teach me. I only wish I could return the favor."

He could—if he kissed her.

Charlotte had only been kissed by that despicable viscount who slobbered all over her. She thought she'd never want a man close to her again. Never want a kiss if that's what it was like. But now, here, suddenly everything had changed. Danforth Grayson caused so many conflicting emotions within her. She wanted to throw herself at him. She *wanted* to kiss him.

"I am grateful for how you've cared for the children," he said softly, his blue eyes drawing her in.

"I . . . am only doing what I was hired to do," she said breathlessly.

"No," he contradicted. "You might have been hired to teach grammar and history but you are doing much more for them. You show interest in them as people. You make them see their worth after no adult has done so." He smiled gently. "I would say you love them, Miss Nott, and that they love you."

She swallowed hard, her gaze locked with his. "I do my best. And I do love them," she admitted. "They are sometimes a mess but all three are loveable in their own way."

Something in his eyes changed and she sucked in a quick breath.

He was going to kiss her.

And he did.

It was nothing like Viscount Waverly's kiss had been. This was soft. So soft. Like a gentle breeze brushing against her lips. Warmth flooded her. Then he stopped. His lips moved to her brow and pressed against it tenderly. His hands fell from her face and he stepped back. Dazed, Charlotte looked up at him.

And saw regret.

"I'm sorry, Miss Nott," he apologized, his body stiffening. "I'm not sure what overtook me. I merely wished to show you my gratitude for all you have done for my nephew and nieces." He paused. "I'm not like the men you spoke of. I would never—"

"I know," she said, placing a hand on his forearm. "I take no offense, Mr. Grayson." She dropped her hand. "We care for the children. We have that in common. I'm pleased to see you concerned for their welfare."

"It won't happen again," he said brusquely. "Shall we return to the house? I wish to pen a note to the Duke of Gilford and ask him for recommendations regarding a physician that might come to see Rodger."

"Of course," Charlotte said and turned.

He did not take her arm this time as they returned to the house. She knew he wouldn't again and understood. They'd shared something for a brief moment that would never be repeated. Her heart ached but she couldn't risk her future and this post by giving in to what she was feeling. Begging him to kiss her again. She'd already seen the remorse he carried and wouldn't trouble him.

"Let the duke know of the earl's frequent shortness of breath and coughing, especially at night. That his chest tightens and pains him, especially when he is wheezing."

"That's good to know. I'll be sure to let His Grace understand the severity of Rodger's complaints."

They entered the house and Charlotte said, "Good night." She quickly made her way up the flights of stairs until she reached the floor where the schoolroom was. Her chamber was just beyond it. Opening the door, she entered and closed it, leaning heavily against it. The tips of her fingers touched her lips. Where his lips had been. As tears streamed down her cheeks, she gave in to the tremendous yearning that ran through her. She went to the bed and curled up, her fist against her mouth, keeping the sobs inside.

She would think about this once only and never again.

WHY THE BLOODY hell had he kissed her?

Gray sat at the desk, pulling out parchment and ink, cursing himself.

He shouldn't have kissed her. He didn't mean to. It had just happened. Without thinking, his hands had gone to her face. The smooth skin felt like silk and he longed to caress it. To caress more than her face. He wanted to see what lay beneath the shapeless, colorless gowns she wore. He longed to run his hands along her gentle curves. Kiss his way from her head to her toes and back up again.

Their kiss had been chaste. A mere brushing of his lips against hers. And a moment of reverence as he kissed her brow. Gray longed to taste her and had fought those urges. He'd promised her he would be a gentleman and yet the first time they were truly alone, he'd been the exact opposite.

He wondered if she could ever trust him again. She'd been gracious. Understanding. She hadn't seemed panicked by his actions or outraged. She'd been the one to reassure him. It felt as if he'd betrayed her and yet at the same time, he wanted more. He wanted all of her. Which was ridiculous. He couldn't compromise the family governess.

He'd have to marry her if he did and Gray never wished to marry. He never wanted to feel responsible for a woman. Didn't want one clinging to him, wanting his protection. Wanting his love. Wanting more than he had to give.

He had nothing left to give. All emotions had been left on the battlefield. He was at Gray Manor to see to the running of the estate and that the children were in good hands. They were, with Miss Nott. She would not only feed their minds but their souls. She would lavish the love on them they desperately needed. While Gray liked all three a good deal already, he didn't want to become close to them. Didn't want to care for them. He wanted them to remain at a distance. Not look at him with worshipful eyes. He wasn't worthy of it.

Reaching for a quill, he quickly wrote to Reid's father, explaining the situation from him leaving the army to his new responsibilities at Gray Manor, including the children. He wrote in-depth of his nephew's ailments and how the asthma had worsened since Gray had last seen the boy five years earlier. He begged the duke to help him find a physician that might bring relief, if not a cure, for Rodger.

He sealed the letter, using the Crampton ring he found inside the desk. Gray supposed Seymour had grown too large to wear it and kept it here for convenience. He left the message on a tray in the foyer, where Masters would see to its delivery in the morning. Or Smith, he supposed. It would be prudent to follow up and make sure the message reached its destination.

With that, he made his way to the stables. Though it was growing dark, he thought about riding to Wilton, the nearest village. There he could lose himself in drink.

And maybe a woman.

He reached the stables and the thought of touching someone other than Miss Nott left him with a sour taste in his mouth. *Damn the woman!* He wasn't about to remain celibate the rest of his life. He tried to exorcise her from his mind but her image refused to vanish. Those inquisitive emerald eyes. The soft, full lips. The abundant brown hair. They would not leave him.

Exasperated, he turned away from the stables and set out walking quickly across the grounds. Riding at night was difficult enough, especially with the confusion that raced through him. Better to stretch his legs and walk out his frustration.

Gray walked for several miles and then made his way back in the moonlight. Exhausted, he collapsed atop his bed and fell into a restless sleep.

Chapter Eleven

CHARLOTTE LOOKED AT the two young girls. "Are you clear on everything you need to work on today?"

Harriet sighed dramatically. "Miss Nott, we understand all of our assignments. And that Betsy will look in on us and eat luncheon with us."

Jane smiled brightly. "We'll be fine, Miss Nott." She hesitated. "And I will be a very, very good girl."

"I will, too," Harriet declared. "I haven't done anything naughty in at least three days. Maybe four. Not since before Uncle Gray came."

Unfortunately, Charlotte couldn't say the same. She had done a bad thing by letting Danforth Grayson kiss her. Oh, she understood after thinking long and hard that it wasn't a kiss of desire. It was one of thankfulness. Almost friendship. She had taken care of things for him so that when he'd arrived, he hadn't been greeted by a huge disaster. Lord Crampton's desk, which had been in a muddle, had been neatly arranged. She'd prepared her lists and taken the children in hand, setting up a program of discipline and variety in their studies. The man had been overwhelmed and then grateful—and had showed his gratitude with a sweet, friendly kiss.

She told herself not to expect another one. She'd seen the remorse on his face. He wouldn't repeat the same mistake twice.

Charlotte just had to hope she could stop thinking about it day and night. If she couldn't, she might have to decide to ask Mr. Grayson if they could interview new governesses, as well as the other staff members he wished to hire. Her funds were low, though. She would have to wait until her quarterly salary came due. She wasn't spending anything now. If she could keep this up, she would have enough to travel to London and seek another position. It wouldn't be through The Plummer Employment Agency but she could find other employment agencies in the city. And this time, she would have references. Charlotte knew that Mr. Grayson would feel obligated to write her a decent reference after all she'd done at Gray Manor.

Even if she did leave after only three months' time.

Maybe she wouldn't have to. Maybe she could see him less and less and forget about the silly notions that filled her. Of course, that was difficult, seeing as she would dine with him each night. Last night had taken every bit of courage she had to enter the dining room. At least she hadn't seen him during the day. It pleased her that he responded as if nothing unseemly had occurred between them and they pursued a pleasant conversation throughout dinner. He'd ridden throughout the estate that day, meeting many of the tenants and seeing what items needed to be fulfilled. In turn, she had told him about the children's studies that day.

When dinner had ended last night, Mr. Grayson didn't ask to walk with her. For a moment, Charlotte considered simply returning to her room but she decided there would be no harm in strolling through the gardens. She'd done so, though the peace she usually felt when she returned to the house had been lacking. Her unrest had continued all night and now into today. She must concentrate more on her charges and quit fantasizing about their guardian.

"Uncle Gray!"

She ceased her woolgathering and found the object of her fancy standing in the doorway to the schoolroom. Both girls ran to him, latching on to a different leg.

"Miss Nott has left us work to do while she is with you, Uncle

Gray," Jane informed him.

"It's quite a lot," Harriet confirmed. "I'm not sure if we'll finish it all."

"Betsy will look in on us," Jane added. "We like her."

"Perhaps you might have time to do a drawing for me if you finish your assignments," he suggested.

"I will," proclaimed Harriet.

"I'll try," Jane said, doubt in her voice. "Harriet is a better drawer than I am."

"I'll like whatever you do, Jane. It's the effort behind your art that matters." He looked to Charlotte. "The carriage has been sighted. I thought I better retrieve you for the interviews."

"I was on my way. I'm sorry you had to come fetch me."

"It's all right." He glanced down at his nieces. "Be good and finish all of your work before you start on the drawings."

Harriet scowled but Jane smiled sweetly. Both girls retreated to their seats and opened their books. Once they'd started, Charlotte turned and met Mr. Grayson, who waited in the corridor.

"They were happy to see you," she said.

"Yes, it seemed so. I also looked in on Rodger."

"Have you written to the duke yet?"

"A messenger left yesterday morning. I'm hoping to receive a reply soon. I plan to go personally to London. While I'm there, I'll see to a new wardrobe. I can't keep alternating between my two uniforms."

Charlotte thought he looked dashing in his officer's uniform but then again, Danforth Grayson would look equally impressive in civilian dress.

They reached the foyer, where Smith awaited them.

"I've taken all six to the breakfast room, Miss Nott, as you requested. They're being given tea and cakes." He started to hand her a stack of pages and then gave them to Mr. Grayson instead. "These are the references, sir. Miss Nott said you would look over them before you interviewed the candidates."

"Very good, Smith." He turned to her. "And where might we be doing that, Miss Nott?"

"I'd thought the small parlor just off the breakfast room. It's close and not nearly as intimidating as the drawing room."

"I defer to you. Smith, give us a quarter-hour to peruse the references and then bring in the first applicant."

The footman looked to her. "I'm to bring the women first, isn't that right, Miss Nott?"

"Yes, Smith. Thank you."

They went to the small parlor and seated themselves. He handed her half of the references and then they traded after finishing.

"I already am leaning toward a few," he admitted.

"Don't let a reference totally sway you," Charlotte cautioned. "They can be written to hide deficiencies. You had said experience would be important. There's also the way they will present themselves. Both positions call for someone with good communication skills, as well as a person who can think on their feet quickly."

He chuckled. "I can see you're already far better at this than I ever could be. Since we are interviewing housekeepers first, why don't you take charge?"

Smith announced the first applicant and Charlotte introduced herself and Mr. Grayson. She explained a little about the house and what duties would be required and then asked several questions that would have no wrong or right answer, wishing to hear what the first woman would say. Charlotte concluded the interview by allowing the woman to ask questions of her own, which seemed to startle her.

After they'd spoken to all three women and they were alone again, she asked, "Do you have a preference?"

"Mrs. Cassidy," he responded. "She was confident and articulate. She didn't have as much experience as the others but I liked her manner. She has enough maturity to command respect from the other servants and she seemed eager to find a place she could stay at for many years."

"I agree," she said. "Mrs. Cassidy will be a good fit for Gray Manor." Setting aside the three women's references, she said, "Are you ready for the men?"

"Yes. I do like how you tell them a little about the household and their duties before giving them a chance to speak. I think familiarizing them with us is a clever idea."

Charlotte wanted to say it was an approach she'd first learned from her father but merely smiled.

"Why don't you ask the majority of the questions this time since the post deals with estate matters?"

"I will—as long as you add anything you can think of."

She agreed and Smith went to collect the first applicant. Mr. Grayson asked good questions and then allowed her to add a few of her own. After Charlotte did so, he regarded her with respect and she felt good about what items she had brought up.

"You're most astute, Miss Nott," he said once the first applicant left.

"You did an excellent job yourself, Mr. Grayson." Charlotte referred back to the references in front of her. She thought she'd seen more than admiration in his eyes and knew she deceived herself.

The next man's interview went quite well and Mr. Grayson said the same once the man left.

"It's almost a shame to have to take more time when I think we've settled on our new manager," he said.

"Still, it's only one more applicant. He came a long way and we should give him his due," Charlotte pointed out.

The door opened and Smith led in Mr. Linfield, the last person. As he came closer, Charlotte nearly fainted—because she knew him.

Jeremy. Her friend. The groom that had ridden out with her at Rumford Park for a number of years. Papa had always insisted she have someone with her when she visited their tenants. Jeremy had been the one who accompanied her the most. He was always asking questions about the estate and soaked up everything she told him. He'd left shortly before her father's passing, having an opportunity to work with his uncle at an estate near Dover. Charlotte had not connected the name on the references with the man she'd known.

As he came toward them and caught sight of her, his smile faltered. She gave an imperceptible shake of her head and mouthed "no" to him as he approached. He immediately focused on Mr. Grayson, his smile returning, and greeted him as he introduced himself.

"And this is Miss Nott," Mr. Grayson said. "She is helping me conduct the interviews today."

Jeremy inclined his head. "Miss Nott. A pleasure to make your acquaintance."

The interview proceeded and Charlotte wasn't surprised to find Jeremy well-spoken and informed on numerous aspects of running an estate.

"I began humbly, Mr. Grayson, as a groom at Rumford Park," he told them.

"Rumford Park?" Mr. Grayson frowned. "Is that by chance near here?"

"Yes, sir. It's the other side of Wilton, perhaps seven miles or so away from the village."

"I recall a Lord Rumford coming on a few occasions to visit my father."

Charlotte saw him struggling with a memory. She knew that memory had to do with her. Quickly, she said, "Mr. Linfield, tells us more about your life after leaving your post as a groom."

"I had the opportunity to move into estate management, thanks to my uncle."

He went on to tell them about how he assisted his uncle and then moved into the role of full-time manager after four years, when his uncle suffered from apoplexy.

"I've served as an estate manager for six years on my own now. May I tell you of some of the things I've implemented over the years?"

They listened to the changes he'd made and Charlotte thought Jeremy would be an ideal candidate for Gray Manor.

"May I ask why you wish to leave your present position?" Mr. Grayson asked.

"I've already left it, sir. The viscount died and his son assumed the title. While he was happy to write me an excellent reference, he had a friend from school who'd fallen on hard times and wished to help this friend out by offering him my position. I was given a generous sum of six months' salary so that I wouldn't be rushed while I located my next position."

Mr. Grayson looked at Charlotte and she nodded in agreement. He turned back to Jeremy.

"Mr. Linfield, we'd be happy for you to you come to Gray Manor. When might you be able to start?"

"I would need to return to Canterbury for my things. I could take the mail coach tomorrow and begin upon my arrival."

"Nonsense. My carriage can bring you. Let me tell the other candidates my decision and speak to Mrs. Cassidy, whom we want to offer the post of housekeeper. If she's willing to collect her things in Canterbury and return with you today, the coach could bring you back and have you here before dinner." Mr. Grayson stood.

"That would be excellent," Jeremy declared. He rose and Charlotte followed suit.

"Let's go see the others then." Mr. Grayson strode from the room, telling Smith to inform the coachman of the trip to Canterbury and that he would bring back Mrs. Cassidy and Mr. Linfield.

Jeremy fell into step with her. "Lady Charlotte, what are you doing here?" he asked quietly. "You could've knocked me over with a feather when I saw you."

"I am the governess at Gray Manor."

"But why? It's been almost ten years since I've seen you. I would have thought by now you'd be wed and have children of your own."

"After Papa's death, my brother had other plans for me. He sent me away. There was no Season. No opportunity to wed. I've had to make my own living since I was eighteen."

Jeremy's face flushed with anger. "That's plain wrong, my lady."

"Hush," she urged. "No one knows of my past here, Jeremy. They only know I've been a companion and governess. I'm quite happy with my situation and my charges. Good positions are hard to come by. I want to keep this one—and keep my past private."

They reached the breakfast room and he said, "I'm very sorry, Lady Charlotte."

"Miss Nott," she said.

"Of course. Thank you, Miss Nott," he said and moved away from her as Mr. Grayson thanked everyone for coming and announced who had been awarded the positions.

Charlotte asked Mrs. Cassidy if she would be able to return today after packing her things and she was happy to do so.

"You should arrive in time to join Mr. Grayson and me for dinner," she told the two new employees. "We can further discuss your duties during the meal so you'll be ready to begin in the morning."

She saw Mrs. Cassidy frown and wondered if it was because she would be eating with the master of the house—or that she disapproved that Charlotte did so. She decided this would be her last meal with Mr. Grayson. They would have no further business to discuss each evening. She would be more comfortable going back to having a tray provided in her room.

The six boarded the carriage bound for Canterbury and Charlotte said, "I hope you didn't mind that I suggested they dine with us this evening."

He studied her a moment. "No. It's an excellent idea. I'm sure you need to get back to your pupils."

"Yes, I'll check on Lord Crampton before I return to the girls."

"Do that," he said brusquely and entered the house.

Charlotte felt she'd done something wrong—and had no idea what.

CHAPTER TWELVE

GRAY RETURNED TO the study and tamped down his agitation. No, if he were to be truthful, it wasn't agitation.

It was jealousy, pure and simple.

He'd been aware of Miss Nott and Mr. Linfield speaking privately to one another. It was perfectly natural. She was the type of woman who would make everyone feel welcomed. And yet he'd sensed a connection between them. Some affinity that angered him.

"Ridiculous," he muttered to himself.

He was going to be gone from Gray Manor soon. Especially now with competent people hired, it would be sooner than he'd expected. Miss Nott would be out of his sight and mind. If she chose to develop a friendship with Mr. Linfield after his departure, it was perfectly within her rights. As long as she did her job and looked after the children properly, the rest of her time—and who she spent it with—was her own.

Then why did he feel so resentful?

Gray steepled his fingers. The delectable Miss Nott had gotten under his skin. He'd been foolish enough to barely kiss her. Fortunately, she had acted with grace and understanding and accepted his apology.

But Gray had forced himself to make that apology. He wasn't sorry at all. If anything, the brief joining of their lips had created a maelstrom within him.

He wanted to kiss Miss Nott until her lips were swollen. Until she begged him to touch her. Until he could get his fill of her—which might never happen. It was wrong. Absolutely wrong, especially after what she'd confided in him. That's why he knew he needed to leave soon. Gray had to stay away from her. If he didn't, he'd ruin her—and himself. He couldn't marry. It wouldn't be fair to a woman to be saddled with a man who'd been so hollowed out by war. Miss Nott deserved someone who would please her. Cherish her.

Love her.

That certainly wasn't him.

Frustrated, Gray left the house and, this time, went for the ride that allowed him to escape all thoughts, rational or otherwise. He pushed himself and Titan hard. By the time he returned to Gray Manor, the physical exertion had him trembling as he walked back to the house. He passed Smith and told him to send up hot water for a bath—and Parker. The footman's eyes widened but he scurried off.

Gray arrived at his rooms and fell into a chair, breathing hard. Parker entered tentatively and saw Gray sprawled.

"The hot water is coming, Mr. Grayson. Let me help you."

Without further ado, Gray had a valet. Parker undressed him and saw him into the bath. He scrubbed Gray as if he were a small child and dried and dressed him.

"I'll see your coat brushed, sir." Parker paused. "Might I suggest that you invest in a new wardrobe soon?"

"I plan to. In London. I'm going there soon to find a doctor for Lord Crampton."

"Very good, sir." Parker took the sweat-soaked clothing with him and left the room.

Gray made his way downstairs and to the small dining room. He passed a footman who told him the coach had returned from Canterbury with Mrs. Cassidy and Mr. Linfield and that Miss Nott was showing the pair their quarters.

He entered the dining room and seated himself. His weariness had fled and he felt exhilarated now from the exercise.

The door opened and none other than Masters appeared. The butler wore a sling that supported his plaster but no tailcoat.

"Mr. Grayson, I wanted you to know that I'm back on full duty. My head cold is gone and my broken arm won't prevent me from seeing to my responsibilities. I do apologize for not wearing a coat. Miss Nott let out a few shirts for me so that there's room for the plaster. She's doing the same with a couple of coats."

"Where does she find time for it, Masters? She teaches the children. Runs the household. Makes decisions about the estate. Supervises the staff. And now sews for you?"

The butler chuckled. "I wish there were more Miss Notts in the world, sir. It would be a better place."

"She should run the bloody English army."

With a straight face, Masters said, "I don't believe she's been given that opportunity yet."

Gray burst out laughing. "It's good to have you back, Masters."

"I heard that you've finally accepted Parker as your valet. He's most pleased."

"I have. For now. I'll be leaving for London to live most of the year. I'm not sure if I'll take him with me or not."

Masters frowned slightly. "I see. I would suggest you make good use of Parker, sir. If you must go, he would be a steady servant. There's not much else for him to do here." He hesitated. "Will you leave soon?"

"I want to make sure the new hires are acceptable before I venture to town. I'll also need to visit Seymour's other property. The house near the coast. Are there any others I'm not aware of?"

"No, sir. Only the London townhouse and the place near Dover."

Miss Nott appeared. "Good evening, Mr. Masters. I hope you're feeling well. How is the sling I fashioned working out?"

"Quite well, Miss Nott. Thank you again for all of your help." Masters left.

Gray looked at her. He could stare at her face for hours but it wasn't only her outer beauty that attracted him. It was the goodness that resided within her. She was the most unselfish person he'd ever met.

"Good evening, Mr. Grayson," she said, and her smile stopped him in his tracks.

"Good evening, Miss Nott. Did our two get settled?"

"I showed Mr. Linfield his cottage and gave him the option to prepare his own meals there or join the servants for theirs in the main house. Mrs. Cassidy took the former housekeeper's quarters, which consisted of a room that serves as both an office and parlor, along with a bedroom. She was most pleased."

"That's good to hear."

The door opened and a footman ushered in the pair. He greeted them and had them all seat themselves. Two footmen appeared tonight to wait on them. Gray and Miss Nott spent the entire time discussing duties and expectations for both positions. Miss Nott agreed to give Mrs. Cassidy a tour of the entire house tomorrow morning, while he agreed to ride the entire property with Mr. Linfield.

As the meal concluded, he thanked them for dining with him so that they were clear regarding their responsibilities. Both newcomers expressed their gratitude. They left and Miss Nott stayed behind.

"Now that these positions are filled, Mr. Grayson, I will be taking my evening meal in my own room."

"Why?" Gray asked, his temper flaring.

Calmly, she said, "I see no need for us to meet regularly since you'll be doing so on your own with Mr. Linfield and Mrs. Cassidy. That was the bulk of what we discussed at dinner and those matters are now out of my hands. Of course, you're welcome to stop by the schoolroom any time to see your nieces. I'm also happy to give you weekly reports on their progress, as well as Lord Crampton's. If you'd like to arrange a time to do so, please let me know."

She sounded so damned . . . competent.

"You've taken efficiency to a new level, Miss Nott," he said, his tone edged with anger.

The governess ignored it and said, "Thank you, Mr. Grayson."

"We shall dine every Thursday and discuss the children then."

Frowning, she refrained from speaking a moment and then replied, "As you wish. Good evening."

Miss Nott left and his temper soared. If the two footmen hadn't been present, he would have hurled his wine glass against the wall.

Instead, he retreated to the library, where he planned to get thoroughly soused.

He poured a crystal tumbler almost to the brim with brandy and downed it in one lengthy swallow. The liquid burned a path to his belly, coating him with fire and warmth. He refilled his glass and took it to a chair, where he sat sipping and brooding.

After two more glasses, the giggles hit him as he remembered getting soused with Burke and Reid at a seedy tavern during their first year at Oxford. They'd climbed up on the bar and swayed as they'd sung at the tops of their lungs *My Thing is My Own* and *The Jolly Brown Turd*, much to the enjoyment of the pub's patrons, who egged them on. Those university days had been so carefree. So long ago. Before he'd learned of the horrors of war.

Gray poured himself another brandy and sang a few lines aloud.

The maid she shat and a jolly brown turd
Out of her jolly brown hole,
Quoth she: if you will candle light
Come blow me the same cole.

He couldn't remember any verses beyond that. Something about a friar meeting the maid but his thinking was too fuzzy to remember.

He decided to forgo the glass and let it tumble to the ground as he now took swigs straight from the decanter. More giggles erupted as he remembered writing dirty limericks with his friends and leaving them on the desk for their tutors to find. One, a jovial man with a good sense of humor, had read them aloud to his gathered pupils. Gray frowned, trying to remember his favorite one and stumbled along as he recited to himself:

There was a young sailor from Brighton,
Who remarked to his girl, "You've a tight one."
She replied, "Oh, my soul,
You're in the wrong hole,
There's plenty of room in the right one!"

Gray erupted in drunk laughter, feeling quite clever, and brought the decanter to his lips again, finishing off the remaining brandy. He tried to remember other limericks and found he drew a blank. Bored, he stood unsteadily, the room moving. Or was it he that moved? He couldn't tell as the empty decanter fell from his hand and hit the carpet. His stomach lurched and he realized, too late, that he should have stopped imbibing long ago.

He plopped back down and slowed his breathing as he gripped the sides of the chair while the room swam. He'd been drunk before but not for a good number of years. War was an uncertain time and an officer couldn't afford to be off his game in any way, especially deep into his cups. He'd indulged in a single glass of wine now and then but had avoided strong spirits during the past five years.

He'd better get to his bed. Standing slowly, he took a few steps. Dizziness overwhelmed him, forcing him to drop to his knees. Why had he been so foolish? His head would ache in the morning something awful. He knew at this point he'd never manage to leave this room, much less make it up the stairs and to his bed.

Opening his eyes, he spotted the settee and crawled toward it. By the time he reached it, he hadn't the strength to climb on it. Instead, Gray lowered his head to the floor and curled up on his side. His head swirled with images of Miss Nott, that full, bottom lip calling out to him. He wanted nothing more than to sink his teeth into it and hear her cry of pleasure.

His last thought was of his arms about her, his tongue inside her mouth. He shuddered with pleasure and passed out.

CHARLOTTE DRESSED FOR bed and then unpinned her hair, brushing it one hundred strokes. She plaited it into a single braid and restlessly moved to the window, staring out across the lawn.

The past month, she'd worked every hour of daylight and far into the night in order to be able to accomplish everything that needed doing at Gray Manor. She'd gotten by on very little sleep, falling into bed and going to sleep immediately.

Tonight, she was agitated. Almost without purpose. She'd left dinner and knocked upon Mrs. Cassidy's door. The housekeeper had admitted Charlotte warily but then they'd shared a cup of tea and confidences. By the time she left an hour later, she felt she had a new friend in Mrs. Cassidy. Next, she'd finished letting out Mr. Masters' jackets. She'd split the seams so he'd be able to get his arm inside the sleeve and then stitched it loosely together so it wouldn't flap and get in his way. Once his plaster came off, she would repair the coats. She'd also visited young Lord Crampton and spent half an hour with him. She knew the boy was lonely and tried to see him on a daily basis, varying the times she came. She left him with a footman. A different one had been assigned to stay awake in the earl's chamber each night in case he suffered an asthma attack and needed assistance.

Charlotte paced her chamber, having nothing to do. It was the first time since she'd arrived at Gray Manor that she had a moment to herself. Within an hour of her arrival and hiring, she'd been planning two funerals. Things hadn't slowed since. Though she longed to go to bed, she knew sleep wouldn't come. Her mind raced too much, all of her thoughts centering on Danforth Grayson. She told herself she'd done the right thing by ending their nightly ritual of dining together. It wasn't proper. She was a governess. He was the head of a large household who did the hiring—while she was the hired help. No matter what she secretly wished for deep within her heart, it could never come to pass. The former military man would never be interested in a lowly governess.

She decided to go to the library and find something to read. She hadn't done any reading for pleasure in months and since she was wide awake, she might as well enjoy the large Grayson library. Charlotte withdrew her green silk dressing gown from the wardrobe. It was the finest thing she owned, a gift from the duchess, who told her it brought out the green of her eyes.

Taking a candle from the bureau, she left the bedchamber and went downstairs. As the clock chimed, she counted ten bells. The house was dark and quiet. Gray Manor definitely kept country hours. She entered the library and smelled a candle which must have been extinguished only a short time ago. Charlotte supposed Mr. Grayson might have been here collecting a book for himself. She wondered what he might like to read and then snorted. It didn't matter. It shouldn't matter. She had to stop thinking about the man else she'd go mad.

"Get a book, Charlotte," she muttered to herself and went to the shelves.

She'd only perused the spine of a few books when she heard a low moan and stilled, fear spiking in her. Turning, she called out, "Who's there?"

Most of the room was in shadow. No one answered. She tamped down her nerves and returned to her search, trying to convince herself she'd only imagined the noise.

"No," a voice said, filled with anguish.

Charlotte asked again, "Who's there?" and still received no reply.

Her heart beating, she slowly walked toward the center of the room. Her foot hit something and she bent, retrieving a tumbler.

"You can't. It'll kill them all."

This time, the voice was clear.

And it belonged to Danforth Grayson.

"Mr. Grayson?" she called out, taking a few more tentative steps.

He muttered and then gasped. Charlotte saw a dark shape on the floor and moved toward it, finding him lying on his side. The strong scent of brandy invaded her nostrils and she determined he was drunk. It surprised her since she'd only seen him consume a single glass of wine at night. Then she watched his body twitch and he moaned again as if in pain. He was dreaming of the war. She had no doubt about it but wondered if she should wake him. As words poured from him, he sounded in agony.

Placing the candle and tumbler down, she knelt beside him, touching his shoulder. He shrugged it off. Charlotte brushed the hair from his brow, reveling in its silky texture. She ran her fingers through it several times, massaging his scalp, trying to comfort him.

"Mr. Grayson," she said gently. "Gray?"

He shot to a sitting position, his eyes wide. Charlotte didn't know if he was awake or still in the depths of his nightmare.

Then his hands latched on to her upper arms and yanked her toward him. Their mouths collided.

And everything changed.

CHAPTER THIRTEEN

THIS KISS HAD nothing in common with the brief touch from before. It was hard, demanding, born of need. And greed.

Charlotte's belly tightened and then exploded with butterflies as Gray's mouth devoured hers. The kiss, almost brutal in nature, stirred something dormant within her. Then he was urging her to open to him. She was helpless to resist. His tongue swept inside her mouth, filling her, rocking her to her core. The place between her legs seemed to explode, a sudden pulsing beating within her as he took and took and took. Breathless, her hands found his shoulders and clasped them tightly.

Then his tongue teased her, no longer dominating, as if calling her out to play. Tentatively, she moved hers against his and both of their breaths hitched. His fingers tightened on her arms and she stroked his tongue as he had hers. A low, guttural noise came from the back of his throat and his kiss became more urgent. Suddenly, they were at war with one another, each fighting for supremacy. She would never have understood the thrill of this kind of battle. Of tongues. Of wills. She grew lightheaded and wondered if the taste of brandy from him had her slightly tipsy.

She no longer knew space or time, only Gray's insistent kiss. Her breasts seemed to swell and then grow heavy, her nipples aching with need. He seemed to understand and one hand released her, only to cup her breast through her dressing gown. She gasped at the touch, his fingers kneading it. Her hands slid up his neck and locked behind it as she pushed herself against him. He drew a nail across the nipple and she whimpered. His thumb began circling without touching it, driving her mad. Then he tweaked the nipple, pulling and twisting on it. Desire flared within her.

His mouth left hers and trailed hot kisses along her jaw and to her throat. She murmured his name again and again as the pounding between her legs thumped rhythmically.

She wanted his touch there.

Charlotte sensed her face flaming at the thought. This was insanity.

Gray's mouth returned to hers, nipping her lips and soothing them with his tongue. His arms had gone around her, drawing her against him, her aching breasts mashed against his muscled chest. Her fingers played with the hair along the nape of his neck, teasing it as his tongue teased her.

When her time came and life was at an end, this is the moment she would relive before everything ebbed away. Her body crushed against his. His mouth slanting over hers, again and again. The rush of passion filling her. Need for him singing in her veins. She wanted it to go on and on, knowing somehow she would never be satisfied again with anything in life.

That gave her pause. This was out of control. She prided herself on conducting herself with dignity, always maintaining restraint. With Gray, restraint had flown out the window.

If she didn't stop this, she was unsure of what would happen next. She'd had no mama to inform her of the ways between a man and a woman. As Charlotte's body betrayed her, giving itself over to Gray, she knew if they didn't halt that they were on a collision course from which they could never return. Much as she wanted to remain in this man's arms and keep on with the drugging kisses, nothing good could come of it.

Deliberately, she moved her palms to the broad wall of his chest. His heart beat out of control underneath her fingertips. She pushed against him and pulled back, breaking the kiss.

"Gray, we must stop," she said gently, sounding perfectly in control but knowing her heart beat as fast as his did.

He looked at her in confusion a moment, then those beautiful blue eyes flickered with desire. The yearning she saw almost broke her resolve and Charlotte forced herself to keep from hungrily kissing him again. Instead, she brought a palm to his cheek, feeling the slight stubble against it.

"Are you all right now?"

His hand went to her wrist and encircled it, his thumb slowly stroking the delicate underside, making her pulse jump.

"I would say I'm sorry . . . but it would be a lie," he said, his voice low and rough.

She bit her trembling lower lip, not trusting herself to speak.

His other hand went to her waist a moment and then he pushed himself to his feet, bringing her with him. Her thumb stroked his cheek once, reveling in the feel of him.

"You were having a nightmare," she said softly.

His brow creased. "I can't seem to rid myself of them," he admitted. "There were times I had to follow orders that were given . . . and even times I issued orders myself . . . that caused the deaths of men under my command. It's impossible to let go. I hear the anguished cries of the dying. The dreams can be vivid." He swallowed. "I've tried to stop feeling—because with feeling comes vulnerability. I already hurt so much for those who were lost."

"War is savage. The atrocities you saw may never leave you. But Gray, you and your commanding officers only did what you thought best. The loss of life is inevitable in battle. Please don't keep holding yourself responsible."

He shook his head. "I'm sorry you saw me like this."

"I only hope I brought some comfort to you. I was afraid to awaken you."

Instead, he'd awakened something within her that would never give her rest.

"You did." He paused. "You called me Gray."

"I thought you might respond to that."

His gaze searched hers. "May I know your Christian name?"

"Charlotte."

"Charlotte," he echoed reverently, as if her name were a prayer. "Charlotte."

Pulling away from him, she said, "I wish you a good night," and took the candle from where she'd set it.

She exited the room, leaving him in darkness, only knowing that she must escape. Her body burned with a fever unknown to her. If she stayed, it would be a mistake.

Reaching her bedchamber, she went inside and, for the first time since she'd slept under the roof of Gray Manor, locked her door. Charlotte climbed into bed, her body afire with need. She wanted Gray's hands on her, everywhere. She longed for his kiss. His taste. His touch. It was as if she'd become Pandora and opened the forbidden box, allowing things to escape that she could never put back. She'd had a small taste of carnal knowledge and it would be hard to pretend the hunger within her for Danforth Grayson didn't exist. Yet she must. She was a governess, no longer of his world. If—or when—he wed, it would be to a woman of the *ton*. He was not meant for her.

And yet just like Pandora, who'd slammed the lid of the box she'd opened with only one thing remaining inside, Charlotte was aware that the one thing she would always foolishly cling to—was hope.

AFTER A RESTLESS night, Charlotte rose, washing and dressing. She heard voices and went to the window, where she saw the carriage waiting. After a moment, Gray came striding toward it and she gazed longingly at the muscled legs and broad shoulders as he climbed into it. Parker followed him inside and closed the door and the carriage took off. The servant had shared with Charlotte that he would be able to remain at Gray Manor because Mr. Grayson had accepted him as his valet.

She only wondered where they now went. He hadn't said goodbye and hurt spread through her like wildfire. Which was ridiculously absurd. Why should the master of a household inform a lowly governess of his decision to come or go? She was an imbecile to think otherwise. What occurred between them last night would never happen again and she knew he would be a gentleman and never bring it up again. Now that Gray Manor had its housekeeper and estate manager, Gray would have little to do with her. He would reside in his sphere and she in hers. As it should be.

Charlotte inhaled deeply, smoothing her gown and heading to the schoolroom. This was her realm. This is where she could make a difference in the lives of two little girls. She entered and saw Betsy already there. The servant bathed the girls and dressed them and had stepped in to watch over them when Charlotte had been occupied by other matters. Perhaps she should start overseeing those things now and free up the servant.

Before she could say anything, servants appeared with their breakfast trays, Mrs. Cassidy bringing up the rear.

"Good morning, Mrs. Cassidy," she said pleasantly. "I'm so glad you came to the schoolroom. This is Lady Harriet and Lady Jane, who are sisters to Lord Crampton."

Both girls scrambled to their feet and curtseyed, which pleased Charlotte. The housekeeper also looked happy and complimented the girls on their manners.

"Miss Nott used to be the housekeeper and our governess," Jane said.

"Now we get to have her all to ourselves," Harriet added, smiling.

"A word with you, Miss Nott?" Mrs. Cassidy asked.

"Certainly. Go ahead and begin eating, girls," Charlotte urged and then followed the housekeeper into the corridor. "After breakfast, we have an hour before lessons begin. That should give us ample time to go through the house together. Betsy can watch the children for me."

"Mr. Grayson left this morning for London and will be gone several days," the housekeeper said. "He asked if you'd show Mr. Linfield the estate today."

"I see. Could you tell Mr. Linfield to examine the estate ledgers this morning? I will tutor the girls until noon and then be able to escort him this afternoon."

"Very good, Miss Nott." The older woman paused. "Mr. Grayson seems to put a good deal of trust in you."

"He was Major Grayson until very recently," Charlotte said. "I was present when his brother and sister-in-law passed away on the same day. The major resigned his commission and came to Gray Manor to serve as guardian to the children and estate. He'd been gone many years and I've been able to help fill in the gaps for him. It was difficult when the previous housekeeper and manager left and I stepped in to assume some of those duties. I know Mr. Grayson is happy to have you and Mr. Linfield in service now. I am relieved to solely be the children's governess once again."

"I see. Then I will see you shortly?"

"Yes, Mrs. Cassidy. Let me eat my meal and I'll be downstairs."

Charlotte returned to the schoolroom and asked Betsy to spend the afternoon with the girls.

"Where will you be, Miss Nott?" Harriet asked.

"Your uncle had to go to London for a few days. I need to help Mr. Linfield with some things this afternoon but I will be back in time for our reading hour," she promised. "Let's finish our breakfast. Betsy, would you be able to stay with the girls after lessons today?"

"Yes, Miss Nott."

She ate quickly and then gave Mrs. Cassidy a complete tour of the house. She could see the older woman was impressed. They even stopped briefly to see Lord Crampton but Mrs. Minter told them the earl had had a restless night and was still sleeping.

Returning downstairs, she said, "You have the list of things being done around the house. Mr. Linfield will be supervising that construction. You'll take over everything now, from scheduling duties to planning the menus." Charlotte smiled. "I'm very happy you've come to Gray Manor, Mrs. Cassidy."

"It seems I will have a great deal of freedom within my responsibilities."

"Yes. I hope that pleases you. Were you able to convey my message to Mr. Linfield?"

"Yes. He will meet you at the stables at noon."

Charlotte went back to the schoolroom and gave the girls lessons in spelling, grammar, and penmanship. They were also beginning a study of English history and discussed the reign of William the Conqueror in more depth.

Luncheon arrived and she told the girls she would see them later today.

"Can we start our music lessons again tomorrow?" pleaded Jane.

"May we start them," she prompted. "And yes. I've decided mornings will be spent on academic matters. Afternoons will be devoted to drawing, music, and horseback riding."

"Yes!" cried Harriet, who constantly talked about learning to ride.

"And then we'll finish the day with our reading. Mind Betsy now. You might wish to go for a walk in the gardens this afternoon."

"Yes, Miss Nott," the girls said in unison.

Charlotte changed into her riding habit and joined Jeremy at the stables. Sable already had horses saddled for both of them. The groom handed her up and she told Jeremy they'd ride the west side of the property first. They moved in a large square along the perimeter of the property and then cut through it. She pointed out the tenants' cottages, the mill, the crops, and livestock pens, as well as the pasture where several horses grazed.

"Shall we walk for a bit?" she asked. "I need to stretch my legs."

He helped her from the saddle and they took their reins in hand as they walked. Charlotte told him to ask away with any questions he might have and it surprised her how many he came up with. She answered to the best of her ability.

"You know as much about Gray Manor as you did about Rumford Park," he noted.

"I always enjoyed following Papa when he went out on the estate. It was good to be able to help here while the family was in a bind."

"A footman told me of the deaths of the earl and countess. To be on the same day must have been shocking—and very hard for the children."

"Yes, I suppose it was, though the parents spent very little time with them."

"I'm sure they adore you. Everyone here speaks highly of you, Lady Charlotte."

She frowned. "It has to be Miss Nott and Mr. Linfield, even when we are alone, Jeremy."

"I understand," he said. "Lord Rumford must be turning in his grave, though, seeing how you've come down in the world."

"Papa would want me to be happy—and I am. I've taken to governessing quite well. My pupils are bright and a pleasure to work with."

"May I ask you about the books? Did you have a chance to examine them?"

"I did," she said cautiously.

"Mr. March was stealing from the estate. He had been for a good number of years."

"That was my opinion, as well."

"Does Mr. Grayson know?"

"I haven't told him directly. I asked that he look at the ledgers but he's had so much to do since he arrived from Spain."

"He was in the army then?" asked Jeremy.

"Yes. Major Grayson. He'd planned on making the army his career but came home to care for his nephew and nieces. I think you should be the one to bring up to him the discrepancy in the bookkeeping."

"Do you think he'll want to press charges?"

"It's possible. Then again, it might be hard to locate Mr. March. Just because he said he had a new post in Cornwall doesn't mean he actually did. I don't know if Mr. Grayson wishes to hire a Bow Street Runner to look into the matter or not. You can ask him when he returns from London."

"Why did he go?"

She frowned. "He certainly had no need to tell me of his plans. If I had to guess, though, it would be to bring back a doctor for Lord Crampton. The boy suffers from asthma and it seems to be growing worse. Mr. Grayson was waiting upon a recommendation of a physician from the Duke of Gilford, whom he seems to trust."

"Then I will speak to him regarding the ledgers upon his arrival." Jeremy looked at her directly. "Have you made any friends here, Charlotte? Everyone speaks of you with reverence."

She shrugged. "I've learned that a governess is in a unique position. Not considered a true servant by those who serve in the house and yet certainly not one of the family. I am friendly with many of those on staff but no, I wouldn't say I'm friends with any of them. I'm hoping that might change with Mrs. Cassidy's arrival."

Jeremy took her hand and she hid her shock. "We were friends once. Do you think we could be again?" The look in his eyes told her he might want more than friendship from her.

"I would like to be your friend," she said cautiously and then gently tugged her hand away.

She wondered if Jeremy Linfield had feelings for her. They'd been so comfortable with one another many years ago. She ventured he was about ten years older than she was and wondered if he had his eye on settling down.

With her.

It would be convenient, both of them working on the same property. If they wed, she would share his cottage and life. After years of isolation, it would be wonderful to have the opportunity to wed. To possibly have children. Yet as much as she enjoyed Jeremy's company, she feared she'd been ruined for any man. She'd known Gray's touch and doubted she could ever settle for less.

"Shall we return to the house?" she asked and allowed Jeremy to help her into the saddle.

Charlotte wondered if she should make clear to him her feelings to remain unwed. She was afraid he might think it was because she'd once been a lady of the *ton* and he a mere groom. For now, she would put the matter from her mind. She might be reading more into the situation than was actually there. If the day came when Jeremy pressed for more than friendship, she'd make it clear to him—though she'd never reveal to him or anyone that who she pined for was Danforth Grayson.

CHAPTER FOURTEEN

GRAY GAZED OUT the window as the Crampton carriage returned him from a week in London. He couldn't help but feel a coward, leaving Gray Manor without a word to Charlotte.

Especially after what had passed between them.

He'd gone over in his mind every kiss—every touch—so many times. Each time, it filled him with longing. And then anguish. He was not the one for her. He wasn't good enough for someone as wonderful as Charlotte.

Charlotte . . .

Just thinking her name brought a smile to Gray's face. She'd always been the inimitable Miss Nott. Knowing her first name, as well as the intimacies they'd engaged in, made him wish for so many things to have been different. For him never to have gone to war and seen the ugly side of humanity. To have found himself lacking when, time after time, he couldn't save all of his men. Charlotte needed someone whole and pure, a man who would challenge and cherish her.

Not a damaged soul like the one he possessed.

He would have to leave Gray Manor soon because he couldn't stay in her proximity and keep his hands off her. It was a disservice to her. He'd acted as any rogue, dallying with her body and her emotions. He refused to hurt her any more than he already had. She deserved so much better than him. Gray thought again of the handsome Jeremy Linfield, his new estate manager. That would be a man worthy of

Charlotte. But not him. Never him. The darkness that consumed him would only engulf her, as well, swallowing whole her goodness and light. He thought too much of her to drag her into his mire.

Bloody hell. He didn't think too much of her. That sounded prissy and distant. For the first time, Gray admitted to himself that he loved Charlotte Nott. Loved everything about her from her blinding smile to her patience to her caring nature. She wrapped everything around her into her arms and made it better.

Could she make him a better man?

He doubted it. Even the capable Miss Nott had her limitations.

At least the London trip had proven successful. Gray had received word from the Duke of Gilford, recommending a Dr. Winston. The man now accompanied Gray back to Kent, where he would remain several days and study Rodger's case. He'd also opened the Grayson family townhome, which hadn't been used in several years. After speaking to several acquaintances at White's, Gray learned that once Seymour gained such a tremendous amount of weight, it was difficult for him to travel and he remained in the country. Especially with his countess practically bedridden from her numerous attempts at birthing a second son, the Cramptons hadn't socialized in London anymore.

Gray hired a butler and walked through the townhouse with him. He only wished it had been Charlotte touring the place, making neat, tidy notes on all the things that needed to be done to make the residence livable again. Gray had left the construction to be done in the new butler's hands and it would be completed in a few weeks. Once finished, the butler had the authority to hire a housekeeper, cook, and whatever staff he wanted indoors. Gray had taken a liking to Sable, the assistant head groom at Gray Manor, and thought to take him to manage the London stables. If Sable agreed, Gray would allow him to hire the necessary grooms.

He'd also managed to purchase a new wardrobe, thanks to Parker's help. The valet had an eye for color and patterns and, though buried in the country, he seemed to know about current fashion and what styles would work best on Gray. While the bulk of his new wardrobe would be delivered to the townhouse upon completion, he'd still been fitted for several pieces and brought them back with him. He wondered what Charlotte would think of him outside his uniform and then scolded himself for letting his thoughts stray in that direction.

The carriage turned and he saw they headed up the lane and would arrive at the manor house soon.

Turning to Dr. Winston, he said, "We're almost there. Again, I must thank you for coming to the country in order to evaluate the earl."

"I'm happy to do so, Mr. Grayson," the physician replied. "I plan to spend all afternoon with the boy and will give you an update over dinner."

"If you don't mind, I will ask Miss Nott to join us. She's governess to my nieces and ever since Rodger has been home, she also serves as the boy's tutor. She's directly involved with his care, having Parker bathe and dress him each day. She says even though Rodger is restricted to his room, she believes it keeps his spirits up by going through the routine. She also comes twice a day and helps him walk about the room so that atrophy doesn't set into his limbs."

"Miss Nott sounds like a wise woman."

"She is the most knowledgeable woman of my acquaintance," Gray replied as the carriage slowed and came to a halt.

The men climbed out as the door opened. Masters greeted them.

"What happened to your arm?" the doctor asked after Gray introduced the two men.

The butler shook his head. "A bit of carelessness on my part. Please, come in, Doctor."

Mrs. Cassidy awaited them in the foyer and Gray introduced her, as well.

"Dr. Winston will be with us for several days, observing Lord Crampton and making recommendations regarding his condition."

"Would you like to be taken to your room to freshen up, Dr. Winston?" the housekeeper asked. "Then I could provide a light luncheon for you and Mr. Grayson before you see Lord Crampton."

"An excellent idea, Mrs. Cassidy," the physician declared.

"We will be three for dinner, Mrs. Cassidy," Gray told her. "I want Miss Nott to join us so Dr. Winston might discuss Lord Crampton's treatment with us both."

"I'll let her know, Mr. Grayson."

After luncheon, he went to Jeremy Linfield's office.

"How was your ride through the estate? Do you have anything to add to the list of things that need immediate attention?"

"No, La . . . Miss Nott's list was most thorough. She accompanied me for several hours one afternoon. We rode the entire property. She pointed out everything that should be done. I was in agreement with her opinions. I already have tenants on the estate working on some of the projects. I also went to Wilton and hired a group of men that are involved with the improvements within Gray Manor."

"It sounds as if you have been busy."

"There's plenty to do, sir." The manager paused. "I've also had time to go through the estate's ledgers for the past decade."

"And?"

"Have you looked at them?"

"Briefly. I've had others things demand my time." Gray frowned. "Miss Nott alluded to something she'd found within them and now I feel you're doing the same. What do I need to know, Mr. Linfield? You can be blunt."

"That Mr. March, during his seven years here, siphoned funds from various accounts."

Gray let the words hang a moment before he said, "You mean he stole from my brother."

"Yes, sir. That's exactly what I mean. The amounts were small each month but, over time, it added up to a goodly sum."

He knew how careless Seymour had been regarding business. His brother had probably never looked at the ledgers or merely given them a cursory glance.

"What do you recommend, Mr. Linfield?"

"I have a tendency to agree with Miss Nott. She doubts Mr. March was going to a new position in Cornwall and that he has taken the money purged from the Crampton estate and disappeared, along with Mrs. Penney. It would be very hard to trace him, especially if he changed his name. Of course, you could always call in a Bow Street Runner, Mr. Grayson."

Gray thought a moment. "Did the amount stolen cause tremendous damage to the estate?"

"No, sir. It was only a small portion each month. Of course, over numerous years, it became a substantial amount."

"Since it didn't impact the estate and the cost to find Mr. March might be excessive, I say we write this off to experience. I thank you for bringing this to my attention, Mr. Linfield. I appreciate your honesty."

"You can depend upon me, Mr. Grayson. This is too great an opportunity for me, serving you and your family at Gray Manor. I will be meticulous in my work. Have no fear. I will never cheat you out of a single farthing."

"I do trust you, Mr. Linfield. And Miss Nott. I feel Gray Manor is in good hands with you both."

"Thank you, Mr. Grayson. I appreciate your confidence in me—and Miss Nott. She is a remarkable lady."

Once again, that flare of jealousy shot through Gray. He knew he wasn't the one for Charlotte but he hated the thought of another man touching her. Still, Mr. Linfield seemed of good character. If a relationship developed between the two, Gray would be happy for them.

And miserable for himself.

"If you'll excuse me, Mr. Linfield, I have other matters to attend to."

He didn't but left his manager's presence and the house. After being cooped up in the carriage all morning, he wanted to be out and about, exercising his legs. He also wanted to avoid the house because he didn't want to run into Charlotte. He still didn't know what he would say to her.

Rounding the corner from the stables, he halted in his tracks. It was almost as if he'd conjured her, for there she was, walking Jane about on a leading rein in the paddock. His younger niece sat straight in the saddle, looking as regal as any princess. Gray spied Harriet sitting on the fence, joy on her face as she shouted encouragement at her sister.

"That's good, Jane. Keep it up. You're doing splendid."

He'd already been coward enough as it was. Steeling himself, Gray went and joined Harriet.

"Uncle Gray, you're back!" she cried, her smile wide. "Miss Nott said you went to London."

"Yes, I had business there."

The eight-year-old studied him. "I like that you're wearing better clothes," she said, approval shining in her eyes. "I don't like thinking of you at war."

By now, Charlotte had led Jane in a circle and was headed back in their direction. Jane saw him and grinned. As she started to raise a hand to wave, he heard Charlotte warn her to keep both hands on the reins.

"You're still a novice, Lady Jane. Don't let your uncle distract you. Concentrate on your horse."

They approached and Gray found his stomach fluttering as if an army of butterflies beat their wings against his sides. It was part giddiness and part nausea, as if he were some schoolboy spying his crush.

That's when he knew for certain as he looked at Charlotte that he loved her.

Physically, he was attracted to her. What man wouldn't be? With her great beauty, she would have had to fight off suitors if she'd been a member of the *ton*. Instead of being a governess on the shelf at twenty-six, she would have had her choice of suitors years ago if she'd made her come-out in London society.

But it was more than Charlotte's looks that made him love her. It was her warmth and sweet spirit. Her intelligence and curiosity. The way she managed everything effortlessly. How she loved the children.

She stopped a few feet from him and he slid off the fence.

"Hello, Jane," he called. "And good afternoon, Miss Nott."

He didn't look at her and instead went to Jane and helped her from the saddle. She hugged him.

"I'm so glad you're back, Uncle Gray. I made three drawings for you."

"You did? Then I cannot wait to see them."

"I can ride now. Miss Nott is teaching us."

"My turn!" Harriet called out, climbing from the fence and rushing over.

Jane took his hand and a wave of happiness swept over Gray. He glanced down at their joined hands and back at his niece.

"Let's go watch Harriet, Uncle." She led him back to the fence.

He lifted her to it and then joined her as they watched Charlotte remind Harriet of their previous lesson by asking her several questions.

Gray leaned over to Jane. "Does she always quiz you?"

"Always. About everything. Miss Nott says that a person never stops learning. She says it's good to say things aloud and also you should think about them. When I go to sleep at night, I see myself on the pony and I hear in my head what she's told me to do. That's how I fall asleep."

"That must be a very nice way to fall asleep. Thinking about riding a horse."

While he was kept up nights thinking about riding Charlotte Nott.

The governess took the leading rein in hand and allowed Harriet to circle the paddock several times. Gray saw the confidence and exuberance Harriet exhibited and decided she would make a fine rider.

The riding lesson came to an end and he again went and met the pair, removing Harriet from the saddle.

"Did you see me, Uncle Gray? I love riding. Miss Nott says that, tomorrow, we might be able to leave the paddock. Do you want to come along with us?"

"Oh, I'm sure your uncle will be busy attending to the estate, Lady Harriet," Charlotte said.

"Isn't that what Mr. Linfield was hired to do?" Harriet asked pointedly.

"Your uncle has many responsibilities. They include supervising Mr. Linfield and many others. You can't expect him to join us, my lady."

"On the contrary, Miss Nott, I believe I can work a short ride into my busy schedule," Gray replied.

Harriet and Jane began jumping up and down gleefully, clapping their hands.

"Settle down," the governess said sternly and both girls froze. "We need to take Dandy inside and give both him and Daffodil their treats. Mr. Sable has the apples you brought."

"May I lead Dandy to the stables?" Harriet begged.

"You may. Don't run. Walk at a steady rate."

"I'll help," Jane insisted and stood next to her sister as Charlotte passed the reins to Harriet.

The girls started up and Gray watched them a moment. "I don't know what they were like before you came but I believe you've done a remarkable job with them, Charlotte." He glanced at her in time to see her frown.

"Mr. Grayson, I prefer you address me as Miss Nott." Her emerald eyes cut from him to watch the girls ahead and she began walking.

He fell into step with her. "I feel I know you better than others," he said.

"Kissing me a few times does not give you the right to address me in such a manner," she said, winter in her voice. "I have forgiven you for taking those liberties but I must insist that we keep a proper distance between us from now on, Mr. Grayson. It's for the best."

His fingers caught her elbow, the contact sparking something between them. "I don't mean to offend you. I thought when we were alone, though, that—"

"That's where you're mistaken," she interrupted, jerking away from him. "There is no need for us to be alone. Ever." She began briskly walking and he rushed to catch up to her.

"I know you're unhappy with me, Charlotte," he said and he caught her frown of disapproval. "I left without a word to you. I shouldn't have done that."

"And why not?" she boldly asked. "Why would you tell the family governess your personal plans? I neither expect nor want you to do so. I've told you, Mr. Grayson, that I'm very happy with my position at Gray Manor. I can't . . ." Her voice broke and she cleared her throat and tried again. "I won't do anything to jeopardize it." She stopped and looked him in the eyes. "There can be nothing between us. No friendship. Or more. I hope we can be cordial in our dealings regarding the children but I must protect myself, Mr. Grayson."

He saw a vulnerability in her for the first time and had a hint of what it must be like for her, at the mercy and whim of whatever her employer did or said.

"I understand, Miss Nott," he told her. "However, I would like you to join me for dinner tonight." Before she could protest, he added, "I have brought a Dr. Winston back from London with me. He's spending all afternoon with my nephew and wants to discuss Rodger's treatment at dinner tonight. Since you are involved in Rodger's care, I would ask you be there to hear firsthand everything Dr. Winston says. You'll have a chance to ask any questions of him, as well. Are you willing to do so?"

He saw her wavering and she finally said, "Yes. I will be there for dinner."

"Thank you. I feel you'll have a better understanding of what the man says and how to enact any treatment he suggests."

By now, they'd reached the stables and he saw a groom had taken the pony in hand and Sable joined the girls, producing an apple for each of them.

"Remember how ye're to offer the treat," the groom reminded the girls. "Palm up, with the apple in the center."

"Yes, Mr. Sable," they said in unison.

The girls ran into the stables and Sable greeted them. "Good afternoon, Mr. Grayson, Miss Nott. Did the young ladies enjoy their lesson today?"

"They did, Mr. Sable," Charlotte said warmly, all trace of coldness now gone from her voice. "We'll need both Dandy and Daffodil saddled tomorrow afternoon. I'm going to allow the girls to leave the paddock."

"Very good, Miss," the groom said. "I'll have the ponies and Moonbeam saddled for ye."

"And Titan for me," Gray added. "I'd like to see how my nieces do in the saddle on their first time out of the gate."

"Certainly, Mr. Grayson."

"Miss Nott, I will see you and Dr. Winston at dinner this evening," he said. "Sable, I'd like a private word with you."

"I'll see to the girls," Charlotte said and left them.

When she was out of earshot, Gray said, "I'm opening up the family townhome in London and plan to spend a majority of my year there. I'll need someone to manage my stables. Would you be interested in coming to the city with me, Sable? You would be in charge of the grooms and any vehicles and the drivers."

The servant beamed. "Yes, Mr. Grayson, I'd be right happy to come to London."

"We'll be going in a few weeks. You'll be able to hire the necessary staff after we arrive. I'd also like your advice as I add to the stables. I'll need horses to ride and others to pull the coach."

"Any ponies, Mr. Grayson, or will the girls bring Daffodil and Dandy with them when they visit?"

"The children will remain at Gray Manor," he said brusquely.

Sable looked surprised but nodded and glanced to the ground.

"I'll see you tomorrow then, Sable," Gray said and returned to the house, somehow sensing the groom didn't approve of his future living arrangements. He didn't care. The sooner he left the country—and the tempting Miss Nott—the better for all concerned.

CHAPTER FIFTEEN

CHARLOTTE ENTERED THE dining room and saw both men had arrived ahead of her. She joined them where they were standing.

Gray said, "Miss Nott, may I present Dr. Winston? He is a renowned physician practicing in London and has come to give his opinion on my nephew's case."

They greeted one another. She was drawn to the newcomer's kind eyes and thought the man to be about forty. His temples were graying and small bits of the gray peppered his dark hair, as well.

"I am glad you've come to give us advice on the earl's health," she said. 'He's a delightful boy. I hate seeing him suffer so."

"I spent several hours with Lord Crampton this afternoon. I must say that he thinks the world of you, Miss Nott. He couldn't say enough good things about you. Ordinarily, I would think it was because you were lax and children seem to think that a good thing, but on the contrary, he told me of your studies and how you've challenged him more than his teachers at Eton."

"Lord Crampton is very fond of history. We are reading about the Peloponnesian Wars now, as well as translating some Homer."

"Shall we sit?" Gray suggested and they moved to the table.

The first course arrived and it surprised her that they spoke of everything but Lord Crampton's health, which Charlotte thought was the whole point of sharing the meal together. Dr. Winston had a younger brother who served in the army, as well as a fellow physician and friend who'd joined up, and the two men talked of the war and different battles that had occurred. It puzzled her until she realized just how dire Dr. Winston's diagnosis must be. With two footmen in the room and the household already aware of the earl's delicate health, Gray must be waiting until they were alone for Dr. Winston's full report.

Dinner concluded and their host said, "Would you care to adjourn to the drawing room and continue our conversation?"

The physician readily agreed and Charlotte nodded her assent. The three left the dining room and Masters poured port for the men and a sherry for her before Gray dismissed the butler.

Once the door closed, he said, "Now that we have privacy, Dr. Winston, please share with us what you've discovered regarding my nephew's case."

The doctor cleared his throat. "Do you know much about asthma, Mr. Grayson?"

"Only that it involves coughing and wheezing. When my nephew was younger, it wasn't as severe. Since I've returned from Spain, though, I've witnessed how difficult it is for him to breathe at times. Physical activity is beyond him. He hasn't left his bedchamber since I've returned to Gray Manor."

"Asthma involves inflammation of the bronchial tubes. A sticky secretion is produced within the tubes with people who have the disease. The airways can become inflamed and filled with mucus and even narrow in scope. That leads to the coughing, especially at night when prone."

"I have the earl sleep with pillows propped beneath him," Charlotte said. "He wheezes too much when lying flat."

"That is a very good practice, Miss Nott, and it should be continued," Dr. Winston said. "The same goes for you getting him from his bed and having him move about without exerting himself overmuch. Bedsores are nasty things and we don't want him to develop any."

"He also experiences a tightness in his chest, as if something heavy is pressing down upon it," she added. "When that happens, it seems to frighten him more than anything. I know the fear makes it difficult for him to breathe."

"Does he have any extended period without symptoms?" the doctor asked.

"No, he doesn't," she said regretfully. "The attacks occur on a daily basis. Some last only a few minutes, while others can drag on for several hours. Those are the times I worry the most."

"And you should. Especially if he experiences severe wheezing when breathing both in and out."

Charlotte nodded. "That's happened on a few occasions. The chest pressure bothers him more during those episodes and he has trouble stopping his cough. His breathing also becomes very rapid, as if he's panicked."

"Does his face become pale and sweaty?"

"Yes, Doctor. On a few occasions, his lips and fingernails even turned blue." She remembered the first time she'd witnessed it and how frightened she'd been for the boy. "I've been told the local doctor used leeches to bleed him and Lord Crampton became much worse. I haven't summoned him to Gray Manor since I've been here."

"Good. I'm not one for using leeches with severe asthma. I know some of my colleagues believe strong coffee or smoking tobacco can help alleviate symptoms."

Charlotte snorted. "I put a stop to those, as well, once I arrived. Lord Crampton was being given both. Orders again from our local doctor. I couldn't see how giving either to a child would be beneficial." She paused. "I hope I didn't overstep my bounds."

"Not if you are doing what's best for the earl."

"What course of action would you recommend in the future?" she asked. "I'm willing to help in any way I can."

"We can try a daily teaspoon of mustard seeds. I have had limited success with that. I've also used small amounts of quicksilver or cinnabar, though that was only with adults. The earl is underweight for a boy his age. I would suggest a diet heavy in meat. Venison. Hare. Chicken. Some wine, in moderation. Recently, I have had some success adding small amounts of diluted nitro-muriatic acid to broth two to three times a day. Also, I think fresh air and sunlight would do Lord Crampton a world of good. If a servant could carry him down once a day for half an hour and let him sit in the sun while the weather is still good, it might help."

Dr. Winston sighed and looked to Gray. "I must be frank, Mr. Grayson. These measures can only do so much. The earl's health is very fragile. After speaking with Mrs. Minter about the frequency and severity of his attacks and now Miss Nott, I believe he might make a year at best."

The physician's words were like a knife plunging into Charlotte's heart. She couldn't imagine what this sweet boy was going through and to now learn he hadn't long to live was the worst news of all.

She looked at Gray and realized he would become the Earl of Crampton upon his nephew's death. He would need to wed in order to provide an heir. Charlotte couldn't watch him bring home a bride, much less see the woman's belly swell with Gray's child in it. Her determination to leave Gray Manor increased tenfold. She would wait until the current earl passed and then seek employment elsewhere. The thought of leaving her charges brought tears to her eyes. She would see the girls had a competent replacement and then she would leave Kent and never return.

Dr. Winston said, "When the attacks become more frequent and severe, opium should be used. It will relax his lordship, helping him to breathe, and induce sleep." Looking directly at Charlotte, he said, "I would like to show you and Mrs. Minter how to use it when she returns tomorrow morning."

She nodded. "Anything else?" she asked, her voice tight and

strained.

"No. I wish I had better news to share," the physician apologized. "Lord Crampton should be made to enjoy what time he has left and when things worsen, be made as comfortable as possible."

"Thank you, Dr. Winston," Gray said, his jaw tight with tension.

"If you'll excuse me," Charlotte said, and both men bid her good night.

She went directly to the earl's room. Smith was the footman on duty tonight and he gave her a brief nod from where he sat in the corner.

"Hello, Miss Nott," the earl said, looking small in his bed. Dark circles were painted under his eyes. "Are you here to read to me?" he asked hopefully.

She picked up the novel they'd been reading together for the past week. "I am. I was eager to find out what happened next to Robinson Crusoe. The last we read, he was about to escape enslavement from the Moors."

"With Xury," the earl prompted.

"That's right. I'd forgotten the boy's name. You have an excellent memory for details, my lord," she praised.

Charlotte moved a chair close to the bed and opened to where the bookmark sat and began reading. She'd only read half a page when she sensed movement and, from the corners of her eyes, saw that Gray had entered the room.

"What are you reading?" he asked his nephew.

"It's about the adventures of Robinson Crusoe."

Gray smiled as he took a chair and placed it on the opposite side of the bed and sat. "Ah, I read it when I was a boy. What part are you at?"

The boy said a few words before being seized by a coughing fit. Charlotte handed him a handkerchief and he spit the foul-looking mucous into it. She gave him a sip of broth that always rested next to the bedside and he fell back against the pillows looking drained.

"We can read another time," she said.

"No," he whispered. "Please. Go on."

Reluctantly, she picked back up where she'd left off. As she continued reading, she saw Gray take the boy's hand. Though he said he had no feelings left inside him and nothing to give anyone, Charlotte believed that the children might save him. She'd seen the fond looks he'd bestowed upon Harriet and Jane and saw he was just as taken with his nephew. If Gray would only open his heart and allow love into it, she knew he would be a good parent to these children, as well as a good earl when the time came.

She read until the boy fell asleep and placed the bookmark at their stopping point before setting it on the nearby table. Rising, she bent and brushed a kiss on the child's brow. It surprised her when Gray did the same.

They left the room and he walked down the corridor with her, no words between them.

As she turned to go up the stairs to her room, he took her hand, entwining his fingers with hers and said, "Thank you for not only teaching him—but loving him. I'm afraid he received none from his parents. They were selfish people who should never have had children. You have been a godsend to all three of them, Charlotte."

She wished he would hold her hand forever. It felt so right, better than anything she could think of. She saw his eyes drop to her mouth and her lips tingled in anticipation of his kiss. But that would be wrong. Gray would have a life far beyond the one she ever would. He would become titled and wealthy. He belonged to the *ton*. She had been exiled from it.

In this moment, Charlotte knew she must guard her heart. She stepped away from him, pulling her fingers from his.

"Good night, Mr. Grayson."

Hurrying away, she prayed he wouldn't follow. Her heart was already ragged enough, knowing she would lose the young earl soon, and then she'd be parted from those precious two girls. She couldn't give any more of herself to Gray. She'd already lost enough in her life. Charlotte was strong but she could only take so much.

She reached her bedchamber and entered quickly, shutting the door and leaning her forehead against it, tears spilling down her cheeks. Blindly, she turned the lock and pressed her palms against the door to hold herself up from collapsing.

A soft knock sounded. "Charlotte?"

It was Gray.

She blinked rapidly and saw the handle turn—but the door remained shut and locked.

"Charlotte?" he called again and she heard the anguish in his voice.

It took everything in her power not to open the door and throw herself into his arms. What she wouldn't give for a brief moment of comfort, his arms encasing her, his lips moving against hers. But it would lead to nothing. It would resolve nothing. She'd only be more broken and alone than she was now.

After a moment, she heard him sigh and his footsteps carried him away.

Chapter Sixteen

GRAY FINISHED WRITING his last letter and sealed it. He'd first penned a post to the Duke of Gilford, thanking him for recommending Dr. Winston and giving the duke an idea of Rodger's prognosis. The physician had remained in Kent for three days and had left almost a week ago. Dr. Winston wrote down all of his recommendations, which he'd given to Charlotte.

He'd written separately to Burke and Reid, bringing both men up to date on the situation at Gray Manor. His friends knew how passionately he'd hated Seymour and yet Gray wanted to make things right with his brother's children. He vacillated between wanting to give more of himself to the children and yet showing that kind of vulnerability frightened him beyond measure.

It made him think once again of how he only wanted to be left alone to his bitterness. Retreating to London would solve some of his problems. The irony was that while Gray felt unlovable, at the same time, he yearned for love and tenderness.

With Charlotte Nott.

He didn't know how to get past his pain, though. It had proven easier to withdraw from others, where no one could hurt him. It was one thing to recognize he possessed a wounded spirit and another to learn how to forgive himself and move past the darkness that ate away at him. As long as he remained so conflicted, he had to push Charlotte from his thoughts. She deserved a much better man than Gray could ever be. Catching glimpses of her every day brought more suffering than he could cope with. He looked forward to every conversation with her and then hated that he relived every word of it when he was alone. After accompanying her and his nieces on a riding lesson, he'd chosen to stop participating. It was too hard seeing Charlotte's cheeks bloom with roses and hear her laughter as she urged the girls on.

At least he'd come to the decision to leave in the morning. He'd already informed Masters and Mrs. Cassidy of his plans and had spoken at length with Jeremy Linfield regarding estate matters. Sable was readying the coach and Parker was spending the day packing. Gray knew he must tell the children, as well, though he dreaded their reaction. And Charlotte's.

Rising, he took the letters to the foyer for Masters to post. He was thirsty and thought he'd stop by the kitchen for a cup of tea. As he started down the hall, he paused, hearing music. And then the most angelic voice that must be this side of heaven. It drew him up the stairs.

Gray paused in front of the open drawing room doors and then slipped into the room. At the far end, he saw Charlotte sitting at the pianoforte, playing and singing. Rodger sat in the bath chair that Gray had sent to Canterbury for, a smile on his face.

He slipped into a chair near the door, not wishing to interrupt. Closing his eyes, he lost himself in the music and Charlotte's rich contralto. She moved effortlessly from one piece to the next. Her voice evoked emotions in Gray that he hadn't known still existed and when she finished her last song, he removed a handkerchief from his pocket and wiped tears from his cheeks.

She turned and smiled at the boy, who grinned from ear to ear.

"I hope you enjoyed that, Lord Crampton."

"It was better . . . than going . . . outside," he managed.

Gray stood and walked toward them. "I was passing and heard music. I hope you don't mind that I joined you."

Her eyes grew wary but she nodded politely. "Of course not, Mr. Grayson. This is your home. You should go wherever you wish."

"Isn't Miss Nott . . . wonderful?" Rodger asked.

"She is, indeed," he agreed.

"I thought that Lord Crampton might enjoy hearing some music. His sisters are just beginning their lessons and aren't quite ready for an audience yet."

Parker entered the drawing room. "How did you like Miss Nott's singing, my lord?" the valet asked.

"I did." Rodger yawned. "I'm . . . tired, though."

"Not a problem, my lord. I can take you back upstairs. It's time you had a nap after sitting outside this morning and receiving your own personal concert this afternoon."

"Will you play for me again, Miss Nott? Soon?" the boy pleaded.

"I'd be honored to, my lord," she replied.

Parker rolled the bath chair from the room. Charlotte stood and Gray didn't want her to leave.

"Would you play a song for me?" he asked. "A favorite of my father's. Well, actually, my mother's, but I never knew her. She died giving birth to me. Father told me it was one she loved."

"I lost my mother when I was very young," she revealed.

He told her the title. "Do you know the tune?"

She nodded. "I'd be happy to play it for you, Mr. Grayson."

Seating herself at the pianoforte again, her fingers hovered over the keys a moment and then she began. Gray let himself be swept up in the music, thinking of how his mother enjoyed this song above all others. A miniature of her sat in his chambers now. He looked at it every night, the same as his father had, feeling guilty that his birth had caused her death.

Charlotte concluded the piece and rose.

Gray stood. "Thank you. I only wish my father could have heard you sing and play. Actually, your voice is remarkable, Charlotte. I fear you're wasting your time as a governess. You should be singing for audiences in cities far and wide. Your rich tone only adds to the emotion of your performance."

Her lips trembled and tears glistened in her eyes. Gray didn't know why his words upset her so.

"I'm sorry. Have I said something wrong?" he asked.

"No," she said softly. "My mother. She was a singer. I suppose I have inherited what little talent I have from her."

"It's a considerable talent. And I am serious. You should consider going on stage. You could make a hundredfold what you do as a governess. Audiences would clamor to attend your performances."

Anger flashed in her eyes. "Yes, the life of a singer," she said, bitterness thick in her voice. "The crowds pay to hear and then look down upon you when you are no longer on the stage." Her eyes narrowed. "You have no idea what you speak of, Mr. Grayson. Polite Society thinks a singer or actress no better than a harlot. Forgive me if I prefer respectability over denigration."

Charlotte swept past him, spots of color on her cheeks. Gray reached out and snagged her elbow, halting her forward progress.

"Stop touching me," she hissed. "Stop looking at me as if you wished to kiss me." They stared at one another for a long moment. Her anger cooled, leaving only sadness in her brilliant green eyes. "Please, Gray. Just leave me alone."

He released her and she fled from the room. Gray had no idea what had just happened. He'd only wished to compliment her on her beautiful voice, the best he'd ever heard. Then he remembered that she'd said that her mother was a singer. Had Charlotte heard her mother praised—and then lambasted? No, it couldn't be, especially if she'd lost her mother at such a young age. She would have no memory of such cruel remarks.

How and where did Charlotte grow up? She'd mentioned her father when they'd spoken of gardening and it had seemed to him that she remembered the man fondly. More and more, Gray realized Charlotte Nott was an enigma that he would never solve.

CHARLOTTE WENT TO her room, keeping her head down so no one would see her tears. She entered the bedchamber and shut the door, allowing her hurt to manifest itself as she cried softly.

Her father had encouraged her to sing to him every night, praising her voice and telling her how much she reminded him of her mother and his beloved wife. She'd enjoyed entertaining him as he would sit enraptured by her songs each evening after dinner. She'd grown up cocooned in his love, happy she closely resembled her mother and that she could bring joy to her father with her voice.

Those days of happiness had changed when Papa passed. Charlotte could still vividly recall her final encounter with Barclay, calling her the daughter of a third-rate opera singer, telling her that her mother was a whore. If her brother thought that of her and singers in general, she supposed all of Polite Society did, as well. When Gray praised her voice just now and encouraged her to take the stage, it was like a slap in the face. Though she loved the mother she couldn't remember, Charlotte could never follow in her footsteps and sing professionally. She'd rather no one know her name and remain buried in the country, working with children and the elderly.

Knowing it was time for the girls' afternoon riding lesson, she quickly changed into her riding habit and rinsed her face with cool water before going to the schoolroom. Betsy's smile greeted Charlotte and then faltered.

"Have you been crying, Miss Nott?" Harriett asked, concern in the young girl's voice.

"I have," Charlotte admitted, thinking of a quick lie. "I had something in my eye. It hurt dreadfully and as I cried, it must have come out."

Jane took her hand. "I'm sorry about your eye, Miss Nott."

She smiled gently at the shy child. "Well, I'm all better now. It's time we go to the stables."

Both girls grinned and rushed from the room, Charlotte following on their heels. They reached the stables and a groom had Daffodil and Dandy waiting, while Sable held Moonbeam for her. He helped her into the saddle as the other groom handed up the girls.

They left the area and Charlotte had them walk their horses to the nearby meadow.

"We're going to canter now," she told them. "Remember what we've talked about. Hold the reins firmly. Don't tense your body for the horse will sense if you're fearful."

"We're not afraid, Miss Nott," Harriet informed her. "Jane and I love to ride."

"All right. Follow me."

She nudged Moonbeam and settled into a trot, frequently looking over her shoulder. Both girls kept up well as they went up and down the meadow numerous times. Charlotte finally brought Moonbeam to a halt and turned to watch her charges arrive. They both pulled up on the reins, their faces flushed with happiness.

"That was fun," Jane said. "May we do it again?"

"We've ridden enough for one day," she replied. "Would you like to canter back to Gray Manor?"

"Yes!" both girls cried gleefully.

"Harriet, you may lead. Jane, follow behind but not too closely. I'll bring up the rear."

They rode back to the manor and the stables. Sable and another groom greeted them. Once taken from the saddle, Sable handed each girl an apple.

"No giving it to them until they're back in their stalls," he warned.

"Yes, Mr. Sable," Jane said and she and Harriet followed the two ponies being led into the stables.

"Let me give ye a hand," Sable said and helped her dismount.

"Thank you."

The groom sighed. "I'll sure miss ye and the girls, Miss Nott."

"Have you taken another position, Mr. Sable?"

He grinned. "I have. With Mr. Grayson in London. We're leaving tomorrow. I'll be head groom there and get to hire the others."

Charlotte managed a weak smile though it felt as if she'd been dealt a blow to her belly. "So, you'll remain in London?"

"Yes, Miss. Mr. Grayson says he's already hired a butler, who'll take care of hiring the rest of the staff. We'll be there most of the year."

"I see."

A shadow crossed his face. "I thought ye might bring Lady Harriet and Lady Jane to London to visit Mr. Grayson but that doesn't seem to be the case."

"No. Keeping children to a regular schedule is important," she said, though her words sounded far away.

Gray was leaving.

And he wasn't coming back.

Chapter Seventeen

GRAY BREAKFASTED EARLY and knew he couldn't put off talking to the children any longer. He went first to his nephew's room, almost hoping the boy was still asleep. Instead, he found him awake and eating a soup filled with chunks of chicken and onions.

"Uncle Gray." Rodger sighed, the words seeming to take all the strength from him.

"I've brought you a book," he said, handing over a leather-bound copy of *Gulliver's Travels*. "I read this when I was a little older than you are. It's got quite a bit of satire in it. Are you familiar with that term?"

"A little."

"Miss Nott will be able to help you understand it."

"Miss Nott knows a lot."

His throat tightened. "She certainly does. I hope you'll enjoy this."

Rodger coughed some and Gray handed him the handkerchief that sat on the bedside table as he'd seen Charlotte do countless times. His nephew spit the phlegm into it and then spooned more broth into his mouth. The coughing ceased.

"Will you also talk about it with me?" the boy asked hopefully.

Guilt flooded him. "Not in person but you can write to me in London. I'll be spending most of my time in the city. Masters has the address."

"Oh."

His nephew looked so forlorn that, for a moment, Gray questioned whether he ought to go or not. Then he stiffened his resolve.

"The book is broken into parts. Four voyages. In the first, Gulliver travels to Lilliput. Perhaps you could write after you've read each section and let me know what you think."

Rodger nodded and Gray saw resignation in the lad's eyes.

"I'll be off within the hour. I just wanted to come tell you goodbye."

His nephew lifted his hand and Gray shook it. "Goodbye, Uncle Gray."

"Goodbye, Rodger."

He left the room. There was no saying he hoped the boy felt better because Gray knew he wouldn't. The next time he set foot at Gray Manor would most likely be for his nephew's funeral.

Next, he went to the schoolroom where Harriet and Jane would be at breakfast with their governess. He took a deep breath and then entered the room, smiling broadly.

"Good morning, girls," he said pleasantly. "Miss Nott."

Harriet and Jane jumped up to greet him, hugging him tightly. Jane took his hand and led him back to the table. As he sat in the small chair, his eyes met Charlotte's.

She knew . . .

It shouldn't surprise him. Servant gossip was the lifeblood of any house. In her eyes, though, he saw disapproval. And disappointment. He looked away.

"Do you want me to draw you a picture today?" Jane asked.

"Will you go riding with us during our lesson today, Uncle Gray?" Harriet pleaded.

"I am going to London today. I leave in a few minutes. I've come to say goodbye to you."

"When will you be back?" This from Harriet, who eyed him warily.

"Not for quite a while," he said truthfully. "Now that I've hired good people to run Gray Manor and care for you, I will be spending most of my time in the city."

"When will we come visit you?" Jane asked shyly.

"It's important you remain at Gray Manor and keep to your lessons," he said, his throat closing as reality set in.

Harriet glared at him. "When will you be back?" she growled.

"I plan to visit once or twice a year to see how things are being managed."

The girl sprang to her feet, her tiny hands fisted. "I knew it. You only pretended to like us. I told Miss Nott that you wouldn't like me. That you wouldn't like us. I've tried so hard to be good—and it wasn't enough. No one likes us. No one cares for us."

Her face grew red and she said, "I hate you, Uncle Gray. I hope you never come back."

Harriet ran from the room. Jane burst into tears and followed her sister.

Gray sat there numbly.

Charlotte rose, her displeasure obvious. "I never would have figured you for a coward, Gray," she said, her words cutting him to the quick. "They are orphans. They *need* you."

He stood. "They have you and Betsy to care for them."

"That's not enough and you know it," she said, anger sparking like fire in her eyes. "You are their blood kin and you are abandoning them. Would you have abandoned your men on the battlefield?"

"Never."

"Then why would you walk away from these helpless children? And don't tell me you don't feel anything for them. You do. I know you do. I've seen how fondly you look at them."

He crossed his arms. "I've told you I'm no good to anyone, Charlotte. I'll do my duty to the estate. See my nieces and nephew have the best care possible. But I can't be there for them emotionally. I don't have anything to give them."

"You're right. You don't." She scowled at him. "You aren't the man I thought you were, Danforth Grayson. You are beyond selfish. You're putting your own needs above helpless children. Children who worship the ground you walk upon. When you leave, you are abandoning them in every sense possible. The damage will be irreparable."

"You are exaggerating, Charlotte. I don't even have that much to do with them now."

Tears welled in her eyes. "You are a fool and have inflicted worse upon them than their own parents did. Your coming home gave them hope—and now you've snatched that away."

He saw she trembled with rage now and longed to reach out to touch her but knew he would be rejected.

"You've wounded them as surely as if you'd run one of your bloody bayonets through their hearts." Charlotte paused. "Harriet's right. It would be better if you never came back."

She hurried from the schoolroom, leaving him alone. Silence surrounded him and his heart ached more than when he'd seen death claim his own men. Gray knew he brought harm everywhere he went. It renewed his resolve to leave, knowing he did what was best for what was left of his family. It would be hard for the children for a short while but, in the long run, they were better off without him. Charlotte would see the destruction he'd brought pushed aside. She would be the balm for their souls as they slowly healed.

Gray left the schoolroom and went to the stables. Parker told him the carriage was loaded. Sable had Titan saddled and ready.

"I'll ride ahead. The two of you take the coach. The driver knows to return with it so it will be at the family's disposal should they need it. I'll purchase another one once we reach London."

"Very good, sir," Parker said and he and Sable climbed inside the vehicle.

Gray nodded at the coachman waiting atop the carriage and he flicked the reins. For his part, Gray urged Titan on and galloped away from Gray Manor.

And a life that could never be his.

CHARLOTTE WENT TO comfort Harriet and Jane, knowing how raw their feelings were. They had openly given their affections to their uncle and he had let them down in the worst way possible—indifference and his absence from their lives. She would have to pick up the shattered pieces of their hearts and try to mend them somehow.

And not think of her own heart that would never, ever heal.

How could she love a man who would do something so hurtful?

She stopped in her tracks, sucking in her breath. Tears stun her eyes as she realized she loved Gray. Despite his tremendous faults. Despite the fact that he now abandoned them. Of all the idiotic, stupid things to do. She'd gone and fallen in love with a man so broken, so flawed, that the only thing he could successfully do is run away from the very people who loved and needed him.

Charlotte resolved to put every thought of Danforth Grayson from her mind. She refused to mope—and she certainly wouldn't let the children do so, either. She would guide them as they all turned the page and entered a new chapter of their lives.

One where Gray played no part.

Brushing the tears from her cheeks, she knocked softly on the closed door and received no reply. Opening it, she found Harriet and Jane sprawled face down on the bed they shared, both girls weeping into their pillows. Charlotte went and sat on the bed, where she stroked each girl's hair and let them cry it out. They would be spent physically but feel better emotionally.

The tears finally subsided and Harriet nudged Jane. Both girls turned over and stared at her.

"He's an awful, awful man," Harriet said, her jaw setting as stubbornly as her uncle's.

"Your Uncle Gray is very confused and unhappy," she began.

Jane's eyes went as round as saucers. "He is? But I thought he liked it here."

Harriet snorted. "I told you he wouldn't like us."

"Hush, Lady Harriet. That's not true," Charlotte said. When the girl started to speak, Charlotte shook her head. "The war hurt your uncle."

"Did he get shot?" Jane asked.

"No. But it's as if he did. Your uncle was an officer, in charge of a great many men. In war, men are killed. Your uncle, though he was following orders from above, feels responsible for his men dying."

"But he didn't kill them himself," Harriet pointed out, the wisdom of her eight years only seeing in black and white and not the varying shades of gray of real life.

"We know that but he still hurts as if he did kill them."

"Can't we make him feel better?" Jane asked. "I would give him a drawing every day."

"Uncle Gray is broken inside," Charlotte said. "And no one can fix him but himself. He needs to go away and see if he can figure things out."

"Will he?" Harriet asked softly, doubt in her eyes.

"I hope he can. If he doesn't, we'll have to make the best of things. You are very lucky. You live in a wonderful, large house. You don't have to worry about not having enough food to eat."

"And we get to learn from you, Miss Nott," Jane said brightly. "And ride horses and play the pianoforte."

"You do. Not every young girl is lucky enough to do so." Charlotte paused. "I think we will put aside our lessons today."

"Can we go riding?" Harriet asked eagerly.

"I have something better in mind," she told them. "You both are in need of new clothes since you're growing so fast. I'd also like to see riding habits made up for you. We'll go into Wilton today and see the seamstress there."

"Yes!" cried Jane.

"After that, we can eat at the inn."

"What will we get?" Harriet asked eagerly. "We've never been there before."

"We'll have to see what they're serving today. We'll also go to the store and see if they have drawing paper and art supplies. Why, I'll even buy you each some new ribbons."

The smiles on their faces warmed Charlotte.

"We'll leave in half an hour. I want to go see your brother first. I'll meet you in the foyer downstairs."

She left them and went to the earl's room. Mrs. Minter nodded from her chair and Charlotte went to the bed.

"What are you reading?" she asked, not familiar with the large tome in his lap.

"It's *Gulliver's Travels*. Uncle Gray gave it to me. He said you could help me understand it. I'm to write him when I finish reading about each voyage."

"That was nice of him."

The boy frowned. "He won't be coming back for a long time."

"I know. He told your sisters the same thing just now."

Rodger wheezed a few times and then asked, "Is there something wrong with us, Miss Nott? Father and Mother didn't like us. I thought Uncle Gray did."

"He does, my lord. He has many responsibilities, though, since your father died. He must see to all of them. I'm going into Wilton with your sisters. Is there anything you'd like me to bring back to you?"

He thought a moment. "What about a sticky bun? Mr. Masters

brought me one once."

"I'll see to it. And we'll talk about what you've read once I return."

Charlotte smoothed the boy's hair and kissed the top of his head. She retrieved her reticule from her room and checked to see that she had ample money to feed them before going downstairs and seeking out the butler.

"Mr. Masters, I'm taking Lady Harriet and Lady Jane into Wilton. They need new clothes. We also plan to eat at the inn and look for new art supplies. They are going through the drawing paper I brought rather quickly."

He gave her an approving smile. "This will brighten the young ladies' spirits, especially with Mr. Grayson leaving today. Tell the seamstress to send the bill to Mr. Benjamin Bonham in Canterbury."

"Lord Crampton has requested that I bring back a sticky bun for him. Could you tell me where to purchase one?"

"I can. Let's go see Mr. Linfield."

She accompanied him to Jeremy's office and Masters explained what the proposed outing entailed. He asked that the manager use some of the funds kept on hand so that Miss Nott could pay for a meal and miscellaneous supplies while in town.

Jeremy reached into a box. As he did, he said, "There are a few things I need in Wilton, as well. Would you mind if I accompanied you and the young ladies, Miss Nott?"

"That would be wonderful, Mr. Linfield." She knew what a happy person Jeremy was. It would be good for the girls to be around someone who was eternally optimistic.

He slipped an envelope he withdrew from the box into his pocket as he rose. Smiling, he said, "Let's go enjoy this fine day."

Chapter Eighteen

Charlotte told Jeremy that the girls were down in the mouth about their uncle's departure for London and that was why she had suggested the outing to Wilton.

"Then we'll do our best to cheer up the young ladies," he promised. "I was surprised by Mr. Grayson's quick departure. You could have knocked me over with a feather when he told me he'd only return once every year or so. Now mind you, I don't mind the responsibility and am grateful Mr. Grayson has enough trust in me to run the estate. I'm to send him monthly reports."

Gray hadn't even mentioned to her to do the same regarding the children's progress, which only added to his list of sins.

They met the girls in the foyer and Charlotte told them Mr. Linfield would accompany them to the village.

"I hope you don't mind me going with you. I have a few errands I need to run and I can't think of a better day to do so or more delightful company."

She could see him already charming the two. Harriet's scowl lessened and Jane looked at Jeremy hopefully.

"Come, let's go to the stables and see if there's a cart."

"There is, Mr. Linfield," Harriet told him. "I don't know if we'll all fit, though."

Jeremy had a groom bring out a cart, pulled by a pair of horses. The bench where the driver sat would hold another passenger and if they squeezed together, one of the girls.

"Here, we'll have a few blankets brought out and Lady Harriet and Lady Jane can ride in the back. Miss Nott may ride up front with me."

The girls seemed excited and Charlotte got them settled before she allowed Jeremy to lift her to the bench. He climbed in behind her and took up the reins.

The September morning weather was sunny with a slight breeze. Kent was still green as far as the eye could see. Charlotte breathed in the fresh country air and tried not to think of Gray riding Titan toward London. He would only be about seventy miles away but she knew from experience what a wide gulf separation represented. When they arrived in Wilton, she'd be only a handful of miles from where she grew up—but the distance between her old life and current one was vast.

As the horses trotted away from Gray Manor, Jeremy said, "I think it's a fine time to sing."

"Oh, yes," Harriet said. "Miss Nott sings very well."

He gave her a sly grin. "Does she, now? Well, Miss Nott, would you care to sing along with me?"

"Please, Miss Nott. Sing with Mr. Linfield," begged Jane.

Charlotte shrugged. "You begin," she told him. "I'll join in."

"Here's one you'll know."

He began with the first line of *Lord Randall*. She let him sing for a moment by himself and then slipped in, allowing him to sing the melody while she harmonized.

When they finished, the girls clapped enthusiastically and Harriet called, "Again!"

"The same song?" Jeremy asked, laughing.

"Yes. I like it. But this time let Miss Nott start out."

He glanced at her. "I'm not sure I can harmonize as well as you," he said, turning his eyes back to the road.

"I don't think they care," she said gaily and began again.

Jeremy let her sing the first verse and then jumped in. She thought he had a pleasant voice and did a fine job.

"Do another one," Jane insisted.

"Let's do one together," she suggested.

They sang several songs and before long, the village of Wilton appeared in front of them.

"That was so much fun," Harriet said.

Charlotte was glad the girl seemed to have put her foul mood behind her. She wanted this day to be special.

"You can drop us at the dressmaker's," she told Jeremy. "We'll be there a good hour or more."

"That will give me time to accomplish what I need to do. I will call there for you once I'm done."

He slowed the cart until it came to a halt and then handed her and the girls down before driving away with a merry wave.

"Mr. Linfield is nice," Jane said.

"I like him better than Uncle Gray," Harriet said, a stubborn set to her mouth.

Charlotte gave her a warning look. "No mentions of your uncle, Lady Harriet. We're to enjoy today."

She'd only been in the dressmaker's shop twice that she could recall, many years ago. One of her father's tenants had a way with a needle and had made all of Charlotte's clothes. She'd been promised a London-created wardrobe when it came time for her Season, a time that never arrived. She wondered if the shop owner would recognize her, the first hurdle to jump during this trip to Wilton.

Harriet pushed the door opened and a little bell rang to signal customers had arrived. Charlotte closed the door behind them as a young woman close to her own age appeared.

"Good morning, Lady Harriet, Lady Jane."

"Good morning," they responded and then Harriet said, "This is Miss Nott. She's our governess. Where is Mrs. Castle?"

Sadness filled the woman's eyes. "My grandmother died last month. I have taken over the shop for her. But don't worry. I have been sewing clothes for our clients for a good decade now. Grandmother's eyes grew foggy so I took over for her." She smiled at Charlotte. "It's a pleasure to meet you, Miss Nott. I'm Miss Castle."

"I'm happy to make your acquaintance, Miss Castle. Does your mother also work here?"

"No. Mother died when I was five. It was my grandmother who raised me. What brings you in today?"

"We're growing," Jane said solemnly. "Our gowns are too short."

"And we need riding habits," Harriet added.

"Oh, you'll look right smart in a riding habit, my lady," Miss Castle said.

Jane frowned. "What you wear can make you smart?"

Miss Castle laughed. "No, it means that you will look fashionable." When Jane still looked puzzled, she said, "Pretty. You'll look pretty in your new riding clothes." Turning to Charlotte, she asked, "What else do the young ladies need, Miss Nott?"

"I've looked over their wardrobes and made a list." She withdrew it from her reticule and handed it to the seamstress. For a moment, she could see Gray's smiling image and hear him tease her about her endless lists. Charlotte pinched herself, willing all thoughts of Gray to go far away.

Miss Castle's eyes skimmed the page. "Yes, I'll be able to do all of these. If you'd like to look around the store, Miss Nott, I'll take the girls in the back and measure them. It won't take long." She held out her hands and Harriet and Jane took them.

Charlotte wandered through the store, her fingers brushing along different bolts of material. She wished she could order a new gown for herself but she needed to save every penny. The day would come when Gray became Lord Crampton and she didn't wish to remain if he took up residence at Gray Manor. She hoped that wouldn't be too soon. She still wanted time to help these children heal from the wounds their parents—and Gray—had inflicted upon them.

The bell chimed again and she dreaded turning around, thinking it might be someone who would recognize her. It would be rude, though, to keep her head down and not acknowledge another's presence. Charlotte glanced up and saw Dr. Pittman's wife. The physician had seen to her father at his sudden end, not able to prevent or delay the illness. He'd also been the one who'd bled Lord Crampton, trying to help his asthma. She didn't know if Dr. Pittman's wife would know her.

"Good morning," she said cordially and glanced back, fingering some material.

The woman came toward her. "Do I know you? I'm Mrs. Pittman, the doctor's wife."

Charlotte saw the cloudy eyes behind Mrs. Pittman's spectacles and knew she suffered from cataracts, which would impair her vision.

"I don't think so. I am the governess to Lady Harriet and Lady Jane Grayson at Gray Manor."

At that moment, the girls came rushing out, both talking at once in a torrent of words.

"Girls," she mildly cautioned and they fell silent.

Immediately, they curtseyed and Charlotte said, "This is Mrs. Pittman."

"I'm Lady Harriet Grayson and this is my sister, Lady Jane."

The old woman smiled. "It's very nice to meet you. My husband has come to Gray Manor. He's Dr. Pittman."

"Hello, Mrs. Pittman," Miss Castle said. "I have your dress. Would you like to try it on to see if I need to make any adjustments to the hem?"

"Yes, dear."

"I'll be right back," Miss Castle promised and took the older woman's arm, guiding her to the back.

"We got measured," Jane said. "Miss Castle says I have grown almost two inches. Harriet's grown one."

"You are younger," Charlotte said. "Your body is trying to race and catch up to your sister's height."

"I think I'll always be taller," Harriet said loftily.

"No, I will," Jane said stubbornly.

"Let's look at some material. I've picked out a few bolts that I think you'll like."

Miss Castle rejoined them and they quickly chose fabric to match the various gowns to be made up. For the riding habits, Charlotte suggested a hunter green for Harriet and a midnight blue for Jane.

"You have good taste, Miss Nott. You've made excellent choices."

"Miss Nott does everything well. Especially sing," Harriet said.

Charlotte sensed her cheeks heating. "When might you be finished with the garments, Miss Castle? I think the girls are most interested in having their riding habits first."

"If you come back in a week's time, I'll have those and two gowns each completed. It will take another couple of weeks before I can fill the rest of your order."

"Shall we come back to Wilton next Thursday?" Charlotte asked.

"Yes!" the girls cried.

"Thank you, Miss Castle. We will see you then. Let's go outside," she suggested.

The timing was perfect. Jeremy was pulling up in the cart, which had several items placed in the vehicle's bed.

"Is anyone as famished as I am?" he asked.

Charlotte laughed. "I think we all are."

"Then it's off to The Dancing Duck!"

"The what?" Harriet cried.

"The Dancing Duck. It's the inn where we'll dine. Surely, you've seen ducks that dance, Lady Harriet?" he asked, a teasing light in his eyes.

"Never."

"I have," Jane said.

"You have not," Harriet said.

"I have so."

Charlotte intervened. "Girls, enough. What's waddling to one person might very well be dancing to another. You're irritable and fighting because you're hungry. That can easily be solved by us going to The Dancing Duck for something to eat."

Jeremy added, "It's bad luck to argue on a sunny day."

Harriet started to say something and then thought better of it. She stuck her tongue out at Jane. Her sister mimicked the gesture. Charlotte gave them a warning look and they both went to the cart, where Jeremy lifted them to the bed and then assisted her into the seat next to him. They drove a few blocks to their destination and the girls scrambled down without help.

"You're good with them," he said, offering her a hand.

She took it. "It's what I'm paid to do."

"Have you ever thought of having children of your own?" he asked.

Charlotte knew she wouldn't be at Gray Manor long enough to begin—much less develop—a relationship with Jeremy. She needed to let him know but realized it must be done gently.

"No. I like working with children and then moving on to the next post."

A flash of disappointment crossed his face, which he hid quickly.

They reached the girls and Jeremy opened the door. He requested a private dining room upstairs and the girls had fun ordering different dishes from one another. Charlotte guessed they'd never taken a meal outside the schoolroom.

Their luncheon passed quickly and after Jeremy paid the bill, he asked, "Are we ready to return to Gray Manor?"

"We have two more stops," Charlotte told him. "Lord Crampton requested a sticky bun be brought back to him, while the girls need some additional art supplies purchased for them."

"Then you'll want to go to Simmons' store. I'll collect the sticky buns from the bakery, one for all of us, and then wait for you in the wagon." His look of distaste let her know the gossiping Mrs. Simmons must still be working alongside her husband.

"We won't be long," Charlotte promised.

She and the girls walked across the street and entered the store.

Charlotte pointed to her right. "The ribbons are over there. I'll pick up the drawing paper."

Harriet and Jane scampered to one side of the store and she went to where she remembered parchment and pencils were stocked. She found sketch books and pencils and decide to add some charcoal to the mix. Then she spotted watercolors and thought Harriet, in particular, would enjoy them.

Suddenly, a chill ran through her and she knew Mrs. Simmons must be lurking behind her. Charlotte didn't turn to see if she was right and took her purchases to the counter. Quick footsteps sounded behind her and Mrs. Simmons came to stand behind the counter.

"I thought that was you, Lady Charlotte. Whatever are you doing in Wilton? Does Lord Rumford know you are here? We heard you had a huge falling out."

Ignoring all of the questions, she said breezily, "Hello, Mrs. Simmons. Would you mind ringing these up for me?"

"Who are those girls that came in with you?" the woman demanded.

"Lady Harriet and Lady Jane Grayson, daughters of the late Earl of Crampton. I am their governess."

The woman's eyes lit with malice. "Wait until Lord Rumford hears you're back. Marching in here as if you owned the place. He won't be happy to hear you're back."

"I'm only at Gray Manor for a short time. I leave soon for a post in

York. I'm merely filling in until a new governess can be found," she lied smoothly, hoping if the woman thought her gone soon, the gossip's impact would be lessened and spread more slowly.

Disappointment filled the woman's eyes. "I see. Well, Lady Charlotte, I'll—"

"Excuse me."

She turned to help the girls and found Jane at her elbow and wondered how long the girl had stood there. Taking her hand, she pulled her away from the vindictive shopkeeper.

"Is your name Charlotte?" Jane asked solemnly.

"Yes, it's my given name."

Jane cocked her head to one side and studied her a moment. "You look like a Charlotte."

She chuckled. "And you look like a Jane." They reached Harriet. "Oh, what pretty ribbons. Have you chosen one you like, Lady Harriet?"

"I think this one." Her nose crinkled. "Do you think it will go with my new riding habit, Miss Nott?"

"Yes, it's very close to the same shade of green. Jane? Are there any you like?"

"I can't decide." She shuffled a foot back and forth.

"Then show me your two favorite ones and I'll help you choose."

Jane pointed to a pale blue and a much darker blue.

"Hmm. Either will bring out the blue in your eyes but the darker one would match your riding habit."

"I think I want this." Jane pointed to the darker shade.

Charlotte pulled the spools of ribbon from their place. "I'll pay for our goods. Why don't you join Mr. Linfield outside?"

She watched them leave the store and took both ribbons to the counter.

Mrs. Simmons gave her a sly look and with venom in her voice said, "Don't want the little ladies to know how you've come down in the world, I see. You used to be one of them, didn't you, and now look at what you've become. A no one. No better than the rest of us. I can't wait to tell—"

"I suppose I will have to speak with the estate manager at Gray Manor and report to him how poorly you treated me and the young ladies," Charlotte smoothly interjected. "I wonder how many goods he orders from your place of business. It would be a shame if he decided to take his business elsewhere. But then again, I am sure you can afford to lose that business, Mrs. Simmons, else you wouldn't treat your customers in such a loathsome manner."

"You are threatening me?" the woman snarled.

Charlotte smiled benignly. "I would never threaten anyone, Mrs. Simmons."

She sputtered, "Don't you dare say a word, my lady. Not a word."

"I won't—if you won't." Charlotte's threat hung in the air. "If I hear that you have mentioned my name, especially when I will be leaving in a very short while, then I will speak to the steward before I depart, Mrs. Simmons. You can count on it."

The color drained from the older woman's face. "Since you'll be off to York soon, I suppose there's nothing to tell," she said meekly.

Charlotte gave the woman a knowing look. "I am glad that we understand one another."

Taking up the ribbons, she indicated how much she wanted of each. Mrs. Simmons cut it and added it to the other goods and told Charlotte what she owed. Jeremy had given her money beforehand and she used it to pay the woman.

As Charlotte gathered the items, Mrs. Simmons gave her a sly look. "What if Lord and Lady Rumford are invited to Gray Manor? Will you hide from them?"

She gave the busybody a stern look. "That won't be necessary. The family is in mourning, thanks to both Lord and Lady Crampton's passing. By the time they are entertaining again, I will be long gone.

Good day, Mrs. Simmons."

Charlotte walked away, knowing by the end of the day all of Wilton would know she'd returned to the area. It would only be a matter of time before the gossip spread to the servants at Rumford Park. She wondered if one of them would let slip to the earl or countess that Lady Charlotte was serving as governess for the Earl of Crampton's orphaned children.

Handing her items to Harriet, Charlotte allowed Jeremy to help her into the cart.

"Was the old witch there?" he asked softly.

"She was." Charlotte shuddered. "She gets more malicious with each passing year."

He flicked the reins and the horses began moving.

"Did she recognize you?"

"Of course."

Jeremy tucked the reins into his left hand and with his right covered hers, which sat in her lap. "Don't worry, Charlotte. Your brother can't hurt you anymore."

"Let's sing!" Jane called out.

As the wagon left Wilton, Charlotte wondered if she would ever be able to leave her past behind.

Chapter Nineteen

GRAY STRODE DOWN the busy London street, the sharp November wind hitting him square in the face. For the two months he'd been in the city, he'd taken to long walks, wandering aimlessly with no set destination. He'd also ridden a great deal, often on Hampstead Heath.

He had nothing to do. He'd tried going to White's a few times and had seen a few acquaintances at the club but he had nothing in common with those men. They had been people he'd known from his school days. None of them had seen war and its atrocities. He preferred spending his time alone, walking or riding or reading when he finally ventured home.

The townhouse wasn't home, though. It never had been. He'd always preferred the country to the city. The residence seemed cold, like a mausoleum. It needed a woman's touch.

He yearned for Charlotte's touch.

Cursing under his breath, he continued to make his way home before darkness set in. He'd written to her once he'd reached London since he'd forgotten to ask her to send a monthly report to him regarding the children's progress. She'd done so at the beginning of both October and November. She wrote separate ones for each of the three children, very detailed, but nothing personal. Gray wanted to know how Harriet's art was progressing. Did she need a drawing master yet? And he wondered how Rodger had liked *Robinson Crusoe*, especially the ending. His nephew had written him twice, once each time he'd finished one of Gulliver's voyages.

Then nothing.

Gray wondered if Rodger's health grew worse.

He reached into his pocket and unfolded one of Jane's drawings that he carried with him. His niece had not one iota of artistic talent but Gray carried the page with him faithfully wherever he went, wondering if she was growing out of her shyness. He missed the children. He missed Gray Manor.

Most of all, he missed Charlotte.

Doing what was best for everyone had been his only course of action, though. Leaving Gray Manor let all of them once more fall into a predictable routine. Hadn't Charlotte been the one to stress to him the importance of a routine for children?

He reached the townhouse and entered, peeling the gloves from his hands. The butler took his coat and hat and told him mail awaited him on his desk. He went straight to his study and closed the door, pouring himself a brandy before sinking into the leather chair behind the desk. Flipping through the stack, he paused, recognizing the familiar handwriting from her many lists which he'd read again and again.

A letter from Charlotte . . .

It was the third week of November, much too early for one of her reports. Gray took a healthy swallow of his brandy and opened her note, knowing what it said before even reading it.

Mr. Grayson –

Lord Crampton has taken a turn for the worse. Rather than summoning Dr. Pittman, the local physician, I sent word to Dr. Winston in London. He has come and gone, doing all that he could.

I believe it's important for your nephew to see you one last time. I urge you to return to Gray Manor with haste.

Miss Nott

A cold seeped through him, more bitter than the wind he'd spent the last several hours in. Rodger lay dying. That bright, eager lad. So smart. So amiable. He'd never live to adulthood. Never finish his education or wed.

Dread filled Gray. Not only was he losing his nephew, but he would become the new Earl of Crampton. He shuddered, thinking of even more duties that awaited him.

Including providing an heir.

If he didn't, the title would go to some distant cousin who lived in the West Country. He'd never met anyone from that branch of the family. He owed it to his father to wed and have a son. His father had been such a kind gentleman and had wanted his sons to be the same.

Suddenly, what had seemed an enormous burden lifted from him. Gray was the same man he'd been moments ago—and yet everything had changed as he thought of his father. Instead of letting the war consume him in a raging inferno, it struck him he must put the past to rest. It was time to step up and become the man his father would have expected him to be.

To be a man good enough for Charlotte to wed.

He would admit to her how much he'd missed the children—and how much he needed them—and her—in his life. He could return to the country, where he'd always been happiest, at least before Stinkin' Seymour had ruined everything for him. He would care for the land and his tenants. He would marry Charlotte and she'd become a countess, never having to work again. They could have children. Fill Gray Manor with children.

And love. He would tell her how much he loved her. Gray would make sure his children—and Harriet and Jane—knew they were loved. Not spoiled but given the right amount of attention. Even a little coddling.

He glanced at her note again, guilt filling him at the happiness her news had brought. A child's death was a high price to pay for such happiness. Gray would always remember his nephew. He would go to him now. Remain at Gray Manor for a while. And when an appropriate amount of time had passed, he would speak to Charlotte of his feelings.

Leaving the study, he returned to his suite of rooms and rang for Parker. The valet appeared within minutes.

"You need to pack our things, Parker. We are returning to Gray Manor."

"For how long, Mr. Grayson?"

"Indefinitely. I plan to spend a good portion of the year there from now on."

As the new earl, he would take his place in the House of Lords and thus be expected to spend some months in London. The very parties and balls he dreaded would now become events he wished to attend, his beautiful wife on his arm. Charlotte would love London. She and the girls would thrive here.

"Very good, sir. When will we leave?"

"First thing in the morning. That should give you plenty of time."

"I'll start at once," Parker said.

Gray left and returned downstairs. He spoke to the butler and housekeeper, explaining that he would be spending several months in the country and not return to the city until spring. He assured them they would remain on, as would the staff currently in place. If his family were to spend part of the year in London, it would help to keep the servants employed year-round.

Going to the stables, he found Sable and told his head groom he'd be returning to Gray Manor in the morning and wanted the coach and Titan ready.

"I'll be gone for a good while, Sable. Make sure that all of the horses are exercised at regular intervals."

He doubted he should keep on the coachman but knew the single salary wouldn't be a problem. Better the man have a roof over his head and be in place to serve than trying to locate a new one whenever he returned.

Gray dined alone and then went to the library. Perusing the shelves, he took two volumes to his room. One told of Arthurian legends and the other was a history of the Roman Empire. He would bring these to Rodger. If the boy was too weak to read them himself, Gray would read them aloud to him.

By the time he returned to his chambers, Parker had everything ready to go for tomorrow's travels. The valet left and Gray climbed into bed. For the first time in many months, no nightmares came.

CHARLOTTE SAT AT Lord Crampton's bedside. He rested peacefully now, thanks to the dose of opium she'd administered several hours ago. The boy grew weaker each day. He'd asked her to write to his uncle and let him know about the situation. She did so, knowing Gray would come at once. She thought she'd prepared herself for his arrival.

Until he entered the room.

Her body stilled, aware he was there, the hairs standing up on the back of her neck. She felt his presence. Smelled his cologne. Wanted to reach out and touch him. How foolish she'd been to think she could lock her heart away. Where Gray was concerned, she had no strength. No willpower.

Charlotte rose and slipped her hand from the boy's. She crossed the room to where Gray stood inside the doorway.

"He's resting peacefully now. Dr. Winston has prescribed opium to help him sleep. It's the only thing that quietens his cough."

Gray looked to his nephew and back to her. "How long does he have?"

"A few days is Dr. Winston's best guess."

The stoic features gave way to a brief sadness and then once more he was in control of his emotions.

"I'll leave you with him. Mrs. Minter is here if you need anything. I need to return to the girls and their lessons."

She watched him move slowly toward the bed and take the seat she'd vacated. Gray took Rodger's hand in his. The other caressed the boy's brow tenderly.

Knowing the earl was in good hands, Charlotte returned to the schoolroom. Betsy quietly slipped out and Charlotte sat, looking over the work the girls had completed during the last hour of her absence. While Jane busied herself correcting spelling errors by writing the words ten times, Charlotte helped Harriet solve a difficult multiplication problem.

"How is Rodger?" Jane finally asked.

"The same."

She'd allowed the girls to briefly visit their brother each day and now said, "Your brother is very ill. I know it's upsetting to you. If you don't wish to see him anymore, it's all right."

Harriet grew thoughtful. "It hurts my heart, Miss Nott, when I seem him struggling to breathe. But I think we should go see him at least one more time. To say goodbye."

"I think that's a wise decision." She paused, knowing she needed to prepare them regarding Gray's return. "Your uncle has arrived this morning."

Harriet slammed her palm against the table. "Why? He doesn't care about Rodger."

Charlotte placed her hand over the girl's. "You're wrong. I think he does. A great deal. He is hurting just as you and Lady Jane are."

"Do I have to talk to him?"

"I won't have you behaving rudely, Lady Harriet, especially to your own flesh and blood." She softened her tone. "You should politely answer any questions he asks you but you don't have to initiate conversation with him."

"Good." Her bottom lip stuck out in a pout.

"We'll go see Lord Crampton after luncheon then as we usually do," she suggested.

"Can I be nice to Uncle Gray?" Jane asked. "I want to talk to him." She glanced to her sister and then looked away.

"If you wish," Charlotte said.

Harriet glared at her sister but Jane merely went back to her spelling corrections.

Charlotte wondered if she would be able to keep a fragile peace in the house so young Rodger could pass without obvious conflict.

CHAPTER TWENTY

GRAY HELPLESSLY WATCHED as Rodger continued to cough. Nothing seemed to give the boy relief. He tried giving his nephew something to drink but he only choked on it. His breathing was rapid and his eyes reflected pain. He didn't know how much more Rodger could take. Mrs. Minter had offered more opium but the young earl refused to take it.

"Why?" Gray asked the older woman.

"His sisters come to visit each day around this time," Mrs. Minter revealed. "If he takes the opium, he'll sleep through their visit."

"Want . . . to . . . see them," Rodger wheezed and began coughing again.

"Is there nothing else we can do?" he asked, frustration building within him.

The woman shook her head sadly. "No, Mr. Grayson."

He wondered how his nieces would react to his presence. Surely, Charlotte would have warned them he had returned to Gray Manor. In particular, he worried about Harriet. She was the spirited one, much more volatile than her quiet sister. If she grew angry, Gray would leave the room so as not to agitate her or Rodger.

Minutes later, Harriet and Jane arrived with Charlotte. His older niece refused to meet his eyes but Jane came and wrapped her arms about his waist as he stood. He smoothed the girl's hair and kissed the top of her head.

"I'm glad to see you, Uncle Gray," she said.

"I am very happy to see you, Jane."

Harriet's gaze cut to them. She glared at her sister as if she were a traitor and then gave Gray a hard look before turning back to her brother.

By now, Charlotte had come close to the bed, standing with Harriet on the opposite side from where he and Jane stood. She stroked Rodger's hair lovingly.

"Hurts," the boy managed to say.

"Your chest?"

He nodded.

"And your neck?"

He wheezed what Gray thought was a yes to her question. The wheezing sounded when he breathed both in and out and the coughing continued.

Charlotte sat on the bed and began kneading his neck. She said, "Your brother's neck and chest muscles hurt. Dr. Winston called this retractions. I'm hoping massaging them will help."

"I can help." Jane put her tiny hands on Rodger's chest and rubbed.

Gray saw his nephew smile, his eyes now closed.

Harriet took Rodger's hand and told him as soon as he was better, they would all sit around the fire in the drawing room since it was much too cold for him to go outside. Gradually, the coughing tapered off and the boy's breathing became regular again. His eyes opened and he smiled.

Jane removed her hands and said, "You look much better, Rodger. I'm glad we came to visit you."

He nodded, words seemingly beyond him.

"We love you, Rodger," Harriet said, a fierce look in her eyes. "Never forget that."

"I won't," he whispered.

"Would you like some of the medicine now, Lord Crampton?"

Charlotte asked. "It will help you sleep."

Rodger nodded and Mrs. Minter came over.

"I'll be back later, my lord," Charlotte promised. "It's time for your sisters to have their music lesson. When you are stronger, perhaps you'd like to join them in those lessons."

Jane's eyes lit up. "Yes, Rodger. I love it. We could play together. That's called . . ." Her voice trailed off and her face scrunched up. She looked to Charlotte. "What is it, Miss Nott?"

"A duet."

"That's it. We can learn a duet, Rodger."

He smiled wanly and Charlotte ushered the girls from the bedchamber. Gray decided to follow them to the drawing room.

Once they arrived, Jane noticed he'd accompanied them and asked, "Are you going to listen to us play, Uncle Gray?"

"If I'm allowed."

"I don't mind," the girl said. "But Harriet might."

He looked to his other niece. She shrugged her shoulders and went to sit at the pianoforte.

Jane pulled on his sleeve and Gray leaned down as she whispered, "I think she wants you to stay."

"I will," he whispered back.

Charlotte had Harriet warm up with some scales and then she placed a piece of music in front of the girl. Knowing she hadn't played but a short while, he was surprised with how well his niece did. She played two more short pieces and Charlotte stopped her a few times, having her work on certain passages.

The girls switched places. Jane oozed confidence. She played the same scales her sister did and then Charlotte placed different music in front of her. Gray could tell it was more complex than what Harriet had practiced as Jane's small fingers danced across the keyboard with ease. She played a second piece with no instruction from Charlotte and then a third, this time singing as she played.

When she finished, her gaze went immediately to him and he rewarded her with a smile.

"You both are doing very well," he praised. "I'm surprised at how much you've learned in such a short amount of time."

"Jane plays better than me," Harriet said. "I don't mind. I draw better than she does."

Jane nodded. "I love the pianoforte," she said dreamily. "I want to sing and play like Miss Nott someday."

"I'm sure you will surpass me, Jane," the governess said crisply. "Harriet, you need to practice a bit more on what we worked on before. Jane, why don't you start the new piece during your practice time?"

"Yes, Miss Nott," they said in unison.

"I'll be across the room with your uncle. Take turns."

Charlotte moved to far end of the room and he followed, sitting in a chair next to her.

"Harriet is right. She's a far better artist than Jane will ever be. I've started her on both charcoals and watercolors. She thrives whenever she can express herself through her art."

"I'd like to see some of her work. My father could draw quite well. I'm sure that's where her talent comes from."

"As far as Jane goes, she enjoys drawing but she excels at music. She's already far ahead of her sister regarding the complexity of the pieces she can play. While I believe Harriet will play adequately with continued practice, Jane will most likely enjoy playing her entire life and entertain at gatherings."

He thought of the future and could see others gathered around Jane as she played. Hopefully, it would include her cousins. His and Charlotte's children. "It's good to know they thrive in different areas. What about their schoolwork?"

"Harriet enjoys mathematics and geography. She's very practical. Jane likes to write stories and has excellent penmanship, though her spelling can be atrocious at times. Both girls enjoy history."

Charlotte paused, listening to Harriet for a moment, and then said, "Rodger hasn't been able to continue his studies due to his condition. I did read the rest of *Gulliver's Travels* to him and we discussed Swift's use of satire."

Her mouth trembled slightly and Gray longed to reach for her hand. He forced his to remain on the arms of his chair.

"I am glad you came to see him," she finally said. "He talked of how he missed you. You left quite an impression on him."

"I never should have gone away, Charlotte," he admitted. "I was wrong to leave you. And the children."

She swallowed and he saw she was trying to maintain control of her feelings.

"Harriet still harbors resentment toward you but I'm sure you can win her over again—if you invest time in a relationship with her."

He stared at her until she finally met his gaze. "And you, Charlotte? Will I ever be able to win your approval again?"

She bit her lip and Gray wished he were the one who sank his teeth into its plumpness.

"My approval or disapproval is irrelevant, Mr. Grayson. I am merely the governess."

"Charlotte," he began and stopped, seeing her tense.

"Miss Nott," she prompted.

"Charlotte," he said more firmly, "there are things we need to speak of. Not now. But in the future."

"I'm happy to discuss the children and their progress with you at your convenience, Mr. Grayson." She rose abruptly. "I'll be with Lord Crampton while the girls practice."

She quit the room and he knew how deeply he'd hurt her—and the children.

Gray pledged he would do whatever it took to get back in her good graces.

CHARLOTTE SPENT HALF an hour with Lord Crampton. He slept restlessly and she told Mrs. Minter when he next woke to administer another small dose of opium.

She returned to the drawing room after changing into her riding habit and told the girls they'd practiced enough and it was now time for their daily ride. They scurried off to change and she suggested to Gray that he return to his nephew's room, avoiding looking directly into his eyes. She left quickly and headed for the stables. After an hour's ride with the girls they returned to Gray Manor and changed again. Once the hour devoted to reading ended, Betsy brought up their dinner. Charlotte retreated to her own room, where a tray awaited her. She picked at the food and then left most of it untouched as she returned to the earl's room.

As she suspected, Gray still sat with the boy. Mrs. Minter was putting on her cloak and she gave Charlotte a brief report of how the boy had done that afternoon.

"Thank you, Mrs. Minter. I will see you tomorrow morning."

As the woman left, a footman arrived to take her place and Charlotte excused him, telling him she would remain on duty tonight.

Because she thought this would be Rodger's last night on earth.

Pulling another chair to the opposite side of where Gray sat, she said, "If you would like to leave and have some dinner, I will stay with him."

"I couldn't eat anything," he said. "Not with Rodger in such poor condition."

She saw the pain and regret in his eyes and silently forgave him for deserting them. He had demons to fight which she would never know. Charlotte only hoped that Gray would emerge the victor in this battle for his soul.

"I was the same. It's hard to manage an appetite at a time like this."

He stroked the boy's hair. "Do you think . . ." His voice faded as his gaze met hers.

She nodded, no words necessary.

"Do you mind if I stay with you?" she asked.

"You have every right to be here. You love him."

"Thank you."

Charlotte took the boy's cold, pale hand and wrapped both of hers around it. They sat in silence, listening to the ragged breathing.

An hour later, she noticed the earl's face changing. Sweat beaded around his hairline and then began streaming down his face. As she wiped it away with a cloth, she noticed his lips turning blue and his breath quickening. The coughing started again, racking his thin body. His eyes flew open as he gasped for air, wheezing in and out rapidly. She saw panic fill his eyes as his bronchial tubes must be closing, making it difficult to breathe. His lips darkened, the blue standing out against his pale face. She turned his hand and saw the fingernails were also blue.

"Do something," Gray hissed as he lifted the boy from the pillows and thumped him on the back.

"Stop," she said and he eased his nephew back. "It's the end," she mouthed.

A calm descended upon her as she climbed onto the bed and wrapped her arms around the young earl. Gray did the same from the other side, squeezing his eyes shut, misery on his face. Charlotte brushed kisses along the Rodger's temple, murmuring soothing words as he struggled more and more to inhale and exhale.

Then he made an odd noise and gasped. She tightened her arms about him and felt him still. His struggles to breathe ceased and she gently kissed his forehead and pulled away from him.

Gray did the same and they stared at the lifeless body. For the first time since she'd been employed at Gray Manor, Charlotte saw the child was at peace, his features softened, making him look even younger than his twelve years.

She stood. "He fought valiantly. He wrestled death time and again."

Gray kissed the boy's head and rose. "Rodger was braver than any soldier I fought with."

She smiled wistfully. "He would have liked that. He told me he wanted to be a soldier. Just like his Uncle Gray."

Gray collapsed on the chair and began sobbing. Charlotte circled around and came to stand next to him. She placed an arm about his heaving shoulders and petted his hair in an attempt to soothe him. He wept for some minutes as she did her best to comfort him.

Finally, his tears subsided. He stood and brushed his hand over Rodger's face, closing his eyes, and then brought the sheet up to cover him. He looked at her with red-rimmed eyes.

"I need a brandy. Will you join me?"

Charlotte nodded.

They left the room and went downstairs to the library. A cheery fire burned in the grate, the only light illuminating the room. Gray poured each of them a generous amount and then handed a tumbler to her.

He raised his. "To Lord Crampton. A very brave boy who would have been a good man. May he now receive the peace he deserves."

She tapped her glass to his and swallowed the contents. A river of fire burned her throat, straight to her belly. Warmth spread through her.

Gray took the crystal from her and set both aside. Without a word, he enfolded her in his arms, his lips meeting hers.

It was like coming home.

CHAPTER TWENTY-ONE

CHARLOTTE HAD YEARNED for Gray's kiss for so long. She'd dreamed of it ever since he'd left. But her memory of it was a weak imitation of what she now experienced.

He kissed her with aching tenderness, his lips molding to hers. His hands moved up and down her back and she clasped his shoulders, kneading them. The kiss became more urgent, tinged with hunger and desperation. His tongue danced along the seam of her mouth, encouraging her to open to him. She did and it slid inside. Instantly, it was as a match being lit. Fire spread through her every limb. Her heart beat rapidly and she clutched him more tightly.

The kiss went on and on. Moving her. Branding her.

As Gray's . . .

Her core began pounding fiercely, calling out for his touch. She couldn't help but think it wicked—and yet she longed for it all the same. Need rippled through her and Charlotte had no idea what to ask for from him, trusting he would lead them in the right direction.

Gray suddenly swept her into his arms and strode to a large chair, never breaking their kiss. He sat, with her in his lap, and continued his assault. She grew dizzy and hot as she pushed her fingers into his hair. He groaned as she played with the silky strands. He finally broke the kiss and then covered her face with light, butterfly kisses. Her cheeks. Her eyelids. Her brow. His lips went lower as he scorched a path along her jaw and then dropped to her neck, licking, nipping, kissing his way.

Delightful shivers ran through her at each touch.

The onslaught of kisses continued as his hand found her breast and caressed it. Charlotte heard herself whimpering at his touch. Gray pulled her gown down and captured one breast, freeing it from its restraints and taking it hostage with his mouth. He burned fiery kisses onto it before his mouth found her nipple. His tongue encircled it, teasing her, and she cried out his name. Charlotte could feel his smile against her skin. Then he sucked on it, long and hard, causing a dampness to come between her legs. He sucked until she thought she would go mad.

His mouth sought hers again and the long, drugging kisses went on forever. She stroked his face with her fingers, the slight stubble rough beneath her fingertips. His hand slid along the curve from her waist to her hips and even lower. Gray captured the hem of her gown and tugged it up. His hand slipped under it and glided sensually from her ankle up her calf to her knee. It traveled higher and arrived at where she'd wanted it.

He cupped her and she moaned.

Breaking the kiss, he murmured, "You want me, Charlotte. You're ready for me."

"I don't know what I want," she said, tears spilling down her cheeks. "I only know I want whatever I can have of you."

It was true. She knew he was damaged from his time at war. She was willing, though, to have any part of him that he would give her.

"You can have all of me," he said huskily and his mouth took hers again in a searing kiss.

She kissed him back with everything in her heart, knowing she loved this flawed man—and would never love another.

As he kissed her, his finger began caressing the seam of her sex and new ripples of heat traveled through her. His pushed a finger inside her. Charlotte thought she should be horrified but she craved his touch too much to protest. He stroked her, his finger mimicking his tongue, and her nails dug into his back. Another finger joined it and Gray slowly began driving her toward madness. She heard sounds coming from her that she'd never uttered.

His lips dropped to her throat again, circling where her pulse beat wildly. His fingers continued their dance, urging her toward a destination she'd never known existed.

"Almost there," he said, his voice low and rough.

His fingers moved and pushed against something inside her that made her breath catch. He slowly circled and then toyed with it. Charlotte felt a wave about to break within her and gasped.

Gray stroked it again, murmuring against her throat, "Come, Charlotte. Enjoy your release."

She bit her lip. "I'm . . . afraid."

He lifted his head, those blue eyes piercing her soul. "I'm here. You need never be afraid again."

With that, he kissed her tenderly and suddenly she exploded. An unimaginable pleasure washed over her, spilling from her, as intense waves erupted. She cried out, the sound swallowed by Gray as he devoured her once more in an endless kiss. She shuddered and then went limp, spent.

He broke the kiss and pressed his lips to her brow, his arms like a wall that kept out the rest of the world. Charlotte's head dropped to his chest, her cheek burrowing close, feeling the pounding of his heart beneath it. Gray stroked her hair lovingly as she tried to understand what had happened.

"Are you all right?" he asked, his voice rumbling against her ear.

"Yes," she said breathlessly and raised her head to meet his gaze. "What was that?"

"It's called an orgasm. Or release."

"It was amazing," she said, reverence in her voice.

"It can be even better."

She chuckled. "I don't see how." Then she frowned. "How can I make you feel the same?"

He kissed her. "Ah, the ever-thoughtful Miss Nott, always wanting to do for others."

"No, Gray. I'm serious," she insisted, her arms looping about his neck, her fingers playing with the hair along his nape. A wave of energy rippled through her and she suddenly felt she could climb a mountain without pause.

His eyes grew hooded. "Come to my bed and I'll show you."

Could she do that?

It would be terribly wanton. Something only a married couple should do. But Charlotte knew she would never marry. And she wanted to take a part of this man with her when she left Gray Manor.

She smiled. "Then let's make a memory together. Just for us."

He stood, bringing her with him. "Just for us," he echoed and carried her across the room.

As he reached for the doorknob, she said, "You'll need to put me down."

A wicked gleam flashed in his eyes. "What if I choose not to?"

In her best governess voice, Charlotte said, "Gray, put me down. There will be servants we will pass. I can't be seen with you carrying me about."

He eased her to the floor, only to push her back against the door, his body pinning her against it. His hands captured her waist, holding her in place as his mouth ravished hers. Her head spun and she was grateful he held her up because her own two feet certainly would have been unable to do so.

"Gray?" she murmured against his mouth.

"Hmm?" he asked as he continued to kiss her.

Charlotte turned her head to the side and reminded him. "The bed?"

He pressed a soft kiss under her jaw. "Yes. The bed," he agreed and released her, stepping back.

She swayed slightly and his hands caught her waist again. "Are you certain I shouldn't carry you?" he asked, one corner of his mouth turning up with mischief.

"Give me a moment," she said and took a deep breath. "All right."

"You're sure?"

"Yes."

Gray removed his hands and watched her. Charlotte turned and grasped the door handle to steady herself. After a moment, she opened the door and took a few steps from the room. He followed. They went up the stairs, only seeing one maid, and then turned right. Reaching his suite, she looked up and down both sides of the corridor as he opened the door and nudged her inside.

The massive bedchamber reminded her of her father's at Rumford Park. Candles had been lit and a fire roared, casting off heat. But not as much as Gray's body. He'd felt like an inferno next to her and his kisses had only heated her further.

He entwined his fingers with hers and led her across the room, pausing when they reached the bed. Then raising their joined hands, he pressed the softest of kisses upon her knuckles. The gesture moved her and Charlotte had to blink away the tears that sprang to her eyes.

"May I undress you?"

She should feel ashamed of her behavior but she wanted the feel of his skin against hers.

"Only if I may return the favor," she replied, not bothering to hide her smile.

His brows shot up and a devilish grin emerged. "You may do anything with me that you like, Charlotte."

Her cheeks burned and he laughed softly as he removed her gown, setting it on a nearby chair. With ease, her petticoat and corset joined it, leaving her in her chemise. He bent and pulled her shoes from her feet, followed by the stockings. Then he eased the pins from her hair and it tumbled down her back. He ran his fingers through it numerous times, a pleased look on his face.

"Would you help me now?"

She undid his starched cravat and cast it aside before pushing his tailcoat from his shoulders and pulling his arms from it. She unbuttoned his waistcoat and it joined his pile. Her fingers loosened the buttons of his shirt and he helped by pulling it over his head.

"Oh!"

Charlotte gazed at the broad, muscled chest in wonder. Did all men look like this? She doubted it for if they did, they would never hide themselves in layers of clothes and parade about bare-chested for the entire world to see.

"Do you like what you see?" he asked softly.

"Yes."

Her fingers reached out and glided from his belly to his throat. Gray shuddered at her touch. She swirled her palms over him, feeling the muscles move beneath her hands. He emitted a growl and captured her wrists, stilling her hands, and kissing her long and deep. She moved closer to him, pressing her body against his, only the thin chemise between them. She felt her nipples harden and her breasts grow heavy.

"Help me with my boots."

Gray sat on the bed and Charlotte turned her back to him, grabbing the heel of the right boot in her hands. She yanked hard and the boot came off. Repeating the action, she removed the left. He stood and quickly ditched his trousers and stockings as she gaped at him. His erection was something she'd never seen before and curiously, she stretched out a hand and encircled it. He sucked in a quick breath.

"Is that good?" she asked. "Like when you touched me?" She stroked the hardened shaft to its rounded tip.

"Yes," he hissed through gritted teeth and lifted her hand. "That can come later."

"How much later?"

"Patience."

By now, she had none. Her body raged as a furnace being fed a steady diet of coal. Charlotte reached for the hem of her chemise and pulled it up, over her head, and tossed it aside. Gray gazed at her lovingly. He might not love her as she did him but she knew she affected him deeply.

"Charlotte," he said huskily, taking her in his arms again.

His erection pressed against her belly as he kissed her until she was breathless. He walked her backward until the back of her knees hit the bed and pushed her down to the soft mattress.

"I plan to explore every inch of you."

She shivered in anticipation. "Then I will do the same to you." She would see what he did first and imitate him since she had no idea what he meant.

She soon learned.

Gray's hands and mouth probed everywhere on her body. No place was left untouched. Sensations Charlotte had never known came and went, an electricity between them that built to a fever pitch. At first, she merely lay there and enjoyed it but as desire flickered within her, she wanted a more active role. She began touching and tasting him as he did her and they soon lost themselves in a world of their own making.

His fingers found her sex once again and teased her until she panted. She took his rod in hand firmly and moved her hand up and down it, enjoying the groans that came from him.

Gray eased her fingers away. "Almost time," he said, as breathless as she was, and then found the place he'd touched before. "Your sweet pearl," he murmured, rubbing it until all rational thought vanished.

"Charlotte, I must tell you that this will hurt the first time," he warned. "Are you sure it's what you want?"

"Yes," she whispered.

What was a little pain when she had this beautiful man's body covering hers?

He increased the pressure and she erupted, the pleasure so intense that she screamed. His mouth covered hers, swallowing the noise, and his fingers left her. Suddenly, something large and hard pushed into her and she shoved his chest, trying to knock him away from her. It didn't move and neither did he.

Breaking the kiss, he said, "Just get used to me. I'm sorry it hurt so much but you were so tight."

The sharp pain had already subsided and something unnamed built within her. She felt the urge to move and pushed up against him.

"Ah, you're ready to begin."

"Begin? What have we been doing until now?"

"Getting started."

Gray pushed deeper into her, filling and stretching her. It felt foreign and somehow wonderful at the same time. They both moved and it felt even better. Somehow, their bodies communicated with one another and they began a rhythmic dance. Each thrust brought an exhilarating rush and the pressure inside her built again. She understood it this time, knowing he pushed her toward and over the precipice, where she would fall—and he would catch her.

They moved faster and faster until Charlotte thought they might be flying and then they were, soaring higher as their bodies came together as one. She moaned. He gasped. They continued until both were spent and he collapsed atop her, driving her into the mattress. She welcomed his weight, her arms tightening about him, never wanting to let go.

Gray pivoted until they were on their sides, still joined, facing one another. His hand cupped her face and he kissed her sweetly.

"Charlotte," he said, her name like a prayer coming from his lips. His forehead touched hers and she inhaled the scent of sandalwood soap, wafting up from his heated skin. It surrounded her. She would never smell it again without thinking of Gray and this moment.

She kissed him. It would complete the memory of their time together. She tasted him and wished things could be different. That she could spend the rest of her life in this man's arms.

It was impossible. He was now Earl of Crampton. She was a lowly servant. He would wed a lady of the *ton* and they would make a life together. His wife would give him his heir. And hopefully, he would come back to being the man he'd left behind. Charlotte could only hope that tonight, what had happened between them, was the beginning of his healing.

She broke the kiss. "I must go."

His arm tightened. "No. Stay."

"Gray, please. I won't have your valet find us naked in your bed. Besides, sometimes Jane has a nightmare and comes to me for comfort."

"All right. Give me a moment."

He rose and came back with a small basin and towel. He dipped the towel in the water and touched it between her legs.

"What are you doing?" she demanded, suddenly embarrassed at this intimate gesture.

"You have a little blood on your thighs from where I pierced your maidenhood. I am sorry I had to hurt you, Charlotte. It never hurts after that first time."

But there would be no other times between them. She already knew she was hopelessly in love with Gray. The sooner she left, the better. With Rodger's death, changes would happen quickly. She might even suggest that he take the girls to London for a change of scenery. There, she could find another employment agency and hopefully gain another position quickly.

He yawned as he finished bathing her and moved the cloth and basin aside. She thought this the best time to approach him, when he'd be more amenable to her suggestion.

"The girls are going to be very upset about their brother's death."

"I will break the news to them in the morning. Will you be there with me?"

"Yes. I know you hadn't planned for them to ever come to London but it might do them good to go there for a week once the funeral is over. Get away from Gray Manor and the memories here."

He nodded. "I do think it a good idea. I have a few things I need to do there."

She knew she'd called him away from his responsibilities.

"You will come, too?" he asked, a sliver of doubt in his eyes. "To help with them?"

"Yes, I'll accompany you and the girls to London."

"Good." He bent and kissed the tip of her nose. "Let me help you dress again."

He stood and offered his hand, pulling her from the bed. She allowed him to dress her, enjoying the feel of his hands on her body. Charlotte decided she would burn in hell for her actions tonight.

And didn't care.

Once he had her dressed, he threw on a dressing gown and belted it, moving to the door and through it.

"Get back inside," she said and he stepped back in as she closed the door. "You're not going to escort me to my room, Gray, especially in nothing but your dressing gown. Remember, the servants?" she prodded.

He grinned sheepishly, his hands spanning her waist. "You push every rational thought from my head, Charlotte."

She couldn't help but laugh. "The feeling is mutual."

Gray's lips touched hers again in a gentle kiss. He lifted them, his breath warm against her skin. "Good night, Charlotte Nott."

"Good night."

Charlotte pulled away from him and opened the door again. Without a backward glance, she shut it behind her and hurried to her room. She'd done the unthinkable. Lay with a man.

And she had no regrets at all.

CHAPTER TWENTY-TWO

GRAY SURPRISED HIMSELF by sleeping a few hours. When he awoke, he pushed his nose into the pillow next to him and inhaled deeply, smelling Charlotte on it. He sighed.

She was everything he could possibly want in a woman.

He only hoped she would commit to him. She had to, else why would she have made love with him? He'd started to pull out and spill his seed on her stomach and changed his mind at the last moment, in part because he'd been so caught up in their lovemaking. He needed their bodies joined together in that final, climatic moment. It had been magical. Different from all his encounters with other women. Gray knew exactly why.

Because he loved her.

He'd yearned to tell her when she'd been nestled in his arms, her abundant brown hair spilling across his chest. Something told him it wasn't the right moment. Not so soon after Rodger's death. Gray had always been a man who held his cards close, never revealing his emotions to others. He doubted even Reid or Burke knew how adversely the war had affected him. The only emotion he'd ever been open about with his friends was his intense hatred for his brother.

He would wait for the right time to tell Charlotte of his love for her. They needed for the funeral to be behind them and some time to pass—then he would speak his heart to her and they could plan for their future together. With Harriet and Jane. Those girls were already so dear to him. They would be their first children and he would drown them in love, hopefully making up for the lack they received from their parents. He wanted others, children with Charlotte. She would be the best of mothers.

Rising, he washed and dressed himself since it was too early to call for Parker. As he made his way to his nephew's room, he decided her suggestion to take the girls to London was a sound one. They'd never spent a night anywhere other than Gray Manor. A trip to London would be a unique experience for them and hopefully help keep their sadness at bay.

Gray arrived at Rodger's room and entered. Darkness blanketed the bedchamber so he left the door open. He also opened the curtains and would watch the sun rise. He slipped into the chair he'd sat in only hours ago and kept vigil over his nephew's body. An hour later, the sun made an appearance, a sliver that grew as it rose from the horizon into the sky.

He sensed a presence and turned, finding Masters in the doorway.

"Our young earl is gone," the butler said sadly.

"Yes. Can you see to the preparations? I'll stay with him until someone else arrives."

"Were you with him in the end?"

"Yes. With Miss Nott. We both held him close as he slipped away."

Sadness filled the older man's face. "That's good. The poor little earl." He shook his head and turned away.

Gray stayed until Mrs. Cassidy and two maids arrived with buckets of water.

"We'll take care of things now, Lord Crampton," the housekeeper said.

Her words startled him. He would have to get used to a title.

Leaving, he knew it was still too early for the girls to be up so he went downstairs for some breakfast. A footman served him and once Gray finished, he made his way to the schoolroom. Harriet and Jane were eating and chatting happily. Charlotte's tray hadn't been touched.

"Good morning, girls," he called. "Miss Nott." He took a seat next to her, opposite his nieces.

"Good morning, Uncle Gray," Jane said with enthusiasm.

She elbowed Harriet and the girl mumbled, "Good morning."

"Continue eating," he said. "Miss Nott has told me of your academic progress. Her expertise with music will help Jane but I think it's time we hired a drawing master for you, Harriet."

She looked at him, her head cocked. "You would do that?"

"Yes. Miss Nott says you're already using watercolors and charcoal. There are other mediums to be explored, as well. We'll look for someone to come to the house after the new year arrives."

Jane looked pointedly at her sister and Harriet got the message.

"Thank you, Uncle Gray."

By now, they'd finished their breakfast and he said, "I've come to talk to you about something."

Harriet opened her mouth and then snapped it shut.

"Is it Rodger?" Jane asked, her voice small.

"Yes. Your brother has gone to heaven."

Jane burst into tears. Gray rose and sat next to her. He gently lifted the girl into his lap and she buried her face against his chest. Harriet sat stoically, staring out the window. Charlotte rose and took a seat beside her.

"It's all right to cry, my lady," Charlotte said.

"It's so unfair," Harriet said, her voice hard.

Charlotte smoothed her hair. "It is. I've never understood why children become ill and are taken."

"Rodger was very good," Harriet insisted. "And he was smart."

"Yes, he was both. He loved you and Lady Jane very much."

"He'll miss everything," Harriet said, her bottom lip quivering. "He won't ever return to school. Or go to university. He won't have friends. We'll never see him again." She burst into tears.

Charlotte wrapped her arms around Harriet. "He isn't suffering now, my lady. You know how hard it was for him to breathe. How much he hurt. He's in heaven now and he'll watch over you and Jane the rest of your lives. You'll see him again one day, far in the future. He'll be waiting for you and introduce you to all the angels, who will be his friends."

"Do you really think so, Miss Nott?" Harriet asked.

"I do. Lord Crampton will see you wed. He'll watch from heaven as you each have children of your own. You'll tell your children about their uncle. What a kind, wonderful person he was. Maybe one of you will even name your boy after him."

Harriet looked to her sister and held out her hand. Jane took it and they shook.

"The first boy will be Rodger," Harriet said.

Jane nodded. She looked back to Gray. "Is there a funeral?"

"Yes. We'll hold one tomorrow."

"Can we go?"

He looked to Charlotte, far out of his league.

"The girls did not attend their parents' funeral," she explained. "I felt they were too young and they showed no interest." She looked at each one. "Would you like to go to this one?"

They nodded solemnly.

"Will you come, Miss Nott?" Jane asked.

"Of course. Why don't we take a break from our studies today? I've always felt a good, long walk or ride helps me feel better when I'm blue."

Jane giggled. "But you're not blue, Miss Nott."

"It means if you're sad."

"I'd rather ride than walk," Harriet said.

"Then we'll ride."

Gray spoke up. "Miss Nott and I have an idea. After the funeral, it might be nice to go somewhere. How would you like to come with me to London for a week?"

Jane's eyes grew as round as saucers and Harriet couldn't contain her smile.

"You can see the Grayson family townhouse. There are museums we can visit. Parks to see."

"Will Miss Nott come?" Jane inquired.

"Yes, of course she will."

"Then Jane and I will go," Harriet said, deciding for the both of them. She stood. "Let's put on our riding habits."

Jane scampered from his lap and the girls left the schoolroom.

He looked at Charlotte. "You think allowing them to go to the funeral is wise?"

"I think they would regret not being there. It was . . . . different with their parents."

"You mean they had no connection with them," he said flatly.

"True. How are you?" she asked.

"I went and spent a few hours with Rodger. I didn't want him to be alone."

"That was thoughtful of you."

He warmed at her praise. Reaching over, he took her hand. Immediately, she pulled it from his.

"There are eyes everywhere, Gray. Especially at times like these."

"I understand," he said, though he longed to touch her. Taste her. Have her in his bed again.

Charlotte rose. "I must change into my riding habit. I'm sure you have things to see to."

With that, she left the schoolroom.

THE LATE NOVEMBER morning was cold but the wind had died away.

Charlotte was glad the bright sunshine shone down on them. She would have hated for it to be gloomy. Rodger Grayson had been such a sweet, easy child, his nature as sunny as today.

She allowed Gray to hand her into the carriage and Harriet and Jane followed. She would ride with them to the church and then sit at the back with the other Crampton servants. As the carriage pulled up in front of the stone edifice, the bells rang ten. Gray helped them down and both girls took one of her hands, holding on tightly. Gray went ahead of them, opening the door and allowing them to go inside.

The church was filled. Gray joined them and she tried to release the girls' hands.

"Take your uncle's hand," Charlotte urged. "You must go to the front where the family pew is."

"Aren't you coming with us, Miss Nott?" Harriet asked.

"No, my lady. I will sit with Mrs. Cassidy and the other servants."

"But I want you with us," Jane whined.

She knelt and put her hands on the girl's shoulders. "It's not my place, my lady. Go with your Uncle Gray now."

"No," Jane said, her eyes filling with tears.

Gray patted her head. "You're right, Jane. Miss Nott must sit with us today."

She shot to her feet, shaking her head at him. "It's not proper, my lord."

"It's what's best for the girls," he said firmly and took Jane's hand. She grabbed on to Charlotte's with her free one and Harriet took her other.

The four of them walked up the aisle together and the whispers started at once. Charlotte looked straight ahead, knowing there was no way to stop the gossip. As they approached the front of the church, her footsteps faltered when she spied a familiar profile. The head swung around and her half-brother glared at her with such malice that she shivered. His wife stared hard at Charlotte, as well, and then whipped her head back around.

As Gray held out a hand for them to seat themselves, she numbly took her place, her eyes locked on the clergyman before her. She could feel Rumford's eyes boring into her. At least the crowd had settled down.

The service began and she did her best to focus on the reverend's words. When it ended, Gray rose. She followed suit and they led the girls from the chapel and back to the coach. Only family would be going to the gravesite for the burial and no one had been invited back to Gray Manor. Gray thought it would be better for the girls that way. Thank goodness Lord and Lady Rumford wouldn't come as mourners.

Charlotte had no idea they would be here today. They hadn't attended the services for Lord and Lady Crampton, which she'd planned. They were rarely in Kent, preferring to spend their time in town. It surprised her they'd come today.

The vehicle stopped and they sheltered in it for a few minutes until the reverend arrived, along with the wagon bearing the former earl's casket. A brief service followed and then the coffin was lowered into the grave.

Gray stepped forward and knelt to the ground, scooping up a handful of dirt.

"Do the same, girls," he said solemnly.

Harriet and Jane bent and scooped up some soil into their palms and Harriet asked, "What are we doing, Uncle Gray?"

"Everyone is born of this earth, Harriet, and when we die? Our bodies return to the earth. We are Rodger's family and loved him best. We will say something nice about him and then sprinkle the dirt atop his casket."

"Why?" asked Jane, puzzled.

"It is a way we show solidarity in our mourning," Gray explained. When Jane frowned, he added, "Our gesture shows we stand together as we are paying our final respects to Rodger."

"Oh," Jane said. "May I go first, Uncle Gray?"

"Of course," he said gently.

"May Miss Nott also help?" demanded Harriet.

His gaze met Charlotte's. "Yes. Miss Nott also loved Rodger."

She swallowed and knelt, her fingers capturing some dirt. Charlotte rose and nodded to Jane.

"Rodger, you were a very nice brother. You always liked my drawings. I'll miss you."

Gray gestured and Jane sprinkled the earth atop the casket. She stepped back and Harriet moved forward.

"I am sorry you died, Rodger. You were very smart and nice and you would have been a good earl. I'll miss hearing your stories. I love you."

Harriet dribbled the dirt across the casket and then looked to Charlotte to see if she'd done well. Charlotte nodded and Harriet smiled. She took her sister's hand.

"You go next, Miss Nott," Jane urged.

Charlotte fought the knot in her throat as she said, "I was privileged to know you, Rodger, even if it was for a short time. You were a good, kind boy and always protective of your sisters. I will never forget you."

She released the dirt in her hand, scattering it across the casket. Her eyes turned to Gray and her throat grew thick again. It melted her heart that he had included the girls in the burial ritual, making them a part of the ceremony as Rodger was laid to rest. It was thoughtful and sweet and she knew doing so brought Harriet and Jane comfort.

He moved to the grave and looked down at the coffin, blinking back tears.

"I will only have one nephew, Rodger, and I am glad that you were mine. You demonstrated great courage in the way you lived. I am proud—and humbled—to have been your uncle. I hope I can learn to be as good a person as you were. I promise to take care of your sisters for you. I will never, ever forget you."

Gray's voice broke on the last word and he raised his hand, the dirt falling into the grave.

"Rodger can now rest in peace," he told his nieces. He touched his chest. "And don't forget—he will always live on in our hearts and our minds."

Jane sniffled. Gray reached out and took her hand and then Harriet's. Harriet motioned to Charlotte. She stepped closer and Harriet linked Charlotte's fingers with hers. The four of them returned to the carriage. As they passed the church, she saw no carriages remained but still held her breath until Gray Manor came into view. No carriages sat in front. Thank the heavens that her mean-spirited brother and his spiteful wife had not come here to berate her.

Gray had told them they would leave for London in the morning. For Charlotte, the dawn couldn't come soon enough.

CHAPTER TWENTY-THREE

RIDING IN THE Earl of Crampton's carriage was far different from Charlotte's previous travel experiences. The journey was remarkably smoother. The seats much plusher. And her companions were far superior to any of the travelers that had been packed into the mail coaches that she had taken to her various posts.

Harriet and Jane had scrambled into the coach and claimed a place next to different windows so they could look out. She found herself sitting across from them with Gray. Having been intimate with him made her even more aware of him. The spice of his soap. The heat that radiated from him. His size, which crowded her just a bit—and which she didn't mind at all.

She'd packed all of her meager belongings, intending to remain in London when Gray took the girls back to the country. Her reticule contained her sizable amount of funds. When she'd received her quarterly salary last month, the amount shocked her. She'd quickly written to Mr. Bonham, the family solicitor in Canterbury, alerting him to the fact she'd been overpaid. His reply informed her that Mr. Grayson had adjusted her salary, thanks to the many tasks she'd taken on at Gray Manor over the last few months. Though she'd been angry at Gray at the time for leaving the children, his kind gesture softened her feelings toward him somewhat. Now that she would be searching for a new post, she had more than adequate funds to see her through in case a suitable position took some time to acquire.

"What's that?" Harriet cried, pointing up ahead.

"Canterbury," Gray told her.

"I've always wanted to go there," she said wistfully. "Some of our supplies that can't be found in Wilton come from there. And Mr. Bonham lives there. He's nice."

They reached the walled city and the girls couldn't contain their excitement as the carriage rolled past.

"It's so big," Jane said in wonder.

Gray chuckled. "You think it's large? Wait until you see London. It's many times the size of Canterbury."

They both clapped their hands in glee, bouncing up and down on the bench seat.

"Have you been to London, Miss Nott?" asked Jane.

"I have. The Plummer Employment Agency is located there. They have aided me in finding my positions."

"Do you like London?" Harriet asked.

Though she'd spent most of her years in the country, Charlotte had gone to London with her father through the years. She had looked forward to living there during her Season. As a young woman with no visible means of support, though, the city had been not to her liking.

"As all places, London has its good and bad qualities."

"Spoken like a true governess," quipped Gray, his eyes lit with amusement by her prim response.

"Do you like being a governess, Miss Nott?"

"I do, Lady Harriet. Especially when I have such bright and well-behaved charges as you and Lady Jane."

"I think I'm going to be a governess when I grow up," Jane said.

"No," Gray said, "you are a lady, Jane. You will go to London and have a Season or two and find your match."

Charlotte swallowed. Without him knowing, Gray's words cut her to the quick. She had been a lady who'd never gotten her Season.

Jane frowned. "What does that mean?"

"You will go to live in London and make your come-out. You'll attend balls and routs and garden parties and meet all kinds of handsome young men. Hopefully, one will appeal to you and you'll decide you wish to wed him and he wishes the same. You'll marry and have children of your own."

Jane thought a moment. "Could I be their governess?"

"No," Gray said emphatically.

The girl looked at Charlotte. "Will you be governess to my children, Miss Nott?" she asked innocently. "I might have a Rodger, you know."

"That's far in the future," Gray said, closing the matter.

Then out of the blue, Harriet asked, "Will you get married, Miss Nott?"

She gripped her hands in her lap. "I know of no governesses that are wed."

"But you could if you wanted to," Harriet prodded.

"I'm quite happy as I am, my lady."

Harriet wasn't ready to let the matter drop. "You could always marry Mr. Linfield. He likes you."

Charlotte's face flamed at the suggestion.

"He likes everybody, Harriet," Jane said.

Harriet gave her sister a knowing look. "He especially likes Miss Nott. I've seen him smile at her. In a special way. And they sing so well together."

"What's that called, Miss Nott?" Jane asked.

"Harmony. Harmonizing," Charlotte managed to say.

Jane nodded. "That's it. Uncle Gray, you should ask Miss Nott and Mr. Linfield to sing for you in harmony. It's when the notes are close together and they get along, isn't it, Miss Nott?"

"Yes, my lady," she said and turned to look out the window. She sensed Gray stiffening beside her.

"Tell us what we'll do when we're in London, Uncle Gray," Harriet begged.

As he began talking about different activities, Charlotte kept her face averted until the evidence of her embarrassment had faded.

The rest of the trip went by swiftly and they arrived in the city just after eleven o'clock, the second carriage pulling in behind them. Parker and Betsy got out and footmen appeared to carry their luggage inside. Gray introduced them to the butler, Mr. Roy, and housekeeper, Mrs. Purcell. The woman led them upstairs to their bedchambers. Harriet and Jane would share one. It was in shades of yellow and blue and both girls exclaimed how pretty it was.

Charlotte turned to Betsy. "Would you unpack for the young ladies?"

"Yes, Miss Nott."

Mrs. Purcell led Charlotte down the hall and opened the door to a very large room decorated in a soft moss green shade.

She frowned. "I thought I would be nearer my charges."

"His lordship said to give you this room, Miss Nott. Betsy is to stay in the room next to them. Lord Crampton said she will see to the young ladies' needs."

"I see."

"Shall I unpack for you, Miss Nott?"

"No, thank you, Mrs. Purcell. It won't take me long and I know you have other duties to attend to." She paused. "May I ask what agency you came from?"

"The Hammond Employment Agency, Miss. So did Mr. Roy and several of the footmen and maids."

"I used The Plummer Employment Agency," she said, not wanting to arouse suspicion.

"I've heard of them but I've found employment three times with Hammond's now. Oh, luncheon will be in half an hour, Miss Nott. Lord Crampton asks that you and his nieces join him. I'll return shortly to bring you downstairs."

A maid entered and the housekeeper added, "Ah, here's your hot water to freshen up."

Charlotte removed her hat and gloves and washed her face and hands. She was a little uncomfortable, being treated more as a guest than the family governess, but she wouldn't dampen the girls' spirits. Already, they seemed to have a burden lifted from them. She knew this brief respite from Gray Manor would be good for them.

Luncheon consisted of roasted chicken and vegetables, with a toffee pudding to end the meal. Charlotte had to ask Harriet not to dip her finger into the bowl.

"But I'm trying to get every last bit, Miss Nott. It's so good," she protested.

"Good manners mean using a spoon to eat your pudding, my lady. No fingers."

The girl looked to her uncle in hopes he might be on her side.

"Miss Nott is always correct, Harriet. Haven't you learned that by now?"

"Could we have toffee pudding again while we're here?" she pleaded.

"I'll tell Mrs. Purcell how fond you are of it. I'm sure that can be arranged," Charlotte said.

"I hope you've saved room for something special," Gray told his niece, his eyes twinkling. "No trip to London is complete unless you've gone to Gunter's for an ice."

A lump formed in Charlotte's throat. Her father had always taken her to the shop bearing the pineapple sign outside it. Gunter's had been their favorite place to visit.

"Even though the day is cold, there's no wind to speak of," Gray continued. "I thought we could ride in the barouche and see the city's sights." He looked to her. "What do you think, Miss Nott?"

"I think the young ladies would enjoy that quite a bit. Maybe the trip to Gunter's could occur at the end of the tour."

"A splendid idea. I'll let our driver know and have Mrs. Purcell locate plenty of lap blankets to keep us warm."

Half an hour later, they were seated in the barouche, piled with blankets. Gray sat next to Charlotte, their bodies touching from their shoulders to their calves, heat from him more than enough to keep her warm. He slipped one hand underneath the blankets and wrapped his hand around hers. Even through both of their gloves, she sensed the spark between them. They rode through the city as he pointed out various places, telling the girls they would visit some of them during the upcoming week.

As promised, the last stop was Gunter's. Usually, Charlotte had been to the sweet shop in much warmer weather and she and her father had eaten their ices from their carriage. This time, Gray escorted them inside and the four of them enjoyed ices and biscuits at a small table.

After her first bite, Harriet declared, "This is better than toffee pudding!" and then added, "But I'd still like more of that, too."

They returned to the townhouse and though Charlotte had suggested they suspend lessons this week, Gray asked if they could do their usual reading hour. His nieces readily agreed and he led them into the library, where a cheery fire burned in the grate.

"Let me find something," he said, going to skim the shelves.

Charlotte sat on a settee and Harriet plopped close to her. Gray returned with a book and took the place on her left. Jane scrambled into his lap and wiggled around, trying to get comfortable. She pushed against his pockets.

"Watch out, Jane," he said, pulling a paper from his pocket. "You might crush one of my prized possessions."

"What's that, Uncle Gray?" she asked.

He unfolded it. "You should recognize it."

Her eyes lit with pleasure. "It's one of my drawings. Why is it in your pocket?"

"Because I always carry it with me. To remind me of you." He smiled at her fondly.

Charlotte could see that the page had been folded and refolded many times. She wondered if he'd looked at it each day he'd been in London, separated from the children. Warmth spread through her, seeing how touched Jane was.

And melted her own heart.

This was a good man. He was trying his best to do right by his nieces. He would become the father they never had. It also strengthened her resolve to leave soon so the three could get on with creating a life together.

All four of them read aloud, the girls first so Gray could hear how they were doing, then he said he wanted to read to them. His voice was deep and clear and mesmerized his nieces, not to mention Charlotte herself. Then he passed the book to her.

"Your turn, Miss Nott."

She took the volume and picked up where he left off, reading until the end of the chapter. As the clock struck six, she closed the book.

"It's time to see to your supper," she told them.

Mr. Roy entered the library. "Mrs. Purcell has asked that the young ladies come and eat. Betsy will supervise them."

They rose from their seats, Charlotte with them.

"I was hoping you might dine with me tonight, Miss Nott," Gray said, his face serious but his eyes dancing with mischief.

By now, the girls had left the room with Mr. Roy.

"Lord Crampton, I think—"

He took her wrists and pulled her back to the seat she'd just vacated. "That's your problem. You think far too much."

His hands cupped her face. "Although thinking can be good. I've thought about this all day."

He lowered his lips to hers and it was as if a powder keg exploded.

Charlotte surrendered to the kiss, reveling in his taste and touch.

When he finally broke it, he said, "You *will* dine with me."

Rising, he took her hand and helped her to her feet. They moved to the small dining room where they'd eaten luncheon with the girls. The meal was as delicious as the first had been and Gray was in a good mood, talking about his friends Burke and Reid and sharing some of their antics growing up. When dinner ended, he asked if she would accompany him to the drawing room and she agreed, reluctant to part from him.

He poured himself a brandy and asked what she might like.

"Brandy," she told him, remembering how she loved the taste of it on his tongue.

They sat side by side, sipping their drinks, a congenial silence between them.

Then Gray asked, "Would you play for me, Charlotte?"

"If you'd like."

"I would. Very much so."

She went to the pianoforte and sat, deciding to play Beethoven for him because she found it soothing. As usual, Charlotte lost herself in the music, forgetting he was even there—until Gray came to stand behind her, placing his hands lightly on her shoulders.

She finished the piece, having to use all her concentration to make sure her fingers hit the correct keys. She placed her hands in her lap and gazed up at him.

Gray sat on the bench beside her, his back to the instrument. One arm encircled her waist.

"That's was lovely," he said softly. "You are lovely."

She knew he was going to kiss her and opened to him the minute his lips touched hers. His other arm went around her and they kissed for a long time.

"Will you come to my bed now?" he asked.

Charlotte shouldn't but she knew she'd most likely have a new post within the next few days. Telling him she was leaving and the fallout she expected wasn't something she looked forward to. Gray was a man used to getting his own way.

She decided tonight would be their final time together and that she would enjoy every minute of it.

Placing her palm against his cheek, Charlotte said without hesitation, "Why don't you come to mine?"

CHAPTER TWENTY-FOUR

GRAY ACCOMPANIED CHARLOTTE to her bedchamber. He'd made sure she'd been given one far away from his nieces for this very reason. He'd spoken to Betsy and told her that Miss Nott had been working very hard lately and she deserved a bit of a holiday. The servant agreed with him completely and said she would bathe and dress the girls and supervise them in order to give Miss Nott some much needed relief.

Charlotte opened the door and breezed in. Everything she did was with grace and assurance. He quickly closed the door behind him and came to her before she turned, wrapping his arms about her and pulling her against him. His lips found the nape of her long, elegant neck and he kissed it tenderly. She shuddered against him and Gray sensed the depth of emotion running through her.

He turned her to face him and his mouth was drawn to hers. He could kiss this woman until the end of time and it would never be long enough. Her arms looped around his neck and she pressed her body against his.

Gray deepened the kiss, ravishing her mouth now, already growing hard and longing to be inside her. Her fingers tugged on the hair along the nape of his neck while his pushed into hers. Pins spilled everywhere as he combed his fingers through her luxuriant, thick hair.

"I want you," he murmured against her lips and dragged his own down to her throat. Her pulse pounded violently there and he licked it, matching the rhythm it beat to.

Charlotte whimpered, the sound increasing his desire to please her. To make her his. Always. He scooped her into his arms and carried her to the bed, which a maid had already turned back. Placing her on it, he stepped back and stripped off his clothes as quickly as he could. He enjoyed watching her watch him do this, her eyes dilating with desire.

She pushed up on one elbow when he'd finished, arching one eyebrow.

"Care to help me do the same, my lord?" she said suggestively.

"You little minx," he growled and grabbed her wrists, pulling her from the bed and kissing her long and hard.

Her hand came between them and began stroking his erection.

"Not yet," he said. "I want to see to you first."

Nimbly, he removed her layers of clothing until she stood naked before him. Not shy as he'd thought the governess in her would be. Instead, Charlotte was all woman and proud of it.

His arms enveloped her and he kissed her until her lips were swollen. Releasing her, he playfully pushed her back onto the bed and she laughed after hitting the mattress. Gray climbed onto it, his body hovering over hers, and then bent and took her breast into his mouth.

He explored her leisurely, not leaving anyplace untouched, until she panted beneath him, begging for him to enter her.

"Remember, it won't hurt," he reminded her.

"I wouldn't care if it did. Just hurry," she implored.

He pushed inside her until he was completely sheathed by her body. Charlotte gasped, her nails digging into him. Slowly, he withdrew and surged forward again, enjoying the noises coming from the back of her throat. As before, they found a rhythm—their rhythm—and the ritual of lovemaking seemed something they had invented. Their secret. Their joy.

They reached their climaxes at the same time and he kept himself from roaring in triumph. This woman was his. Now. Forever. Always.

He rolled to his back and brought her with him. She sprawled atop him, totally spent. Her breathing evened out and he knew she dozed.

He gave her an hour. The only thing that kept him from awakening her was enjoying the feel of her against him. He stroked her back, the skin like velvet beneath his fingertips.

Finally, he could wait no longer and began kissing her shoulder, nibbling and licking as he went. Charlotte stirred and the fire lit between them again. This time he took her, hard and fast, and it was over quickly.

When it ended, he cradled her in his arms. "Was I too rough?"

Her throaty laugh caused him to relax. "Not at all. It was different. But I liked it. Very much." She raised her head and smiled at him.

Gray pushed her head back down to his chest. "Sleep," he ordered.

Twice more during the night he awakened her to make love to her. Each time was different yet special. When dawn approached, he rose and dressed as she watched.

He came to sit on the bed and kissed her again. "Thank you."

"I should thank you," she replied, her fingers joining with his.

"I hope we have enough stamina today for two very active girls."

"Gray, I think you should spend the day with them. Alone."

"Alone?"

"Yes. They need attention from you. I think it would be special if they had a day with their uncle all to themselves. Harriet, especially, would thrive having quality time with you."

"I'm not sure I can handle the two of them without you," he admitted.

"Major Grayson, you had how many men under you? I don't think two small girls will be a problem."

"Soldiers are one thing. Young, unruly nieces are something entirely different."

"You'll be fine," she told him.

"What will you do?"

"I have a distant cousin in the city that I haven't seen for some time. I may call on her. Or I may see about having a new gown made up."

He brought her hand to his lips and kissed it. "Your wardrobe is atrocious. It hides all of your luscious curves."

"It's fitting for a governess," she said primly. "I'm not a part of the *ton*. I dress for my station in life."

Gray kissed her hand again, anxious for the day he could dress her as his countess.

"At least come to breakfast with me and the girls," he urged.

"All right."

Gray went to the door. She looked so appealing, the sheet drawn to her waist, her full breasts exposed, her hair tumbled about her. It took all his willpower not to return to the bed and love her again.

"I'll see you in a few hours."

He returned to his own suite. He would spend today with his nieces and when they arrived back at the townhouse, he would speak with Charlotte about their future as man and wife.

CHARLOTTE BREAKFASTED WITH Gray and the girls and he told her they would return by five o'clock so they could all read together again. She went to her room after eating to retrieve her cloak, hat, and reticule. A maid was about to make up the bed.

"Here, let me help you."

"Oh, you don't have to do that, Miss."

"I don't mind. I make mine every day at Gray Manor."

She went and tossed the sheet up, thinking how she and Gray had tangled in them all night. She should be exhausted from their numerous bouts of lovemaking but felt energized instead.

"Did you come from The Hammond Employment Agency as Mr. Roy and Mrs. Purcell did?"

"Yes, Miss Nott. Did you?"

"No, I've found my posts through The Plummer Employment Agency. Have you heard of it?"

The girl nodded. "My cousin used it. It's two blocks down from Hammond's."

Charlotte fluffed the pillow, having received the information she needed.

"I'll come back," the maid said.

"No, please stay. I'm going out and will be gone a few hours so you're free to stay and tidy up."

"Thank you, Miss."

As the servant took up her duster, Charlotte pinned her hat to her head, thinking of how she'd had to scrounge even under the bed to find the hairpins Gray had loosened last night. She wrapped her cloak about her, trying to push away memories from the long, sweet night.

For now.

She left the Mayfair townhouse and, from yesterday's explorations, knew it was a little over a mile from The Plummer Employment Agency. Though the wind was brisk today, Charlotte decided to walk. It would save the hansom cab fare and she always did her best thinking when she walked. She went over in her mind what she would say during her interview, hoping she would leave with a position secured, despite a lack of reference from her current employer. She also thought when would be the best time to notify Gray of her departure. Alone—or with the girls present so that he would better control his reaction to her news.

Turning the corner, she spied The Plummer Employment Agency on her right. She would have to walk in each direction a few blocks in order to locate her destination.

Then her heart skipped a beat. Heading her way in the opposite direction was none other than Mr. Plummer himself. It was too late to change her course because she saw he recognized her.

"Why, Miss Nott, whatever are you doing in London?" he asked, eyeing her with disdain. "Don't tell me you expect me to find you another position, even though you've held this last one longer than I would have expected."

Tamping down her true feelings, she said sweetly, "Lord Crampton decided to bring his nieces to London, Mr. Plummer. Naturally, as their governess, I accompanied them. Lady Harriet and Lady Jane are delightful young girls and I have enjoyed working with them."

Her reply startled him. "Oh. I see."

"It was lovely to see you, Mr. Plummer," Charlotte said airily and continued down the sidewalk, despising the odious man.

She was glad when The Hammond Employment Agency appeared on her left. Crossing the street, she was granted entrance and directed to a clerk behind a messy desk.

"May I help you?" he asked, adjusting his glasses.

"Yes, sir. My name is Miss Charlotte Nott and I am seeking employment as a governess or companion and would like to sit for an interview today."

"You're fortunate. Mr. Hammond has an opening half an hour from now." He indicated two chairs to his right. "You may wait there."

"Thank you."

Charlotte reminded herself how confidence was the key to a successful interview and she went over again what she would say to Mr. Hammond.

A door opened and a man emerged. He nodded to the clerk, who rose and entered the office. Moments later, the clerk returned.

"Mr. Hammond will see you now, Miss Nott."

She rose. "Thank you."

Once she entered the office, she closed the door and came toward the desk. Mr. Hammond was a small man with silver hair and thin lips.

"Have a seat, Miss Nott. Please tell me about yourself."

This was the one occasion where she would use her story. She knew her lineage set her apart from most applicants.

"My father was Lord Rumford of Kent and he believed in giving me an outstanding education. After his death, my circumstances changed. I have made my own living ever since I was eighteen."

She withdrew a folded sheet from her reticule and handed it to him.

"I was companion to the Dower Duchess of Exbury for several years."

"Hmm."

Charlotte paused as he read her reference from Bernice.

"Very impressive. The duchess speaks of you in glowing terms."

"She was a wonderful lady. I am currently governess to Lord Crampton's two nieces. I know the earl has hired several employees from your agency. Mr. Roy and Mrs. Purcell suggested I seek my new post through your services."

"Do you have a reference from the earl?"

"I'm afraid not."

Charlotte knew she was skating on thin ice here and must be careful how her story unfolded.

"I was hired by Lord and Lady Crampton to tutor their son, who was ill, and their daughters. Unfortunately, both of them passed away rather quickly and Viscount Warren, who was twelve years of age, became the new earl. His health was very poor and he also passed away recently.

"The new Lord Crampton, formerly Major Grayson, came home from the war to act as guardian to the children and handle the Crampton affairs. I'm afraid Lord Crampton barely knows me, which makes me reluctant to ask him to write a reference for me. As you know, the new earl has spent most of his time in London, while I have been at Gray Manor in Kent with the children."

She paused, letting Mr. Hammond digest this information.

"May I ask why you would seek a new post, Miss Nott?"

"Lord Crampton plans to spend the majority of the year in London. He's become very fond of his nieces in a short time and wishes them to stay here, as well." She wrinkled her nose. "Frankly, the city does not appeal to me, Mr. Hammond. I am a country girl at heart and prefer to hold a position away from town."

Now that she had him hooked on her line, Charlotte needed to reel the man in carefully.

"Of course, Lord Crampton will need a governess to replace me. He's been most happy with your agency and hopes you would be able to provide a suitable governess for the girls. They've been through so much lately, with the passing of their parents and their brother, whom they adored. Do you have anyone available? And any posts I might be suitable for?"

She hoped he would overlook her only having one reference and think he had the possibility to earn a commission on not only her but another applicant he was trying to place.

"I have an excellent governess who's just become available. Miss Wight has recently concluded a lengthy stay with a viscount's family. She has almost twenty years of experience working with children."

"If you personally recommend her, Mr. Hammond, I'm sure Lord Crampton will find Miss Wight most suitable. Could she come at ten o'clock tomorrow morning to meet with him? I know he allowed Mr. Roy to hire most of the staff on his own, but the earl is eager to engage with the potential new governess in person."

"Yes, I can see that she's available." Hammond paused. "As for you, Miss Nott, I have two positions that would be a good match for you."

Charlotte smiled, thinking of how Gray had explained the word to Jane. She supposed her job was like a marriage and hoped this man had a place in which she could be happy. One in which she could forget Gray.

"The first is in Lincolnshire, where you would serve as companion to a dowager countess. She recently lost her husband and both daughters have wed and live far away. Her son is the new earl and she wishes to remain near him. She's moved to the dower house."

"How is her health?"

"Relatively good. Because of that, she is seeking a companion who could be with her for many years. The other—"

"I accept."

"You don't wish to hear about the second post?"

"Not when this first one meets my needs. I'm looking for somewhere I can stay for a good length of time. If you think I would suit the dowager countess, I would be happy to accept the position."

"I will write to her today then," he said, a satisfied smile on his face. "When might you be able to start?"

"If Lord Crampton deems Miss Wight is fit for his nieces, then I can leave immediately. On tomorrow afternoon's mail coach."

"I'm certain his lordship will hire Miss Wight. She has an impeccable record regarding her employers."

"Then would you please direct me to the nearest mail coach office so I might purchase a ticket? I'm eager to leave London and return to the country."

He gave her directions and took down some information about her for his office records. Charlotte agreed to pay the agency's fee and took the amount from her reticule. Mr. Hammond seemed surprised.

"Usually, I ask for a percentage from your first salary. Will you . . . have enough to purchase your ticket north, Miss Nott?" he asked, clearly uncomfortable.

"I do, Mr. Hammond, and thank you for your concern. I'm happy I'm in a position to give you your entire commission now."

She promised him she'd be on the afternoon mail coach the next day and left the agency, heading directly to purchase her ticket for transportation to Lincolnshire. She wasn't looking forward to the colder winters, which she'd experienced while serving as companion to Bernice, but the further away from Gray she was, the better.

Now would come the hard part—when to tell him of her imminent departure.

Chapter Twenty-Five

CHARLOTTE DECIDED TO splurge while she was in London and went to a dressmaker's shop. She purchased two new dresses, both made of wool and already made up. They would be more appropriate for the colder climate. She also chose a chemise and corset. It had been several years since she'd bought new ones. Her last acquisition was a pair of gloves. If the dowager countess liked to walk or ride, they might be spending quite a bit of time outside. Charlotte wanted to be prepared for the colder weather, especially since her current pair of gloves had seen better days.

She passed a bookstore and went in, drawn to the used books section. She thought to buy something for Gray, as a parting gift. Finding the autobiography Benjamin Franklin had written, she thought it might be something he would find interesting. She paid for it and then walked back to Mayfair.

Shortly before five, she left her room and went downstairs to the library. The girls were already there with their uncle.

Gray came toward her. "First of all, I managed them quite well today."

Charlotte smiled. "As I knew you would."

"Whenever I had a doubt, I would think to myself, '*What would Miss Nott do*', and magically the right words came to me."

"I'm sure they behaved beautifully for you."

He grinned. "They did. And you were right. Spending time with them was what we all needed. They are growing to love London."

"I'm pleased to hear that. But I know they enjoy their time with you even more so."

He shrugged. "I must leave after we read. While out, we ran into an old army friend of mine. He lost a leg and sold his commission two years ago. I think he's a bit lonely and would like to talk over old times. I promised to have dinner with him and attend the theatre after."

"Then I hope you enjoy your evening together."

Gray gazed at her longingly. "I'd rather dine with you."

"Let's read, my lord," she said and joined the girls.

Once Gray left to go upstairs to dress and the girls went to have their own dinner, Charlotte found Mrs. Purcell and requested a tray be sent to her room. After she ate, she decided she would tell her charges of her departure tonight to better prepare them. In the morning, she would tell Gray that the new governess was expected. She knew she was glossing over the situation, not wanting to think of his ire.

She also dreaded telling Harriet and Jane she was leaving. She'd grown to love these little girls in her time with them but it would be for the best for her to move on. It struck Charlotte that she was doing the same thing to the girls that Gray had done earlier, abandoning them on short notice. He'd thought Harriet and Jane would be better off without him in their lives and she had resented him mightily for it. He had disappointed all three of them when he'd up and left for London. She'd known it was wrong of him to wash his hands of the children and was terribly grateful that he had returned and seemed truly invested in the girls.

How could she justify doing the same thing by walking away?

She wasn't family, though, and never would be. This time, Harriet and Jane would have their uncle to depend upon. He would help them get through this difficult time. Gray would be the constant in their lives that they could depend upon.

Though she feared hurting them, especially knowing the losses they'd already suffered, Charlotte knew just how resilient children could be. Besides, she wouldn't be much of a governess to them once Gray wed. She refused to pine away for a man she could never have, while staying and seeing him build a life without her would be foolish. It was best that she leave now. Gray's new wife could give the girls the love they needed. As time passed, Charlotte doubted Harriet and Jane would even remember her. Her time at Gray Manor had been short, after all. Their memories of a governess who'd only been with them a few months would fade.

Charlotte went to their room and saw Betsy tucking them in for the night.

"I'll finish," she told the servant.

"You must tell us a story, Miss Nott," Harriet said. "A long one."

Harriet had never been one who liked going to bed. Jane, on the other hand, usually fell asleep quickly.

"One story. Of medium-size," she said, and proceeding to invent a tale of a girl and a fawn.

By the time she ended, Jane was yawning. Harriet said she liked the story and wanted to hear another one at bedtime tomorrow evening.

"I know Betsy has been putting us to bed but I want you to do it from now on, Miss Nott."

She smoothed Harriet's hair, knowing her next words would hurt the girl—and herself.

"I'm not going to be able to do that, my lady. I'm leaving for another post."

"What?"

Both girls sat up and Jane asked, "Where are you going, Miss Nott?"

"I've been asked to help someone else who needs me very much. She has lost her husband and is very sad."

Defiance loomed in Harriet's eyes. "We lost our brother. And our mother and father," she said, as an afterthought. "We need you more."

"But this nice lady has no one else, Lady Harriet. I'm to be a companion to her. You are very lucky to have your uncle in your lives now."

Harriet wrapped her thin arms around her legs and rested her chin on her knees. Her mouth set stubbornly. Jane's eyes welled with tears.

Charlotte continued. "Remember how we talked about how your uncle was hurt and sad from the war? He's getting better—and it's thanks to both of you. He is happier now because of you. You're helping him come back to the man he once was and he's helping you get over your sadness with your brother's death." She paused. "You're becoming a true family who can always depend upon one another. And one day, your uncle will wed and someone new to love will come into that trusted circle."

Harriet's forehead dropped to her knees and she mumbled, "But what about a governess?"

"I've found you a new one. Her name's Miss Wight and she has much experience teaching children. She is very eager to come meet you."

"Who will teach us music?" Jane asked, her voice small. "And riding?"

"Your music lessons will go on. And your uncle would be the best riding instructor you could have. Really, this is for the best. You will be helping your uncle and I will be helping another lady who has no one."

"I don't want you to go," Jane said, tears rolling down her cheeks.

Charlotte brushed them away. "It's always hard to say goodbye." She wanted to add that Jane could write her but thought it best if she severed all connections with her pupils. If she didn't, she feared their loyalty would be to her and not Miss Wight.

Harriet raised her head, meeting Charlotte's gaze. "I don't want you to go, Miss Nott."

"I must, my lady. I will look back on my time at Gray Manor fondly. You girls have been the best pupils I've ever had."

Harriet scooted back into the bed and turned to her side, away from Charlotte. She pulled the bedsheets over her head.

Jane saw what her sister did and burrowed, as well.

Charlotte's throat tightened, thick with unshed tears. She rose from the bed and found her voice, saying, "Miss Wight will be here at ten o'clock tomorrow morning. We'll sit and visit with her and tell her everything you've been working on during my time with you."

Neither girl replied. The only sound was Jane sniffling from under the covers.

"Good night."

Charlotte leaned over and blew out the candle on the bedside. She left the room and returned to her own. She locked the door, not needing any midnight visits from Gray, and then slowly undressed. She donned her night rail and dressing gown and doused the candles in her room. Knowing it would be impossible to sleep, she took a seat in the chair by the window and stared out it, tears streaming down her face.

The knock came a few hours later. Charlotte stilled.

It was Gray.

She couldn't see him now, with her emotions raw and ragged and her eyes almost swollen shut from crying. She waited.

He rapped gently on the door again. This time, he called out her name.

More tears poured down her face as she sat resolutely. Finally, silence came. Charlotte was still here and yet already the distance between her and Gray seemed wider than an ocean.

She got into bed, gripping the bedclothes until her fingers ached. She knew she was doing the right thing—but why did it have to hurt so much?

CHARLOTTE ROSE AND dressed in one of her new gowns, remembering how Gray had called what she wore atrocious. Of course, he would think so. He was used to seeing women of the *ton* in their custom-fit gowns of sumptuous fabrics. She could never be what he desired. Or rather, what he needed in his life. She knew he physically desired her by the look in his eyes and the touch of his hands. But she was not a woman meant to remain permanently in his life. Gray was meant for a lifetime with another woman.

Still, she wanted to look her best as she marched into battle with him, for that's what it would be. He would try to convince her not to leave. Charlotte must stand firm against whatever onslaught came her way. Her heart told her it was what had to be done.

She arrived and saw that neither Harriet nor Jane was present. Gray was, though. He looked up from the newspaper he was reading and lowered his cup of tea, placing it on the table.

Joining him, she sat on his right. A footman placed a dish of eggs and ham before her, along with toast points and a jar of marmalade. A second one brought her a cup of tea, already fixed the way she liked it.

"I must speak to you privately," she said quietly and took a sip of the tea to fortify herself.

"Leave us," Gray said, his voice soft but commanding.

The moment they did, he reached for her hand and kissed it.

"No, Gray," she said, pulling it away.

"I know. The girls. Isn't it about time—"

"I'm leaving," she said abruptly.

He stared at her, wordless, his blue eyes darkening in anger.

"I've accepted a new position as a companion to—"

"No."

"No?" she asked, anger rising within her. "It's my right to seek employment wherever I choose, Lord Crampton."

His fingers latched on to her wrist. "You are not going anywhere, Charlotte. Not after what has passed between us."

She tugged but he refused to yield. Calmly, she said, "That was a mistake."

Hurt filled his eyes, quickly followed by a steely resolve. "You truly think that?" he asked, his voice low and dangerous.

She bit her lip, trying to think of a response. Being firm wasn't working with him. She would have to soften her stance.

"Gray, what we shared was lovely. I will forever treasure the memories of our time together. But you need—"

"What I need is you," he said fiercely.

She strengthened her resolve. "What you need is a wife. You're already a father to two lost, lonely girls. You are helping them to heal, as they are you. A proper wife will complete the picture. She can provide you with an heir."

"What if you are already with child, Charlotte? Have you thought of that? You could be carrying my heir."

The nails on her free hand dug into her palm. How foolish she'd been. Smart, practical Charlotte Nott hadn't even imagined what they'd done would cause her to be with child.

"If I am, it's your bastard," she said coldly. "Not your heir."

Gray stood so fast, he knocked his chair over. He jerked her to him, his face so close it almost touched hers.

"There'll be no bastards, Charlotte. No other women. You are the one I choose. You are the one I love. You will be the mother of my children, including Harriet and Jane."

With that, his mouth came down on hers, hard and angry. She refused to yield to him and he gripped her shoulders painfully. When she cried out, his tongue invaded her mouth.

She tried not to kiss him back. She stood there, not moving, not thinking.

And then she gave in.

Her ferocity matched his, as they fought for domination. He deepened the kiss, one hand cradling the nape of her neck, his arm going about her waist and holding her to him.

As they kissed, she realized he'd said he loved her.

Loved her?

Hope—the hope left from Pandora's box—called to her.

Charlotte went limp, letting him have his way with her, kissing her until she was spent.

Sensing her surrender, he broke the kiss.

"Did you hear me, Charlotte Nott? I love you," he said fiercely. "I *love* you. I want to spend all of my days and nights with you. I thought you understood that. That my body told you though I hadn't said the words. I wanted to tell you but I was afraid it was too soon after Rodger's death to discuss our feelings. To plan for our future together."

Gray hesitated. "Do you feel the same about me, Charlotte? Do you love me as much as I love you?"

She burst into tears and buried her face against his chest. He stroked her hair, kissing the top of her head, murmuring soothing words as his hands ran up and down her back.

Lifting her tear-stained face, she asked, "Is this real? Am I truly hearing the words I dreamed of?"

He kissed her with such tenderness that more tears spilled down her cheeks.

"I love you, Miss Nott. You have changed me for the better. And I refuse to accept your resignation. You are to remain in this family always. Not as a governess—but as my countess."

Gray kissed her again with enthusiasm. "It's such a relief to say the words. To tell you how I feel." He frowned. "But . . . why would you want to leave, Charlotte? Make me understand."

She swallowed, the back of her fingers stroking his beautiful face.

"I've always had feelings for you, Gray, but you ran away to London. I was very angry at you for abandoning the children—and me. Then you became the new earl. I knew you would have to wed in order to get an heir. Why would I think you would entertain the idea of marrying a lowly servant?"

A slow smile spread across his face. "Oh, but you aren't just any servant. You're a governess. The perfect governess. You're our Miss Nott."

He kissed her again.

"I knew as the Earl of Crampton that you would need to marry a lady of the *ton*. One who could be a good example to Harriet and Jane. A woman who was your equal."

"You're more than my equal, Charlotte. You are superior to me in every way."

"Even the way I dress?" she teased.

He chuckled. "Well, that does leave something to be desired. I did note your new gown when you came in though it's as bland and shapeless as all your others are. You have a stunning figure, sweetheart, with beautiful breasts and luscious curves. I cannot wait to get you to a decent modiste so she can let the world see your physical beauty."

Gray kissed her sweetly. "But you are more than that. You are beautiful inside, Charlotte. It's your shining belief in me that has helped me turn a corner. You've also worked wonders with the girls. My nieces will be thrilled when they learn you'll be my wife." He hesitated. "You will be my wife, won't you, Charlotte?"

"Is that your proposal, Gray?"

He sighed and dropped to one knee. Capturing her hands in his, he proclaimed, "You are the woman I want to be my wife. My countess. My everything. Will you marry me, Charlotte Nott?"

Without hesitation, she said, "I'd be most honored to, Lord Crampton."

He sprang to his feet and kissed her enthusiastically. Then breaking the kiss, he looked around. "Where are my nieces? We must share this good news with them."

"They may be sulking," she said. "I told them of my plans to leave last night."

He frowned. "I'm sure they didn't take that well. Harriet would be angry and defiant, while Jane would have sobbed."

"You know them well."

He took her hand. "Come. Let's go upstairs."

"Wait." She reached for her napkin and dabbed at her eyes. "I've done quite a bit of crying."

"But today's tears were ones of joy."

She cupped his cheek. "They were." She sighed and then asked, "Do you really think I might be with child?"

"I hope so," he said, grinning wolfishly. "I've already purchased a special license for us to wed."

His words shocked her. "When did you do that?"

"Yesterday. With the girls. We went to the British Museum. Flew a kite in the park. And stopped by Doctors Commons. They had no idea what papers I requested and paid for. But I have the license. I suggest we wed soon. Just in case you are with child." He kissed her. "Oh, Charlotte, how could you not think I wouldn't wish to marry you after what had passed between us?"

"I suppose my wisdom doesn't extend to bedroom matters."

He gave her a wicked smile. "Oh, I think you're learning quite nicely there, my love. You're even teaching me a few things."

"I am?" she asked coyly, batting her lashes at him.

"Miss Nott is *flirting*!" he proclaimed. He kissed her hand and added, "I cannot wait for it to be Lady Crampton who flirts with her adoring husband."

Charlotte gave him a beautiful smile. "Oh, Lady Crampton will do much more than flirt, my lord."

His arm snaked around her waist. "I'll hold you to that, my lady."

"About that, Gray," she said.

Before she could tell him about her past, a loud rap sounded at the door. She pulled away from him as he said, "Come," and Betsy rushed in. The servant's face was bright red and she looked frazzled. Charlotte worried that Harriet and Jane had gotten into some terrible mischief.

"The girls are gone!" Betsy wailed.

CHAPTER TWENTY-SIX

"WHAT?" GRAY ROARED, fear rippling through him. "What do you mean—gone?"

Charlotte put a hand on his arm and flashed him a look of warning. He tamped down his emotions and allowed her to speak to the servant.

"Betsy, come sit a moment," Charlotte said, her tone soothing as she led the young woman to a chair. "Now, why do you think the girls are gone?" she asked calmly.

Betsy sniffled. "They aren't anywhere. Their beds have been slept in. I saw you put them to bed last night, Miss Nott. But when I went in this morning, they weren't there."

"Did the check the schoolroom?"

The servant nodded. "I've gone all over the top floor, Miss. Then searched the other floors. Where could they be?" she asked, beginning to sob again.

Gray stepped forward. "I'll gather the servants."

He found Roy and said brusquely, "I need every servant in the foyer within five minutes, from scullery maids to grooms and everyone in-between."

The butler rushed off, obviously understanding some dire situation had occurred. By now, Charlotte had followed Gray, Betsy trailing behind her, wiping her face with her sleeve.

He went and laced his fingers through Charlotte's, needing to feel her warmth.

"We'll find them, Gray," she said quietly.

"I know," he said, thinking if he voiced it aloud, it would have to come true.

Her gaze met his. "This is my fault. I told them last night I had accepted a new post. I had no idea they would react this way." Her mouth trembled.

"It's not your fault," he said gently. "You've told the girls actions have consequences. Encouraged Jane not to blindly follow Harriet's lead in matters. They are the ones who left. You didn't push them out the door."

He saw pain fill her eyes. "But now, my actions have resulted in these consequences."

He tightened his fingers around hers. "It's not your fault, Charlotte," though he could see she firmly believed it was. "Let's go to the foyer."

Already, a good dozen servants stood there and within minutes, the remainder of his staff arrived.

As he stepped forward to address them, he sensed himself going into what he called battle mode. He grew acutely aware of his surroundings. His emotions were pushed far away so that only the rational, unemotional side came forward.

"My nieces have gone missing. Or I should say, I believe they have run away."

Gasps filled the air and he heard the murmuring. His look silenced the voices.

"Betsy has already searched the house but I'd like her and Mrs. Purcell to do so again, from the top to the bottom. Look in every room. Under every bed. In nooks and crannies. Even in the stables."

The housekeeper nodded. She motioned to Betsy and the two women left.

"As for the rest of you, I'll be sending you out to search in pairs.

Think of the blocks surrounding us as a grid. I want you to walk where I assign you, looking in every alleyway, talking to everyone you pass. We'll fan out for two miles since we have no idea when they left."

He took a deep breath. "When you reach the limit, do the same as you return, looking just as carefully in the same places because you might have missed them before. By now, they will be cold and tired. Hungry. They may be making their way back. They may have become lost. Keep sharp and alert."

Gray then broke the entire staff into pairs, male and female, knowing they would think to look different places. He assigned the route each should take and they left, two at a time until all were gone.

Returning to Charlotte, he cupped her face and said, "They'll fan out in every direction but I intend to ride beyond those boundaries. I'll visit everywhere we did yesterday, in case they've returned to any of those places."

Her fingers tightened around his wrists. "Let me go with you," she pleaded.

"No. If they return, they'll want to see you. Your place is here."

Tears streamed down her face and he enfolded her in his arms for a brief moment. Then releasing her, Gray strode from the house.

CHARLOTTE TOOK A seat in the foyer, wanting to be close to the door in case Harriet and Jane came home. She berated herself for telling them she was leaving.

Why had they run away?

It frightened her that they were out in a city which teemed with thousands of people. Though the townhouse sat in Mayfair, it was a short distance to seedier neighborhoods. She feared the girls would disappear and never be seen again. If that happened, she would never forgive herself.

And Gray would never forgive her.

Oh, for those few brief moments when they'd been together. When he'd told her he loved her and wanted to marry her. It would be the happiest memory she would ever have, knowing she had gained the love of such a good man.

Charlotte realized even if the girls were found unharmed, she wouldn't be able to stay. How could she, when she'd been the cause of them leaving? Gray would never look at her the same again. She almost wanted to leave now so she wouldn't have to face him. But she was no coward. She had survived other situations and would this, too. She would stay and pray and see the girls safe again before she exited their lives.

Mrs. Purcell and Betsy returned after being gone over an hour. Both women shook their heads, no words necessary. Charlotte hadn't thought the women would find Harriet and Jane but it still caused her heart to ache. Her tears had subsided and she sat numbly, awaiting the return of the search parties. Betsy said she was going out to help and left them.

"Can I get you anything, Miss Nott?" Mrs. Purcell asked.

"No. Thank you," she said dully. "I will wait here."

Another hour passed and several pairs returned to check and see if the girls had returned. When Charlotte told them they hadn't, every servant turned and went out again, promising to scour every street and alley and shop, now that the stores were opening.

A sharp knock sounded on the door, startling her. She rushed to open it and found a woman of medium height standing there, her dark brown hair starting to show a few streaks of gray.

"Good morning. I'm Miss Wight. I have an appointment to see Lord Crampton."

Charlotte swallowed painfully. She'd forgotten Mr. Hammond was sending the new governess around this morning. And that Charlotte herself should be on the mail coach to Lincolnshire in a few hours.

After hesitating a moment, she invited the woman in.

"I am Miss Nott," she said.

"Ah, you are the current governess. I wish you well in your new post. Might you have some time to speak to me about my pupils and their academic progress? I believe they are six and eight."

"Yes. Lady Harriet is eight and Lady Jane is six." Charlotte shook her head. "Oh, Miss Wight, I fear you will want to consider a different position after I tell you what's going on here."

Surprisingly, the woman took Charlotte's hands. It was then she realized her own were colder than ice.

With sympathy in her eyes, Miss Wight said, "Please, Miss Nott. Share with me what's happening. I knew something was amiss the moment you opened the door and not the butler or a footman."

She steeled herself. "The young ladies are missing. We fear they've run away. Lord Crampton and the entire household is out looking for them now."

"I see."

"They're not bad girls," Charlotte quickly said, not wanting Miss Wight to judge Harriet and Jane harshly. "They are merely high-spirited. Very bright. But they received some . . . upsetting news last night. It affected them more than anyone could have realized."

"I know from Mr. Hammond that they've recently lost both their parents and their brother. What else has occurred that would cause them to act in such a drastic manner?"

Tears welled in her eyes. "I told them I had accepted another post and that I would be leaving today," she said bleakly.

Miss Wight's hands tightened on hers. "Then they must love you very much, Miss Nott. It's not your fault." The older woman smiled. "I wouldn't think of going anywhere else. Lady Harriet and Lady Jane sound quite interesting. I look forward to teaching them."

Relief swept through her. This competent, pragmatic woman would take care of her girls, for that is what Harriet and Jane were to

Charlotte.

"I think we should see about getting you a cup of tea, Miss Nott. You could certainly use one."

She didn't protest and said, "Let's go to the kitchen. We may have to fetch it ourselves. Everyone from scullery maids to our head groom is out searching."

They found Mrs. Purcell sitting alone, nursing her own cup of tea. Charlotte introduced Miss Wight to her as the new governess and the housekeeper had them sit, bringing cups to them both. She appreciated that neither woman tried to make small talk as they sipped the hot brew.

She was halfway through her cup when she heard voices shouting. Immediately, she sprang to her feet and raced from the kitchen. As she drew closer, she understood what was being called out.

"Miss Nott! Miss Nott!"

Charlotte reached the foyer and saw Harriet and Jane there, looking a little disheveled but no worse for the wear. She ran to them, falling to her knees in front of them, crying and laughing as she brought them close in an embrace. She never wanted to let them go.

"Miss Nott, you're here!" Jane said.

She released them. "And thank the heavens you are, too. Why did you leave?"

"I had to go with Harriet," the small girl said solemnly. "I know the right thing was to stay. That's what I wanted to do. But I worried about Harriet being on her own. Are you mad at me?"

"No, darling, I'm not mad. You're Lady Harriet's sister. You did what you must to protect her and keep her safe."

"I'm sorry, Miss Nott," Harriet said, her bottom lip wobbling.

"Why did you leave, my lady?" Charlotte asked. "I was so worried about you."

"I thought you'd lied to us."

"What? I would never lie to you, Lady Harriet. Never." She

paused. "What on earth did you think I lied about?"

"That you liked us," Harriet said, her voice small. "You've been the only one who ever liked us. Liked me. And then you said you were leaving and I just knew you hadn't told the truth before. That neither you nor Uncle Gray liked us."

Charlotte gently took the girl's shoulders. "I don't just like you. I love you, Lady Harriet."

"I understand that now," she said, her head hanging in shame.

"Look at me," Charlotte commanded.

The girl did, her eyes brimming with unshed tears.

"You are a person of great worth, Harriet Grayson. So is Jane. I am proud of you every day."

"Are you mad?" Harriet asked.

"Some," she admitted. "But I was more worried than anything. You are very young to be out alone like that. No adult with you. No money."

"It was cold. And we're hungry," Jane said.

"Are we going to be punished?" Harriet asked.

"Yes," Gray said firmly, finally stepping closer. "No toffee pudding for a month."

Harriet started to say something and then clamped her mouth shut.

He knelt so he could look his nieces in the eye. "You will never do anything like this again. You will always have an adult with you at all times. You acted foolishly. Rashly. You've caused a great deal of trouble. You will never do this again. Do you both understand?" he asked sternly.

"Yes, Uncle Gray," they said in unison.

He rose and helped Charlotte to her feet.

"I think we need to see about feeding them," he said.

"I am hungry," Jane agreed. "But we haven't talked about the best part. That Miss Nott is staying." The girl beamed.

"You're going to marry Uncle Gray!" cried Harriet.

She looked at him.

Gray shrugged. "It was the only way I could get them home when I found them."

"Where were they?"

"We went to the museum," Jane said. "Harriet thought we might live there. Have you been, Miss Nott?"

"She won't be Miss Nott anymore," Harriet pointed out. "She'll be a lady."

"She's already a lady," Jane said.

"Well, yes, Miss Nott is a female—but she'll be a real lady," Harriet said.

"She's already a lady," Jane repeated stubbornly. She looked up at Charlotte. "When we were in Wilton. At the shop. The woman called you Lady Charlotte. Remember? That's when I learned your name. I thought you looked like a Charlotte and you told me I looked like a Jane."

"I'm glad you're marrying Uncle Gray," Harriet said. "If you married Mr. Linfield, you'd only be Mrs. Linfield. Now you'll be Lady Crampton."

Charlotte was speechless.

Suddenly, Miss Wight stepped up. "Hello, Lord Crampton. I am Miss Wight, the new governess to your nieces. That is, if you find that agreeable, my lord."

Gray appeared baffled by the woman's sudden appearance and turned to Charlotte, his palms raised.

She quickly said, "Miss Wight has impeccable references. I have examined them thoroughly and find her to be highly qualified to take on the position."

"My organized Miss Nott, leaving no stone unturned," he said, amusement in his eyes. He turned back to the governess. "Miss Wight, I am pleased to make your acquaintance. If Miss Nott says you are a suitable replacement for her, then who am I to argue with her infinite wisdom?"

The older women smiled graciously. "Thank you, my lord. I look forward to working with Lady Harriet and Lady Jane." She glanced at the bedraggled twosome. "Why don't I see that they are fed?"

She turned to the girls. "I am Miss Wight. It's very nice to meet you."

Both girls curtseyed and introduced themselves.

"You have lovely manners. Miss Nott has done an excellent job teaching you. After you eat, we'll go to the schoolroom and you may show me what you're working on." She turned to Charlotte. "And perhaps we can meet later this afternoon, Miss Nott, and you can share with me an assessment of your former pupils."

Looking back to the children, she said, "Come along, girls. And remember—no toffee pudding."

The two willing took Miss Wight's hands and headed toward the kitchen.

Gray turned inquiring eyes on her. "So, Lady Charlotte. Shall we go to the library? You can tell me all about yourself."

CHAPTER TWENTY-SEVEN

GRAY TOOK CHARLOTTE'S arm since she looked as if she might collapse at any moment. He realized how hard this day had been on her. She was the kind to blame herself for any kind of trouble, even that not of her own making.

They reached the library and she broke away from him, immediately going to the fire. She rubbed her hands up and down her arms and he came and stood behind her, wrapping his own about her. She was so cold. He swept her up and took her to the nearest chair next to the fire. Gray cradled her in his lap. He wouldn't force her to speak of her past. He wanted her to reveal it willingly and only then what she felt comfortable telling him.

But he'd known in his heart she was a lady. From the way she moved to the way she spoke. She had an innate grace and presence that couldn't be taught. It had been with her from birth, the result of generations of good breeding.

So why was she a shabbily-dressed governess?

Patience, he told himself.

Gradually, he sensed her warming. Her cheek nestled against his chest and he could tell from the way she relaxed against him that she felt safe. Probably safer than she had for a long time.

Charlotte fiddled with a button on his waistcoat and then she finally spoke.

"I was trying to tell you, Gray. Before Betsy came in and told us the girls were missing. We were teasing one another. Flirting."

"I remember." He kissed the top of her head.

"I called you my lord and you called me my lady. And then . . ." Her voice trailed off. He sensed her stiffen with resolve and she said, "I am Lady Charlotte Nott. I used to be a part of Polite Society."

She fell silent again. Gray had no idea how one un-became a member of the *ton*. He knew of countless scandals but none of them had removed people from society, though a portion might give those involved the cut direct. A few times, when duels were fought and someone was killed, the victor fled to France or Spain—but he was still a member of society. Then a thought occurred to him.

"Was your father a gambler, Charlotte? Did he lose his fortune and estates?"

"Papa? A gambler?" She chuckled, a rich, throaty sound that made him want to take her straight up the stairs to bed. "No, Papa was wonderful." She raised her head. "You met him."

"I did?"

"Yes. He was Lord Rumford. I was raised at Rumford Park."

His jaw dropped as he stared into her remarkable green eyes. "I knew I'd seen those eyes before. You came with him—to Gray Manor—many years ago. You couldn't have been any older than Jane. Or Harriet."

"I did visit Gray Manor. You were very nice to me. Most boys your age tease girls unmercifully and won't have anything to do with them." Her voice softened. "You were different."

Gray tried to reach into the recesses of his mind but the memory of their meeting was only a shadow.

"That's why you know how to run a household. An estate."

"Yes. Mama died when I was very young. I grew up managing the household. I went everywhere with Papa. He taught me all he knew. It was a very good life."

He searched her face. "What happened, Charlotte?"

Her head dropped to his chest again and she began toying with another button. He put his hand over hers to still it.

"Papa died."

In those two words, he heard that event had caused Charlotte's world to crumble. But why? How?

"I'd just turned eighteen. Papa and I were going to London for me to make my come-out. I was excited about having a new wardrobe. Going to parties. Dancing. Meeting new people."

When she didn't speak, he prodded her gently. "And then Lord Rumford passed away?"

"Yes. It was sudden. I remember how cold that day was. It rained as I walked back to Rumford Park. I remember shivering so in my wet clothes."

Anger filled Gray. What was she doing walking back from her own father's funeral in a cold rain? But asking questions might upset her. Keep some of her story buried. And more than anything, he wanted to know it. To know all of her.

Continuing, she said, "When I got home, my half-brother, the new earl, and his wife awaited me. When he told me there was to be no Season for me, I readily agreed. I knew I would be in mourning for Papa and it was only right to delay my come-out.

"I was wrong. There was never going to be a come-out. I'd always known Barclay didn't like me. I'd never understood why, though. He was a dozen years older and I rarely saw him. He spent a majority of his time in London, saying he abhorred the country. Once Papa was buried, though, Barclay let me know in no uncertain terms how deep his hatred for me ran."

She went back to playing with the button and Gray let her, knowing the story would unfold only when she wished it to. After another long silence, Charlotte shifted and looked him in the eyes, her mouth trembling.

"When I tell you this, I'll understand if you no longer wish to marry me. I'm sure you'll think of me as Lord and Lady Rumford do. And others in Polite Society."

He cradled her cheek. "Let me do my own thinking, Charlotte. And as far as not wanting to wed you, you're wrong. Nothing you could do or say would change my mind."

"Not even if I'm the mongrel of a whore?" she asked, her voice flat.

Shock filled him. "What?"

"That's what the new Lord Rumford told me I was. My mother was an opera singer. Papa said Mama was the most renowned singer of her day. I can no longer remember what she looked like but I have vague memories of her singing to me."

"That's where you get your voice from. Your mother."

"Rumford told me that all singers and actresses are whores. He didn't want his children to be tainted by any association with me. That the *ton* would judge me and find me lacking in every way imaginable. I was ordered to leave on the mail coach the next day. He never wanted to see me again. In fact, he said I was dead to him."

Tears had begun streaming down her face. Gray wiped them away with his thumbs, not trusting himself to speak yet.

"The servants were quite kind. They took up a collection for me. And Rumford did pay for my ticket to London. It took a while but I found work through The Plummer Employment Agency."

He thought of her—young, naïve, and alone. Practically penniless. How hard the years had been.

His lips touched hers gently, not in a kiss of passion, but one of sympathy. And reassurance.

"I look just like my mother. Rumford must have seen her every time he looked at me."

He stroked her hair. "When I look at you, I see a woman of great conviction. One of courage. A woman who places others above herself. You are no mongrel, Charlotte. That's what the loathsome

Earl of Rumford is. And I will see that he pays for what he did to you."

Gray wanted to kill the idiot. Instead, he would find a way to ruin him.

"No. You will do nothing of the kind, Gray."

"Charlotte, I cannot let what he—"

"No. Revenge is something that will stain your soul, Gray. I won't let Rumford touch your life—our life—in that manner. Don't you see? What happened is in my past. If you truly accept me for who I am, then you will let it go."

"How can I? You suffered for years. Alone. Destitute. No family or friends."

Her hands cupped his face. "Don't you see, Gray? It was fate. I had to be turned out from my home. Disowned by my family. Taking post after post." She smiled and it was as if the darkness left his soul. "All that of brought me to you."

Charlotte's thumbs stroked his cheeks. "If Rumford hadn't done what he did, I would have gone to London for my Season." She chuckled. "Even if I hadn't married after that first year, I don't think I would still be there, eight years later, unwed and on the shelf. No. By now, I would have a husband. Children. I would never have come to Gray Manor to act as governess to Harriet and Jane.

"I would never have met you."

He knew what she said was true. He still would have come back to England upon Seymour's death and been guardian to his nieces and nephew. His soul still would be buried in hate and despondency. He was a different person today because of Charlotte. She had healed him. Taken a broken, flawed man and made him whole again.

"Do you know how much I love you?" he asked, his voice low and rough.

Again, that beautiful smile acted as a balm to his soul. "I believe I do—but I would enjoy hearing the words again."

"I love you, Miss Nott. Beyond how any man has loved any woman. You give me purpose. Strength. You saved me. I'm sorry you endured all that you have but you are right. It brought you to my doorstep. I love you, Charlotte. So very, very much."

Gray kissed her deeply then, as desire fanned through him.

He finally broke the kiss and said, "If it weren't broad daylight, I'd carry you up the stairs now and lock the door. Make love to you the rest of the afternoon. But I won't do that until after we are wed. Speaking of that, we need to make plans."

"I'll marry you tomorrow," Charlotte said. "Or the day after. I'll marry you every day if that's what you want."

He laughed. "I would marry you tomorrow but it's impossible."

She frowned. "I thought you'd obtained a special license."

"I did. And it's good for ninety days." He grinned. "But sweetheart, I simply cannot marry you in any of the rags you own. I want you to look like the countess you will be. We'll call on the best modiste in all of London tomorrow. She'll be charged with creating a new wardrobe for you, one suitable for your position. I don't care how long it takes to sew but I do ask that one dress be made up as quickly as possible. Preferably in green so it will bring out the depth of color in your eyes. The day it's delivered is the day we will wed."

"I didn't know I was marrying such a shallow man," she teased.

"I want to give you everything, Charlotte. Even the moon and stars. But we'll start with a gown that shows off your many fine attributes." He touched her breast and squeezed it lightly. "It took me getting you out of your shapeless dress before I discovered just how luscious your body truly is. I want my bride to look her best on our wedding day. That means an appropriate gown. And jewels."

"Jewels?" she repeated, acting as if the word was from a foreign tongue.

"Yes, love. Jewels. There's a lovely pair of emerald earrings and a matching necklace that belonged to my mother. It would mean a great deal to me if you would wear them for our wedding."

Charlotte beamed with joy. "I would be happy to do so, Gray." She hesitated and then said, "Might it be possible to go see this modiste now?"

He stood, his laugh echoing through the room as he twirled her in his arms.

"For you, my love, I will make anything happen."

"I love you, Gray. So much it hurts."

He gazed at her. "I love you even more, Charlotte. Even more."

EPILOGUE

Gray Manor—Three years later

CHARLOTTE LOOKED OUT from where she sat on a blanket with Gray, her hands behind her and her legs stretched out in front of her. Harriet sat by the water, sketchbook in her lap, her hand flying across the page as she captured an image. She'd begun painting with oils two years ago and now several of her landscapes hung throughout Gray Manor and their London townhome. Charlotte hoped Harriet would continue to pursue art and was ready to suggest clay to her as the next art form to conquer.

Laughter caught her attention and she turned, spying her two-year-old son and Jane chasing after a butterfly. Charlotte had fretted that the boy would be spoiled from all of the attention his cousins gave him. Gray had calmed her fears, telling her neither love nor attention would spoil any child. They'd given ample amounts to both Harriet and Jane and the girls thrived because of it.

She closed her eyes, lifting her chin and basking in the sun of the warm summer day. Life was good these days, with a husband who worshipped her and their three children.

Suddenly, she felt something trace her lips and caught the whiff of strawberry under her nose. Charlotte opened her eyes and took a bite of the fruit Gray offered her. A bit of juice dribbled down her chin so he quickly leaned over and licked it before kissing her. She'd worried that he kissed her too much in front of the children but he said it was good that they saw affection between their parents. It was a battle she never would have won and, besides, she was the true winner. With each kiss from her husband, she fell more deeply in love with him.

It was time to tell him.

A shadow loomed and she turned, seeing Miss Wight had arrived.

"I'm here to take the children inside," the governess said. "It's time for Viscount Warren's nap. I'll bring him to his nursery governess and then give the girls their music lesson."

"Thank you, Miss Wight," she said, knowing the woman was a treasure and helped life run more smoothly than it should with three active children.

"We'll be riding afterward, my lady. Will you be joining us?" Miss Wight asked.

Charlotte accompanied them a few times a week on their rides but said, "No, I have another engagement this afternoon. Go ahead without me."

Miss Wight rounded up her charges and left. Charlotte lay back on the blanket. Gray did the same, lacing their fingers together, and they watched the clouds floating by.

"I hope your engagement this afternoon is with me," he said huskily.

She pulled her hand from his and propped up on her elbow, facing him. He did the same, though his free hand lightly touched her face.

"Will you love me when my face is lined with wrinkles and my hair has gone to gray?" she asked.

He leaned over and kissed the tip of her nose. "You are the most beautiful woman I know, Miss Nott," he said huskily.

Charlotte smiled. It was in their most tender moments that he still called her Miss Nott.

"I love more than your fair face and figure, though. It's your essence from within that makes you truly beautiful to me. That is what I love about you. Your selflessness. Your compassion." He grinned.

"And that truly inimitable, indomitable, incredibly efficient governess that still lurks deep within you."

"Will you love me if I grow fat?"

Gray laughed. "I doubt you ever will. And even if . . ." His voice trailed off and she saw understanding dawn in his eyes. "Wait. Are you—"

"Yes," she interrupted, ready to share her joy. "Come next spring, Lord Crampton, you will be a father again."

He pulled her to her feet and then framed her face with his long fingers and kissed her, long and slow. Charlotte melted against him.

Gray broke the kiss. "I hope it's a girl this time. A little Miss Nott who will boss all of us around. Especially her papa."

"You don't get enough of that from me?" she teased.

He growled and kissed her again. "I can never get enough of you, my love."

His eyes darkened and she saw the need of her in them.

"I think we should celebrate," he declared.

"And how might we do that?"

"By me doing every wicked thing I can think of to you," he replied.

Charlotte burst out laughing.

Taking her hand, they strolled back to Gray Manor. After they entered the house, Gray swept her into his arms.

"Yes, it's daylight," he told her. "And yes, the servants will see and figure out what we're up to."

"I don't care," she said airily.

"Neither do I."

Her husband carried her up the stairs and to their suite of rooms, locking the door to keep the world at bay.

Their celebration lasted all afternoon—and into the night. When it finally ended, Charlotte thought what a lucky woman she was.

THE END

About the Author

Award-winning and international bestselling author Alexa Aston's historical romances use history as a backdrop to place her characters in extraordinary circumstances, where their intense desire for one another grows into the treasured gift of love.

She is the author of Medieval and Regency romance, including *The Knights of Honor, The King's Cousins, The St Clairs,* and *The de Wolfes of Esterley Castle.*

A native Texan, Alexa lives with her husband in a Dallas suburb, where she eats her fair share of dark chocolate and plots out stories while she walks every morning. She enjoys reading, Netflix binge-watching, and can't get enough of *Survivor, The Crown,* or *Game of Thrones.*

CPSIA information can be obtained
at www.ICGtesting.com
Printed in the USA
BVHW041714061020
590428BV00007B/72

9 798606 321865